THE GRIM AND THE GRAVE

SAMI EASTWOOD

MaileKai Publishing LLC

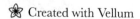 Created with Vellum

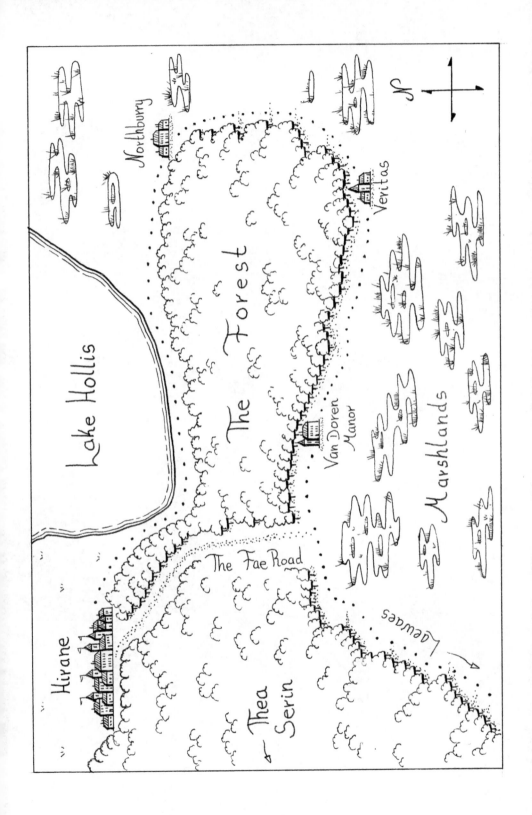

Chapter One

CLOVER GRIMALDI COULD SMELL FEAR. It drifted off the people of Veritas in clouds, making it hard for her to focus. It smelled sharp like rotting metal. It made her nose wrinkle and she delicately wiped at it with her fingers before she stepped into the courier's office.

Mr. Winetrout sat behind the front desk, sorting through a few pieces of parchment in front of him. When he looked up, his watery eyes went wide.

"Percy...go on sorting them letters in the back," he said, turning to his young son, who was sitting behind the counter as well.

Percy looked up with a grimace, but when he saw Clover, he did as his father ordered without protest.

"Parcels for Van Doren?" she requested.

He extended a hand without looking at her. Clover took the iron key wrapped in cloth out of her pocket. She could feel the metal heat up in her hand even through her glove and the cloth. She quickly handed it to him.

While he turned and unlocked the iron box that held Dr. Van Doren's packages, Clover looked around the office like she wasn't interested. Iron bars over the windows, iron doorknobs, iron, iron, everywhere. The simple folk of Veritas feared the fae who lived in the woods just outside their large black gates—iron, of course. The one weakness of the fae, of which Clover was half.

Mr. Winetrout placed the parcels wrapped in brown in front of her. Clover took out a small stack of silver coins and placed them on the countertop before sliding the parcels and key into her bag.

She did not wish Mr. Winetrout a good anything and neither did he wish her.

Rotting metal.

And a fear of what? An overwhelming fear that she would bare her sharp teeth—which she didn't have—and steal their children—which she *definitely* didn't want—and maybe even set their town on fire—which would be far too much trouble than this town and its people were worth.

WHILE THE REST OF THE TOWN TRUDGED THROUGH THE MUD caused by the first rains of the year, Clover's gray leather shoes drifted over the ground as it hardened beneath her. The elements, some of them at least, bent to her will when she could keep her mind clear, but magic within the gates of Veritas was dangerous. She had much more reason to fear the townsfolk than they had to fear her.

Fortunately, there was nothing else to pick up in town today, so she headed as quickly as she could for the western exit of Veritas. The single church bell began tolling the hour, drowning out Mrs. Taverty. The sharp-edged bird-like woman was screeching out a protective folk song in the wide town square. The square itself lay at the threshold of the largest building in Veritas—the church. It stretched toward the sky like it was trying to escape the earth itself. Clover wished it *would* go.

When Clover walked past, the woman quieted slightly, a blessing to all. The orphans she watched over cowered at her feet, kneeling and holding their hands out, begging for donations to the church. What must it be like having a bird of prey like Taverty as a mother?

Clover wondered what her own mother was doing and if the doctor was watching her closely enough. Her mother had a tendency to wander, and the gray clouds overhead were rolling, ready to release another wave of rain.

When Clover reached the western gate, she found it closed. The lock could easily be opened...if you weren't fae. It was a complicated lock of levers and switches that required some strength, but it was made entirely of iron. Clover reached up and tried to move the lock, but the iron began to burn her through her knitted gloves which only covered her palms.

She pulled back, waving her hand through the air to banish the burning sensation. Now what? No one would help her, and the doctor said these parcels were urgent. He would be wanting them soon. She couldn't wait for someone to pass through.

Her heart began to race as she reached up again and grabbed the small lever. It sizzled under her fingers as she tried to push it out of its locked position. Finally, the pain became too much, and she reeled away. Her heel caught a loose stone and she fell hard on her side. Mud squelched between her burning fingers, soothing the pain, but it wasn't soothing her pride, which burned far hotter than iron on her skin.

Clover's head snapped up when she heard snickering. Some children of the village laughed and pointed at her even as they hid around the corners of buildings or behind barrels filled with rainwater. She quickly stood but ducked again as the first of the mud was thrown.

She turned, eyes closed, and blocked Van Doren's packages from the mud with her body. It struck her back, painless and harmless except for what it meant. That she was helpless, powerless against *children* with *mud*. How much more powerless would she be when they grew up and decided to throw something else at her, like pikes or nets made of iron? Clover felt a surge of cold at the center of her chest, but she struggled against her magic even as it swept comfortingly over her skin. She brought to mind her mother's words.

Some snakes only strike after being struck.

There was a slow and painful future ahead for her if she lifted a finger against anyone in the village of Veritas. Even some silly illusion would grant her the same fate as her father —not that she was capable of so much.

"Hey! Get out of here, you little wretches! Go on!"

Clover let out a breath of relief, opening her eyes. "Grant."

"Clover, lovelier than ever," he said. His usually neatly combed hair had a few loose brown curls. His presence filled her with relief, even if she was embarrassed about being covered in mud. Clover flicked the excess muck off her hands and tried to push it off the back of her dress.

Grant's brown eyes were smiling even though his mouth was trying not to. He opened the gate for her. "I see the damage has already been done. Are you all right?"

She tried on a smile. "My pride is hurt worse than

anything else. Did your father send for me? I've taken too long."

"No, not at all. *I* came to get you." He was wearing his dark-brown work clothes, which was odd. He never wore his work clothes into town. "Your mother said something about you being trapped in an iron cage…" He shook his head. "I didn't want to take any chances of that being even remotely true."

Clover smiled. "Well, she wasn't wrong."

He returned her smile before he pressed a hand to the small of her back. "Come on, let's get home before the rain catches us."

The two of them began walking back to Van Doren Manor. Once they were far enough away from the town, Grant took the parcels from her.

"Thank you for rescuing me," she said, watching a smile drift over his features. Clover knew Grant loved being a hero. She was more than happy to let him, since her fae-blood prevented her from saving herself. But she could tell he was disturbed by her treatment, and that he'd been late to the rescue.

He let out a bitter laugh, looking at the mud splattered on the back of her dress and hair. "What good is a rescuer if he comes too late?"

"Considering that you didn't *really* know I was in trouble to begin with, any help is appreciated."

"Little villains," said Grant with a grin. "What kind of person even thinks of throwing mud at someone else for no good reason?"

His tone was teasing, as well it should have been. The same thing that gave them the idea gave it to him when he was younger. The only difference was that Grant grew out of it—

those children might never.

"Oh yes, how could they? No child has ever been so wicked," Clover said with a laugh. She lived for these moments, ones of peace between ones of pain.

Grant continued, "I wasn't wicked, I was…misinformed."

"How unpleasant for *you*." Clover reached behind her and rubbed a clump of damp mud off the back of her neck. Thunder clapped overhead and they both stopped walking and looked to the sky.

"That's a good sign," said Grant.

Clover turned to him. "It's not raining yet."

"Race you back!" he shouted before running off.

Clover ran after him. "Do not drop those!"

Van Doren Manor was far to the west of Veritas, and the farther they got from the city, the safer Clover felt. The dirt road hugged the forest, and a few small gusts of wind blew dry leaves around their feet as they walked. Dark clouds moved toward them from over the marshes to the south.

She noticed Grant didn't mind walking close to the forest like many did. His eyes kept flitting around, the escaped curls brushed the worry lines in his forehead. Grant slowed to catch his breath, but he didn't stop walking. His pace was brisk, and his eyes now held a glint of worry. The smell of fear came back.

"What's the matter?" she asked.

Grant wrung his hands. "I…left in quite a hurry. We really should be going."

"Define, 'quite a hurry'."

"I may have been in the middle of an autopsy."

"Grant!"

"My father doesn't know I've even gone," he said.

Clover scoffed. "So far as you know. Are you off your head?"

"A little. Can we please get back?" he asked.

Clover grabbed his hand, and they began running again. He held her hand tightly and ran beside her even though he could easily outdistance her, as he had shown many times before.

"What about the other patient? The Hallows boy. Did he see you leave?"

Grant shook his head as they ran. "Not a chance, he's been out cold since this morning. Unless he's very good at faking a death-like sleep."

The manor came quickly into sight. It was a hauntingly isolated building. Gray stones streaked with darker watermarks were wrapped with untamed ivy that was dying in the early autumn cold. Steeply pitched roofs made the manor jut out of the horizon like a series of blades.

Clover and Grant both stopped behind the willow tree beyond the view of the high windows.

"Are you sure he wouldn't notice you missing?" asked Clover. She felt a horrible sense of danger coming close. More thunder, and this time, lightning came with it.

Grant nodded. "I'm sure. You know he doesn't move around much when it rains."

"I know. I'll see you at dinner," she said. She took the parcels from him.

"We shouldn't have to sneak around. You deserve better," he said.

Clover's heart skipped a beat, and she smiled.

"The life of a servant is never expected to be one of fair-

ness. You've given that to me, truly, so don't despair so much."
She stepped forward and kissed his cheek.

He frowned. "Don't you ever want more?"

"Do you think we could have this conversation at another
time?" she asked.

"Right, but think about my question," he said. He gave her
a dream-like smile before lunging forward and kissing her.

Clover pushed him off, but she was laughing. "Just go!"

Grant was laughing too as he ran into the forest. Clover
watched him with a shake of her head. Not even a misstep of
hesitation. Most humans didn't know the first thing about the
forest, thus they mistreated it and the fae claimed them. Since
Clover had taught Grant how to respect the forest, he never
feared it lashing out against him, or being targeted by the fae.

CLOVER WAITED A BIT BEFORE SHE COLLECTED HERSELF AND
began her quick walk down the lane. She made a show of
brushing drying mud off her dress and fixing a few flyaway
hairs. The walls around Van Doren Manor were brick. The
red had been washed to a dull brown over the years and the
gates were always open. They had been overgrown in Tangle
Ivy, so she supposed even if one wanted to close them, it would
be nearly impossible. The path up to the servant's entrance
shifted to stone and Clover stomped on it to knock the mud off
her boots. Her mother was waiting for her at the large black
door.

Torryn Grimaldi was a woman in a cage. Her full mind
had died along with Clover's father, and what little remained
was reserved for few things. Acting as a servant to Dr. Van
Doren and caring for her daughter, though even those things

had their limits. Torryn's eyes were currently far away, their blue was pale like her skin.

"Mother?" said Clover. "We should go inside now."

Tears dripped from Torryn's eyes. "It rained then, too."

Clover nodded though she didn't understand. "Come inside." Clover gently took her mother by the elbow and led her easily inside. Torryn didn't try to struggle. She was a frail woman, bone thin from hardly ever eating and hollow-eyed from lack of deep sleep.

The stone corridor leading to their bedrooms, storage closets, and the kitchen was narrow. Clover gently guided her mother down the corridor to her bedroom and sat her down in the chair by the window. Like Clover, she wore the gray dress of the servant, but at least hers still covered her ankles. Clover had long outgrown her dress but getting a new one wasn't a high priority.

Torryn was still crying, lost in some distant memory, or maybe a time and place that had never even existed.

There was no time for Clover to change her clothes. She could clean up whatever mess she made after the parcels were delivered. Clover took the parcels out of her mother's room and to the kitchen. She heard her mother's door open and Clover sighed. Torryn could be anywhere now. Clover didn't have time to search for her.

Clover took the parcels out of the servants' quarters and into the hospital wing. It took up the entire western half of the first floor. She walked through a hallway past the rooms that could hold individual patients. The surgery rooms were the last three in the long line of twelve rooms. At the end of the hall was a door that led to a staircase which would take her up to Dr. Van Doren's office. If Grant had been working on an autopsy, he would be back in one of the surgery rooms.

Clover didn't hesitate to go straight to Dr. Van Doren's office. No place in the house was off limits for her. She had to clean everything, and Dr. Van Doren had nothing to hide other than the fact that he was a hard man, cruel in the blink of an eye. But who couldn't tell that just by looking at him?

She knocked lightly on the door and he grunted, allowing her to enter. His office was a horrible place. The worst room in the house, as it was the only one that didn't have any windows. Not a single one. Just wood-paneled walls. It unnerved her, similar to what she imagined being inside a coffin was like.

The doctor himself was sitting at his desk, writing something. Clover didn't try to see what it was; she already knew. He kept a list of names—names of every patient he ever saw along with their history. When they were born, how many times they'd been ill, and sometimes, their predicted deaths. Grant had explained it to her once—keeping his own records was all part of his apprenticeship.

Clover set the parcels on the worktable that lined the western wall and turned to leave the room.

"Stop," the doctor said.

She did, turning to him and keeping her eyes to the floor.

"What took you so long?"

"The western gate of Veritas had been closed. I had to wait for someone to pass through. My apologies, Master Van Doren."

He looked up, narrowing his stone-gray eyes at her through his circular glasses. His brown hair was tinged with gray at the temples, and though time had weathered his skin a little, he still had the build of a strong young man, similar to Grant. Clover looked down again. He held out a weathered hand. "Key."

Clover gave it to him and waited for her dismissal.

"Where is your mother?"

"The kitchen. Shall I fetch her?" she asked. She could see his hands balling to fists on his desktop and her heart raced in her chest. He was in his later years, but still strong. His hands could easily break any bone in her body. The fae in her had made her thin and narrow. Maybe her bones were a little stronger than those of a normal human, but she didn't want to test them.

"Don't bother." Dr. Van Doren's hands unfurled. "Her mind grows weaker; she loses it even more when it rains."

"Is there something you need me to do, Master Van Doren?" Clover asked.

Dr. Van Doren got up, and Clover held still as a statue. She kept her eyes to the ground and her breathing even as he stood in front of her.

"Why yes, there is something I need you to do." His hand lashed out and struck her hard across the face. Stars exploded behind her eyes, and when Clover opened them again, she was on the floor. Something hot leaked down her face, but she couldn't tell if it was tears or blood. The world wasn't still enough for her to focus. Her breathing was heavy now, with a mixture of sobs and panic. Clover didn't dare get up; she would only be knocked back down.

Dr. Van Doren crouched beside her. "I need you to remember the meaning of urgent." He shifted forward and stepped on one of her hands. "The burning of your hands on the iron barriers of Veritas does not concern me." His foot shifted away. He still needed her to work, after all. He left and Clover still made no move to right herself.

It could be worse, she reminded herself. It could be her mother, as it had been time and time again. After a while, Clover had learned not to rush to her mother's side, because she would only suffer the same fate. And so Clover would have to watch as Dr. Van Doren put her mother in the same position she was in now, and do nothing. She closed her eyes hard enough to cause herself more pain.

Oh yes, it could be much worse.

Chapter Two

A LARGE BRUISE carved a crescent moon on the outside of Clover's right eye. Underneath it was a cut that stung when she moved her face too much. In the smooth metal of the pots that hung from the ceiling, Clover watched the bruise continue to darken. Clover turned away from her reflection and focused hard, the cold of fae magic sweeping across her skin, making the tips of her fingers tingle as her tears floated away from her eyes and into Dr. Van Doren's soup bowl. He could rest his joints during the rain if he wished, but his dreams would not be pleasant. There were powerful magics in the world, but sometimes the simple magics like the ones of emotion were the most useful.

The green sheen of the brassy iveen pots shone in the light of the sconces around the kitchen. The pots were filled with water, waiting to be washed after dinner was over. All the metal in the house was iveen—found and mined in the forest by the fae. Grant had hinted that the house was built with iron, but his crazy grandmother had it all ripped out and replaced with iveen so she could have fae servants. The first in a long and miserable legacy.

Clover stepped back from the sink and waited near the door that led from the dining room to the kitchen. As her mother ate in the kitchen, Clover thought about Grant's question.

Don't you ever want more?

Of course she wanted more. She wanted a good life, a peaceful, safe life for her and her mother, but Clover had no idea what that meant. Where could they go? A sick woman and her half-fae daughter. Ha! No human town would let them live within a league of them, and going into the forest? The fae were protective of their way of life. They would never accept her and they definitely would not accept her mother.

But there was an itch she couldn't scratch, the kind that evaded you, moving to a new place until you've scratched up your whole arm or back. They couldn't keep living like this. She was tired of staying down—no—it was more than that. She was tired of getting knocked down. Yet the question remained: where could they go?

Grant and his father came in, interrupting her thoughts. Clover moved farther into the shadow of her doorway so Grant wouldn't see her face, but she couldn't keep up the charade. Dr. Van Doren waved for her, and she came over, pouring wine into his glass. Out of the corner of her eye she could see Grant shift in his seat. Clover stepped over to pour Grant some wine but he shook his head, so she moved back into the corner.

Grant cleared his throat. "I have a question."

"Go on," his father said, and Clover held back a smirk as

Dr. Van Doren slurped his soup. Cruel dreams for a cruel man.

"Hypothetically, how much blunt force trauma could a person take to the head before they were unable to do the most basic of tasks?"

Clover sighed quietly.

Dr. Van Doren looked up from his soup. "Easy, boy—"

"Don't be cross, sir. It's only a question." Grant eased a smile into his statement. Clover couldn't see Grant's face from here, but his shoulders were tense, spine straight.

"Well then, hypothetically speaking, not nearly as much as I could deliver in a single lifetime," Dr. Van Doren said.

Grant turned to his soup. "It was merely a question."

"You will make a talented doctor, Grant. But you are not a clever man. I suggest you stick to what you're good at," said Dr. Van Doren. "I will treat the servants as I please, and when you are master of this house, you will have the freedom to do the same."

Clover shook her head. She couldn't wait that long. Van Doren would cling to life just to spite her, and what could she do? Kill him? One of her eyebrows went up.

BEHIND HER, THE DOOR TO THE DINING ROOM OPENED, AND Torryn came through. Clover rushed to her. Her heels made an enormous amount of noise in the silence.

"Mother, go back to the kitchen," she said.

Torryn shook her head. "I can't—he was never supposed to be there. He was supposed to leave. Leave us forever."

"Mother, please," Clover whispered, trying to push her

mother back. "Please go back into the kitchen and wait for me there."

"If you cannot contain that woman, I will do it for you." The doctor stood from the table. Grant matched him.

"There's no need, Master Van Doren," said Clover, still pushing against her mother.

Torryn pulled at Clover's sleeves as she slowly began sinking to the ground. "There was only silence. He cried out not once."

Clover held her mother up, keeping her on her feet as she tried to push her back through the door.

"Father, wait!" cried Grant.

There was a sound like something heavy being knocked into the table. A moment later, a heavy hand gripped Clover's shoulder and forced her to the side. She hit the wall of the dining room with a slam. Dr. Van Doren pulled Torryn to her feet by her arm, and she cried out when he twisted it behind her back and shoved her through the door. It closed but on the other side was a loud crashing noise. Clover rushed to the door, but Dr. Van Doren stopped her. Clover's back slammed against the door and he pointed at her.

"Step through that door, and you'll be on the ground for the second time today," he warned before slowly stepping away and back to the table.

Grant was on his knees, holding his stomach. The glasses on the table had tipped over, spilling water and wine every-where. Clover swallowed hard again and again as she forcibly peeled herself off the door and went to the table. She pulled Grant's chair away and he stood. She pushed his chair in and he sat.

The doctor sat in his chair and went back to eating peace-fully—as though he'd never gotten up to begin with. "You should know better than to stand in my way, boy. You're weak, just like your mother."

Clover paused for the briefest moment while she sopped up the spilled wine from the tabletop. Grant's jaw hardened, but not in anger. No, this was sorrow. His eyes peered down at his lap instead of his food and he didn't move a muscle for the rest of dinner. Grant's mother had died in childbirth. Clover knew he blamed himself for it—for a woman he didn't even know.

Dr. Van Doren slurped at his soup, and outside, thunder rolled across the sky.

Torryn's words drifted through Clover's mind as she carted the dishes to and from the now empty dining room to the kitchen. Slowly, Clover realized what day it was.

Seventeen years ago today, Clover's father, Roan, had been murdered. To murder a fae is no easy task. Even when done quickly, nature rises up against humans to protect those that protect it, and when nature mourns, it yields no crops, it pushes bones out of the earth, and the dark fae feel it and come ready to wreak havoc on unsuspecting humans. To this day, Clover sometimes heard about Laewaes, and how things were never good there.

Clover knew little about the events that took place before her birth, only that Torryn Grimaldi was the daughter of the Mayor of Laewaes, highly esteemed and easily offended. When he found out his daughter had not only fallen in love with a fae, but was carrying his child, he retaliated. The people of Laewaes killed Clover's father and banished her pregnant mother.

Torryn's mind never recovered from the trauma. Torryn

hadn't always been this lost, but still Clover sometimes wondered how they both survived and how they had been cursed to end up at Van Doren Manor. But Clover wasn't going to get any answers, so she pulled her bleeding and broken mother off the floor day after day, year after year. This was their life.

"He loved you, he would have loved you," said Torryn as Clover guided her mother to her room after dinner.

Clover raised an eyebrow. "Well, which is it?"

"He wasn't supposed to be there," she said.

Clover helped her mother to bed. "Then why was he there? Why come if he knew it was dangerous?"

"He loved you." The words came out shaky, like she was freezing.

Clover sighed, wrapping her mother in blankets. If he loved her so much, then why hadn't he been smarter? Why hadn't he just stayed away? If he had, maybe their lives would have been different. Maybe if he had, *he* could have told Clover he loved her, instead of her mother yelling it up at her from the bottom of her well of confusion and memories.

THE WHITE LINEN CLOTH CAME AWAY RED FROM TORRYN'S forehead as she laid in bed. When the door opened to the kitchen, Clover tensed. Dr. Van Doren requesting something, perhaps? It was raining out, barely dark, and the doctor had gone to bed a while ago.

She stood and went to the bedroom door, holding the knob, waiting. Clover pressed her ear to the door and listened for what was going on in the kitchen. There wasn't much of anything before the kitchen door opened and closed once again. She didn't want to go in there if the doctor was still there, so she closed her eyes and listened hard. The cold feeling in her chest was nowhere to be found, which meant Soleil would be severely disappointed in her. Clover's magic was never present when she needed it.

She flung open the door to find the kitchen completely empty. In the middle of the table was a small purple flower. It was a little wilted, but when she picked it up, its life returned, and it bloomed beautifully in her hand. Grant's idea of a secret message. She hadn't thought anything could make her smile today of all days, but this did.

Clover went back to her mother's room and made sure Torryn was tucked in and not going anywhere before locking the door behind her. She took her shoes off and left the servants' quarters. Her nimble feet dodged every creaky floorboard, stair step, and door hinge as she made her way from the ground floor to the tower.

The tower was part of the house for reasons unknown. Located at the top of the manor, the tower was a small room just big enough for two people to sit in, with stained-glass windows on all four walls. A ladder, hidden behind a large wardrobe in the attic, was the only way to get there.

Grant opened the door for Clover when she knocked. The rain pattered against the stained-glass windows as Grant sat cross-legged with a wooden box in his hands.

"What's that?" Clover asked, taking the same position. They were both tall and for a while, Clover had worried that they would grow too tall to fit in the room together. Luckily, they'd both reached their limit with a little room to spare.

He opened the box, revealing medical supplies, and she sighed.

"Grant, you shouldn't be taking those things."

He shrugged. "Why not? I'm going to be a doctor, aren't I? These are the tools of my trade. Now hold still."

"Your father will know that you took them," she said. He poured some liquid on a cloth, but she grabbed his wrist. "You're going to get us in trouble."

"He has no right to treat you that way." He took a slow breath, clearly in pain somewhere. "After everything you and your mother do for him, it's unacceptable. Besides, I hid these weeks ago and he hasn't said a thing about it."

Clover let go of his hand and held still.

He pressed the cloth gently to the cut on her cheek. "Who says I'm not clever?"

"Only someone who doesn't know you." Her face scrunched at the stinging pain the liquid brought. "Did he say anything about you being missing this afternoon?"

He shook his head. "No, he didn't notice a thing, just as I said. The cons of having an office with no windows."

"I hate that room," she said.

He took the cloth away and put it in the box before taking something else out.

"So you've told me," he said, pouring something else on another cloth. He turned her face to the side and wiped something on her skin that soothed the stinging. "How's your mother?"

"I've locked her in her room," said Clover. "I think she'll be all right."

He pulled the cloth away. "Should I have a look at her?"

Clover thought about it. What harm could it be to make sure her mother didn't have more injuries than Clover could see?

"I would be very grateful," said Clover.

Grant subtly cleared his throat and tenderly adjusted his

position. Clover nearly rolled her eyes. His patients always came first but who looked after him if he was only looking after everyone else?

Clover's brows pulled together. "Are you all right?"

He gave her a confused look. "What do you mean? I'm fine."

She lunged at him, and he tensed up before wincing.

"Is there anything you won't do to prove a point? It's just bruises—only healed with time." He flashed his perfect teeth in a charming smile and Clover shook her head with a smile of her own.

Grant put the box down and pulled out a pen and a notebook. Clover took them from him.

THE ENTIRE ALPHABET HAD TAKEN HER SOME TIME TO LEARN. Each letter was so different, and it amazed her that these shapes made up the language she had only learned to speak. Dark hairs from her bun escaped and fell against her cheek as she practiced writing her name.

"So have you thought about the question I posed earlier?" Grant asked.

The bones in her fingers began to ache and she stretched her hands. "No." Her hands got stiffer, like they were turning to stone, and an itch built in the center of her chest. Grant only laughed.

"Why do you try to lie if it doesn't come naturally?" he asked. "There's nothing wrong with having dreams."

Clover smiled, scratching her chest with stiff fingers. "Says the dreamer with bright prospects."

"Dreams are for everyone. You could do so much; I don't think you know how special you are."

Clover put down the pen and notebook. "I know very well what I am. It is that very peculiarity that bars me from many different lives I could have if I were someone like you."

"A doctor's son?" he asked.

"I meant human."

"You're human too."

"Is that what you see when you look at me?" she asked, incredulous. How could he think this way after everything? "Do you know what I see?"

"No."

She grabbed his hand and placed it over hers. The different tones of their skin became apparent. It was well known that the fae had "skin like the night" or so the humans described them. Clover was only half, but nothing told people that she was fae faster than the color of her skin, even if it wasn't as dark as full fae.

"I see that there is no place for me in the world of humans," she said. "There never will be, Grant. You only want to think that because you're in love with me and you are optimistic to a fault."

"I don't think I'm *that* optimistic," he said.

She laughed. "You think we can just pick up and go wherever we please? You do realize that your affections for me will change the course of your life?"

"Of course I realize that. How could I not with you constantly reminding me?" A mischievous grin appeared. "You know what I wish you'd remind me?"

"No, though I can't wait to hear."

"Your affections for me," he said.

Clover resisted the smile that bloomed across her lips. She

turned her attention back to her writing and began carefully pressing the pen to the paper, making clear, neat lines.

"What are you doing?" Grant leaned forward to see but she pulled away. "I want to see, let me see."

Clover looked up into his eager face and he grinned. She turned the paper around.

I LOVE YOU, DEARLY

GRANT TOOK THE PAPER, AND HIS GRIN BROKE INTO A FULL, genuine smile. "A perfect script all around." He kept the paper. "You aren't entirely wrong, you know."

"About what?"

"About us going wherever we like. You're right—we can't, but Hirane could offer us more freedom than we'll ever receive anywhere else. The *other* thing you're wrong about is that there are good people in this world, Clover. You just haven't met them yet."

"I think you hold your people in much too high a regard," she said. "You don't know how badly the iron burns."

"You're right...I don't. I'm a doctor, and not just because my father is one. This is what I want to be. But if I choose to believe that I am the only good person in this region—in this world, even—then how can I be a *good* doctor? I want to help people; I have to believe that there is something good inside them. Something that deserves my help."

Clover pressed her hands to her face and resisted the urge to scream. Grant could be so...so...something! She didn't have the right word for this kind of blind faith! Her head hurt. She didn't know if it was from Dr. Van Doren,

Grant's beliefs, or leftover resistance from when she tried to lie.

"Life can be better," Grant said, and she took her hands away from her face to look at him. "It *will* be better. Just be patient."

"For how much longer?"

"Until my father is dead."

Clover looked through the stained-glass window behind Grant. "And how long will that be? He's strong. Never once have I seen him ill, or falter in any way. Silver hair is the only indication that he has aged at all since I was a child, and I'm already twenty years old. How much longer do you expect me to wait?"

"I can protect you." He reached forward and took her hands. Hers were cold and his were very warm. The simple gesture made her hopeful and she wondered if Grant had even the smallest bit of magic in him. "I know I haven't in the past. I know I wasn't able to tonight. But I can—I promise I can."

But that was just it, wasn't it? Clover didn't want him to. Not even Grant was a stranger to his father's abuse. Clover was tired of the people she loved standing between her and the wrath of others. Clover could protect herself and she could protect her mother, maybe not from the humans of Veritas or the surrounding towns—but they were no threat to the fae. She and her mother had no struggle with the fae. If anything, Clover and her mother were victims of the humans as much as any full-born fae. Clover would have to take her chances.

"Grant, I believe you are the only good your people have to offer, and I'm sorry, but you just can't change my mind," she said.

Clover would not be taking this sort of treatment any longer. Grant couldn't leave, since he was bound by laws of apprenticeship. They wouldn't be separated forever, surely Grant would understand that. And Soleil could help them once they got into the forest. Dr. Van Doren's hold on them had its limits, and they began at the edge of the forest. His cruelty was more powerful than her desire to wait out this torment. Torryn and Clover Grimaldi were leaving.

Tonight.

Chapter Three

THE PLAN WAS SIMPLE. Escape Van Doren Manor, go to Thea Serin with Soleil as an escort, and plead to the fae to let Clover and her mother live peacefully in the forest. Then, once they were settled, Clover would come back for Grant. She knew she didn't have any family among the fae. Her father had been an only child and was quickly orphaned, but Soleil said her father was well known and well liked. That had to count for something among them, right? Soleil seemed confident but Clover wasn't sure—she was half human and just look at the result.

There wasn't much of sentimentality to pack. Whatever Dr. Van Doren thought worthless he let her keep. A few little crafts she'd made as a child, a love note from Grant, written when he was fourteen, a bracelet of jade stones that belonged to her father, and a necklace that belonged to Torryn's mother. Clover packed only one spare dress for her, one for her mother, and the red dress reserved for the Blood Solstice. Maybe she could trade it to the fae, or even to the humans. It was the nicest thing she owned. Food wasn't a necessity; the forest would provide and so would Soleil.

Then she left a note for Grant. The writing was as confident as she could make it.

I will come back.

Her mother was tired. The cut on her cheek had been bandaged by Grant only a few hours earlier and it was bleeding again. Torryn was still able to be guided, so that's exactly what Clover did.

The night air was heavy now that the raining was over, and the grass was slippery as Clover gently guided Torryn out of the manor. She stuck to the brick wall that lined the backyard and to the small gate that led into the forest. Both Clover and her mother wore their black hoods reserved for funerals. Once they were through the trees and deep enough into the forest, Soleil was there to meet them.

She was pure fae, almost invisible in the darkness, but Clover could see her. Even though she and Soleil were the same height, the fae girl stood with such strength that she seemed taller. Her clothes were of a make beyond human, earthy yet celestial in color and appearance. They clung to her skin in the patterns of dragonfly and hummingbird wings. Soleil's green eyes pierced the darkness and saw things beyond flesh and bone, just as her ears could hear plants growing from miles away, and her nose could smell the exact moment when the seasons changed.

"I didn't think you were actually going to do it," said Soleil as she looked over them, especially Torryn, whose wide eyes were wandering. Soleil was deathly afraid of humans and going even a single step beyond the forest.

Clover pulled her hood off. "Well, you were mistaken. You'll take us to Thea Serin, won't you?"

"No," said Soleil.

Clover's heart stopped and she stared at Soleil for a few heartbeats before she spoke again.

"Why not? Soleil, we have to leave this place."

Soleil shook her head, her black hair swaying like silk fabric. "There are laws that you're tampering with. I can't let you go because I'm trying to save you."

Clover could smell Soleil's fear mingled with the life of the forest night around them, damp and heavy with natural decay.

"Save us from what? If we stay here, we could die," said Clover.

"And if you leave like this, you *will* die," said Soleil. "You know what happened to my parents."

Clover searched her memory for a moment, trying to remember what happened to Soleil's parents. They broke the law somehow and they died...she didn't remember anything beyond that. Soleil must have seen the blankness in Clover's stare because her face hardened, and her hands clenched into fists.

"There are laws that govern the peace between humans and fae. My parents broke one of those laws, something about trade agreements, it doesn't matter." Soleil closed her eyes. "What does matter is who came for them. The fae call them Veiled Ones, but the humans call them Justice Riders. They came in the night—there was no trial, there was no need. They'd been paid to kill."

Clover shook her head. "Van Doren couldn't possibly value us that much. To pay to have us killed." She walked past Soleil and the fae followed.

"He owns you," said Soleil. "You are breaking the law, and if he didn't value you, then why keep you around? Even humans enslave other humans. They might kill you both.

Maybe they'll only kill her and take you back to Van Doren."

Clover stopped walking at that, and Soleil stopped beside her. They wouldn't kill Torryn unless Van Doren asked them to, would they? What did it matter? They could still hurt her or leave her alone in the forest.

"I'm sorry, but you can't go any farther. I will not take you to Thea Serin. Even if I did, they would not accept her there," said Soleil, but still Clover did not turn back. She looked past Soleil into the forest. Surely the Veiled Ones couldn't make it too deeply into the forest…she and her mother could hide.

Soleil grabbed her arm. "Stop trying to hope for the best. The laws of the fae aren't set in stone. They could choose to take pity on you, or they could reject you entirely. Even if they do let you live here, the dark fae will torment you. At best they'll trick you, at worst they'll lead you or your hapless life-giver to your doom. We're not all light, you know."

Clover had heard all about the dangers of dark fae. Their violet eyes gave them away for what they were and anyone who made a deal with them was sure to die.

Soleil turned and held her fingers over Clover's lips before she could even speak.

"Do you hear that?" Soleil's green eyes glinted.

Clover moved Soleil's hand away before closing her eyes and listening hard. Something was moving closer, pausing every now and then.

"You were followed," said Soleil. "I smell human blood."

Clover turned to her mother only to find her curling up on the ground as though to sleep. She dropped to her knees and grabbed Torryn's shoulder.

"Mother, not now. We have to get up, we have to go."

Torryn closed her eyes. "Where is there to go?"

"He's coming closer." Soleil backed into the trees, her eyes wide with fear.

Clover's heart jumped. Dr. Van Doren had caught up with them? Already? Clover tried to pull her mother off the ground.

She looked at Soleil. "Don't you dare leave!"

"I'm sorry," said the frightened fae quietly before she melded into the darkness of the forest and fled.

Clover gritted her teeth. She wanted to be angry but Soleil's fear was well founded.

"Mother, get up, please!" Clover pulled at her mother, but she wouldn't budge. Clover wanted to cry; she could hear the doctor coming closer even now without using her magic. Clover decided the best thing to do was hide. She knelt beside her mother and from the power the forest gave her, she felt that cold energy sweep across her skin. Small shrubs and stones with lichen on them began to climb over Torryn's body until she was completely concealed by the earth but still able to breathe. Clover herself took shelter in the roots of a large tree nearby and waited.

THE DOCTOR'S FOOTSTEPS CLAMBERED EVER CLOSER, disturbing the forest, so unlike the careful steps of Soleil. Clover closed her eyes and willed the doctor to pass by them and for her mother not to move. She crouched even lower as the footsteps slowed and became unsure. Finally, they stopped, and Clover pressed her hands over her mouth.

"Clover?" a voice whispered and her brow furrowed. "Where did they go?"

Grant?

Clover slowly peered around the tree and saw Grant studying the ground where her mother was covered, though he didn't see her. His white shirt was hastily tucked into his brown trousers and his suspenders hung loosely around his thighs. He stood and ran his hands through his hair, clearly frustrated. She considered staying put. He should go home. She'd left him a note saying she would come back. But he was giving her an opportunity to say goodbye in person. She watched him go over and sit against a tree, looking near tears, and she gave in.

"You shouldn't be here," she said, coming out of hiding, and instantly regretted the words. They sounded too harsh coming from her; she was still tense from thinking it was his father who had followed them out there. She waved her hand and the forest moved away from her mother, though Torryn grasped at it as though she didn't want it to leave. Perhaps the forest held the same sort of energy that Clover's father had when he was alive.

Grant shot to his feet; his anger seemed to crackle off him like lightning. "Me? You shouldn't be out here either. It's dangerous, not to mention—well—selfish! You could have at least said goodbye. Your note was cryptic at best and if I hadn't been looking out my window, I wouldn't have known you'd gone until morning."

"That was the plan," said Clover, sounding too harsh again, and it reflected on the hurt that welled against the bottom of his eyelids. "I didn't want to leave you, but we had to go, you know we did, and I was going to come back as soon as we were safe."

"I said I would protect you and I meant it." He stepped forward and grabbed her by the upper arms. "Do you realize how dangerous this is? You could be killed."

"So I've just learned. Justice Riders? Why have you never told me about them?"

He let go of her. "I didn't want to threaten you into staying. I realize now it simply would have been informative but...I didn't think you would leave without me."

"Grant, I'm sorry. I know how much you want to be a doctor. I know you would have wanted to come with us but then you would be abandoning your apprenticeship and then you'd never achieve your dreams," said Clover. She didn't know *all* the laws, but she knew some of them. If Grant left his apprenticeship now, without having a certificate of completion from his father, then he would *never* be a doctor. He wouldn't even be allowed to start over, and it would be unlikely that any other Trade Master would take him.

He smiled. "It is some small comfort to know you were thinking of my dreams—even if you *don't* trust me to protect you and Torryn."

It always came back to that, but that wasn't the problem—why couldn't he see that? Clover knew he shouldn't even *have* to do that sort of thing.

Clover sighed. "That's not it! I don't want you to have to put yourself between us and your father. It's never ended well."

Clover closed her eyes hard and flinched at how easily she could bring to mind Grant's utterances of pain. She had cleaned up his blood as much as her mother's or her own. No one was safe from Dr. Van Doren. Clover didn't want to hear it anymore.

Grant pressed his hands to either side of her face. "It won't be for that much longer. Less than a year, even! Then as soon as I have my certificate, we'll leave. We'll do what we always talked about."

"Hirane. A city for free fae...we hope." She opened her eyes to look into his big optimistic ones.

He smiled. "We will be free. I know my cousin Warner would help us. We could get married."

She felt suddenly jittery, like he'd touched her with a static shock. Clover loved Grant, and they had talked about marriage before—it never seemed truly possible until now.

"Just like we planned. Only it won't be secret...or illegal...or result in some kind of hideous punishment."

Clover smirked. "Is this your idea of a proposal?"

"Uh, right." Grant looked around before getting down on one knee.

He took one of her hands and gave her one of his charming smiles. "Clover Grimaldi, I have no ring to give you, for now, but I do have all the love in my heart, and I know we can make each other happy. We didn't have a great beginning, but we could have a spectacular ending. Will you marry me?"

Clover was adrift in the starlit sky. She had always dreamed of this moment, but now it was here, all of it before her like the forest presenting a path to her when she was lost. She could never see herself with anyone other than Grant and so the answer came simply.

"Yes."

Grant stood and pulled her into an embrace, since they were in the presence of Torryn, and when they separated, he kissed the back of her hand.

"I'll be finished before you know it and we'll be together. I promise," he said, and Clover believed him—or she wanted to desperately.

She reached up and straightened the collar of his white shirt. "We can make it just a little while longer. But, maybe in the future...only aid my mother. There's no use getting in your father's way for me when I still have the power to pick myself up."

"Never," he said. "I will always protect you; I will always run after you into the woods, I will always rescue you. You must simply get used to it."

Clover let out a laugh, but it mingled so closely with the sob that had gathered in the back of her throat that she didn't truly know which it was. She pulled him closer, and he kissed her forehead, holding her in an embrace. Life for now would continue as it always had—but now there was a light at the end of this path. It could be better as long as they were together. She was still afraid, afraid of Dr. Van Doren, but she could be strong. Grant was right that he had her love, and she had his, and it wouldn't be long before the three of them were long gone. Onward to a better life. To freedom.

❧

GRANT KNEELED AND PICKED UP TORRYN EASILY. SHE BEGAN TO cry softly.

"It's all right," said Grant.

Her mother quieted and reached out with one hand. Clover took the hand and held it firmly as they made their way out of the forest and back to the manor, through the servant's quarters, where Grant put Torryn in her own bed before Clover and Grant left. Clover lit a candle by the kitchen window, which was still dotted with raindrops, before giving it to Grant.

"Why don't you fear the forest?" she asked. His eyebrows went up and she continued, "all humans do. Even with all you know—it could still turn against you. So why don't you?"

"I'm not afraid of you and I figure you and the forest are

one and the same," he said, and it made her smile. She never really asked what he thought of her magic abilities, but it was good to know he had already grown to accept them. "I love you."

"I love you too," she said before kissing him. Love, like fear, had a scent. Like the moment before dawn, when the wind was cool and pure, when all life was coming alive. It was in the air with them now, and she didn't want it to leave. But the actual dawn was coming, and they had to get *some* rest. Clover walked him to the kitchen door.

"Goodnight," he said. "I'll see you in the morning?"

"See you in the morning," she said. "I promise."

He gave the side of her face one last caress before leaving and taking the candle and her heart with him.

Chapter Four

For a while, Grant was right. Things were good and the bruises began to fade while the cuts scabbed over. "Less than a year" seemed much farther away than she realized, but according to Grant, training was complete when Grant could properly treat a patient on instinct without help. No opportunities seemed to be presenting themselves, but Clover was hopeful. Grey Fever season was going to start soon, and the patients would flood in like they always did. To prepare for it, Clover was sent on a familiar mission into town to pick up a replenishment of medicine.

Something was different about this trip into town. The smell of fear was so strong, Clover had to resist the urge to cover her nose. Whisperings were so loud that they echoed down every side street and narrow passage. She hadn't been to town in nearly three days. Something must have happened.

As she was coming upon the Mulligan Grocery, she heard raised voices from within. Clover began walking slowly, stopping below the steps and to one side of the door so they couldn't see her.

Mrs. Taverty and Mr. Mulligan were talking.

"It has to have been her," said Mrs. Taverty. "Lured him into the forest before he could get back to town."

Mr. Mulligan grunted. "She's only half-fae, you don't know she's capable of such magics. Best not go stirring up trouble with the good doctor—if he says it was her, then it was. Until then..."

"So there will be no search? My husband wants to organize one. You can't just expect us to leave Marvin Hallows to the fae, those..." Mrs. Taverty struggled for a moment to find just the right word. "Beasts."

"Father Taverty is free to do so, but don't expect any participation from me, ma'am."

Clover stopped listening. So Marvin Hallows had gone missing. He had a sister if Clover remembered properly. Abigail? Anna? Something like that. Marvin was a nice enough gentleman, which was unusual. He'd been discharged from the manor, healthy and strong only a day and a half earlier. His skin had gone extremely gray during the fever, some of his blond hair had fallen out, causing it to thin slightly, and he hadn't coughed up any blood, but he'd survived. Usually, Clover was sent to call a cart for patients returning to town—many of them didn't prefer to walk the road so close to the forest. But he'd insisted on walking, saving her a trip with what could have been kindness, though she couldn't be sure. And now he'd gone missing.

"There'll be no need of *your* help. The Justice Riders have already been sent for," said Mrs. Taverty, who was no doubt sticking her nose in the air.

At the mention of the Justice Riders, or as Soleil had called them, Veiled Ones, Clover's teeth began to chatter. The cold swirled in her chest as the wind picked up, blowing dead leaves around her boots. She knew she had no reason to be afraid— she'd done nothing wrong. And even if they suspected her of anything, Grant would testify to her innocence. The wind died down.

"Get the groceries and leave. That's all. Just get them and leave," she whispered to herself before smoothing out her features and going up the steps to the door. It opened, ringing a bell over her head.

Mrs. Taverty and Mr. Mulligan stared at her.

"Speak, creature," said Taverty, lifting her nose in the air and straightening her iron spine. "Your lingering presence is unholy."

Clover imagined her face as still as wood. "Order for Van Doren Estate."

"You just wait outside, now. I'll get it for you," said Mr. Mulligan. This was new but expected and Clover went outside the door, leaning on the side of the building.

"Van Doren has kept that girl in check. Her corrupt blood is long subdued."

"Don't be so sure," said Taverty. "Marvin Hallows didn't just vanish into thin air. He was taken. By others like her."

Clover wished she'd brought Grant to town with her. She doubted he could fend all of them off, but they might be less inclined to kill her or attack her outright.

Mulligan made an indeterminate reply. "Van Doren has put that girl in her place. We don't have to worry about her."

Mulligan came out with a stack of boxes which he held out for her. Clover took the boxes and nearly tipped over. They were heavy with food, so she would have to be careful. The clock began chiming and Clover turned her steps toward the western gate.

A HARSH WIND BLEW THROUGH VERITAS, BRINGING WITH IT the smell of the forest. A fetid yawn of dying life as the forest readied itself for winter...but there was something else. Something metallic, like blood. Clover's stomach turned on her way to the gate.

She saw a few boys in their twenties making their way to the gate as well. It was open and moving ever so slightly because of the wind. There were three boys in all, and Clover knew them. Gerard and Walter Vale were twins and the last was Benjamin Freeman. They had been friends with Marvin Hallows. She quickened her pace and so did the boys. Benjamin, the leader of their group, closed the gate and she nearly crashed into him.

She took a few steps back, saying nothing. Fear clenched her throat and seized the words on her tongue. What could she say? *Get out of my way* was far too antagonistic, and *what do you want?* invited conversation, but it seemed they were going to have one anyway.

"We have a few questions for you," Benjamin said. His curly red hair blew around in the wind, making him look insane.

Clover gritted her teeth, staring hard into his red-rimmed blue eyes. "What happened to Marvin?"

"How would I know that?" asked Clover.

Walter and Gerard crossed their arms but only Walter spoke. "We know you lured him into the forest."

"I did no such thing," she said.

Gerard reached forward and grabbed the boxes, while Benjamin held out a hand for calm.

"Easy, boys. Those are on their way to the doctor. No reason to be putting him ill." Benjamin then stood far too close to her. He was big, bigger than Grant, and he could probably pick her up and throw her if he wanted.

"I don't know where Marvin Hallows is." She forced her voice to be steady.

Benjamin smiled. "Now you see boys, here's the trick of the *half*-fae. Full-fledged fae can't lie...but you're not full-fae, are you? Which means she might very well be capable of lying."

"I'm not lying," said Clover.

The scent coming off Benjamin was pure anger. Woodsmoke, acrid and burning in her nostrils, flooding her lungs and mind. It stung her eyes as the iron did her skin.

She struggled for focus. "I don't know what happened to him."

"That doesn't mean you had nothing to do with his disappearance." Benjamin held up a finger. "If she can't lie, she'll try to wrap around the truth with vagueness."

"I had nothing to do with the disappearance of Marvin Hallows." She stepped forward. The boys moved back to keep away from her. "I did not give him to the fae. I did not lure him into the forest. I did not ever use any magic on Marvin Hallows."

Gerard looked at Benjamin. "What do we do now?"

"Now we try a new method." Benjamin looked her up and down, the way you might study a strange weed you've never seen before in your garden right before you rip it out of the ground.

Walter shoved her from behind and Benjamin spun her

and held her as she kicked out toward the twins. Benjamin dragged her back to the gate, and she didn't bother screaming for help because she knew no one would come to her aid. Clover's perspective was turned around and now she faced the iron bars of the gate and she knew where this was going.

"No!" she shouted, kicking her feet out, and they clanged against the iron. Clover breathed hard, her throat tight, forcing whimpers out with every exhale. She couldn't stop the boys, not with physical strength and definitely not with magic. She shouted in fear, but no one would help her. Clover was on her own.

Benjamin knocked her legs down while still holding her and he pushed her forward. Instinctively her hands came out and pressed, sizzling, to the bars. She screamed, using all her strength to push back against Benjamin, who forced her even closer to the gate.

"Did you give Marvin to the fae?" he demanded.

Clover blinked tears from her eyes. "I didn't!" Her fingers glowed red against the iron and despite her answer, he pushed her closer. Her cheek pressed against the iron and another throat-ripping shriek of pain burst from her. The iron began to burn her through the front of her dress as well.

"What is going on—by the Grey!" shouted another voice.

Clover sobbed, trying to get away from the iron that now burned her chest and seemed to be pulling the very air from her lungs. Her teeth clenched so hard her jaw began to ache.

"Did you give Marvin to the fae!?" Benjamin demanded, pulling her off the bars.

Clover took the moment of relief to breathe and answered by shaking her head.

"All right, that's enough, Benjamin," said the same voice that shouted earlier. The nasal tenor told Clover that it was

Constable Gennady, the leader of law enforcement. Actually, he was the *only* law enforcement in Veritas. He was a gangly man with a mustache too big for his face, similar to his ears. "Let her go."

Clover's legs failed her as Benjamin let her go and so her body hit the hard dirt in front of the west gate leaving Veritas. Her body shook uncontrollably from the shock and pain. The fear was gone and the unnatural wrath that took its place scared her. Give her true magic and she could destroy. Give her a weapon and she could kill.

"Those for Van Doren?" asked Constable Gennady.

"Yes, sir, they are," said Gerard.

Clover lifted her head, and when her eyes met Constable Gennady's, he stepped back several paces. He nodded to the gate. "Walter, go on and leave them on the other side. Gently now."

That's it. That's all for the torture of an innocent girl. The cold swirling of magic grew in the center of her chest. Except that's not what had happened. It was the torture of a half-fae, an unholy creature. Subdued. Put in her place. Nothing to worry about. Clover didn't know why she expected anything different. Every day of her life, the world taught her nothing but what she already knew. Most, if not all, humans were scum and Grant was the best of them. They didn't deserve him.

"Get on up, you. Out you go," said Constable Gennady.

Clover grunted. Using the last of her strength, she picked herself up and practically flung herself through the gate. It closed behind her and she didn't bother to turn.

"Hurry on home, get those supplies to Dr. Van Doren," Constable Gennady called through the gate, and it took every muscle in her body to keep the swelling cold threatening to break out of her from doing just that. Still the wind began to blow even harder until nearly every tree surrounding Veritas was stripped of its dying leaves.

Gennady and the three young men behind the gate gave her a look filled with fear and anger before scurrying off and out of the wind. A gentle humming started and Clover turned to the forest, where the boughs of the trees on the edge seemed to open as though ready to embrace her. Accept her. Comfort her. She swallowed sobs at the still-fading pain and picked up the heavy boxes for Dr. Van Doren. She couldn't take the forest's offer. There were other punishments she could still spare herself from and maybe another set of comforting arms to step into.

THE SMELL OF BLOOD STILL THREATENED TO MAKE HER SICK AS she stepped through the doors of the Van Doren Manor, but now there was something different, something in the air that she'd felt only once before. It was like something was grabbing at her clothing and hair and hands and pulling down toward the ground.

"Mother." Clover said it aloud rather than calling it, and she stumbled into the servants' quarters and through to the kitchen, where her mother was staring out the window into the front of the Van Doren property. Clover practically tossed the boxes down before going to her mother and touching her gently on the shoulder.

"Do you feel it?" asked Torryn.

Clover followed her mother's gaze but saw nothing before turning back to her.

"Feel what?"

Torryn closed her eyes. "If you don't feel the Breaking

now, you will soon." She placed her hand over Clover's. There were smears of blood on Torryn's hand.

"What—" Clover's question was cut off by the door to the kitchen opening.

Dr. Van Doren came in. Clover pulled her hand away from her mother's and she pressed her hands together before turning her eyes to the floor. "Is there something you need?"

"Obviously. I need you to come with me," he said.

Clover looked briefly at her mother's bloody hands before following the doctor out of the room without a word. He led her across the manor to the library. The library was a vast room filled with histories and medical information covering two walls. On the third wall was a large window facing east toward Veritas. But the view was not what captured Clover's attention.

Dozens of linen cloths drenched with blood laid in a pile on the floor. She stopped at the door and the doctor grabbed her wrist, yanking her into the room. "These rags need to be washed and hung out to dry. Your mother has already done the hard work."

"What happened?" Clover couldn't manage anything above a whisper. "Whose blood is that?"

For the first time since she was a child, she looked up and met the eyes of Dr. Van Doren. His steely gaze stared back at her, and for the briefest of moments, looked away. She knew then exactly whose blood this was.

ONCE, WHEN SHE WAS A CHILD, A MAGNIFICENT STORM HAD blown a large tree over and right onto that beautiful window facing the town of Veritas. It hadn't broken through instantly.

It struck hard, and over the next few minutes, jagged lines began streaking across the smooth, clear surface of the glass, making little *tick, tick, ticking* noises.

Clover heard this noise now, and she felt like those little jagged lines were etching their way across her chest. It wasn't the same kind of pain as the iron burning her skin, the kind that would fade. This pain was echoing like she was going to feel it every day for the rest of her life.

"Clean up this mess...while I mourn my son." Dr. Van Doren's voice came muffled from far, far away. From the same place where Clover's body began moving quite slowly. Clover's body picked up the blood-soaked rags and washed them one by one. Clover's body hung the clean white rags out to dry. Clover's body took the red water through the gate and dumped it into the forest. Clover's body somehow reconnected with Clover's soul.

Pain rushed through her and the shriek that tore from her burned away the forest she stood before. Stones cracked in half, wind threatened to tear up trees by their roots, and clouds darker than night rolled overhead and released torrents of water on the ground that Grant Van Doren would be buried in.

Chapter Five

"NOTHING WILL GROW HERE AGAIN." Soleil was on her hands and knees with her fingers digging into the dry, cracked soil where Clover had released her despair days before.

Clover was huddled nearby. "Grant can't be dead; I refuse to believe that he's gone."

Dr. Van Doren claimed that Grant had been up on one of the library's rolling ladders, mis-stepped, and fallen backward, where his head struck the edge of one of the tables. The initial trauma had killed him. There was nothing Dr. Van Doren could do.

Emotionally calmed days past the event, Clover now had space to think, and she sensed lies.

"Why do you think differently? You saw the blood…that is another reason life has died here," said Soleil. Her tone was bitter and though Clover was distraught, she was sorry for what she'd created. A cool breeze swept over them, and the tree Clover was leaning against whispered gently. The effect was soothing.

"I don't know," said Clover. "A feeling."

"Feelings are powerful."

"I know—"

"When they're real," Soleil interrupted. "You felt the pulling, death was close."

"But that doesn't mean death was there!" Clover argued a little too loudly. In the bright moonlight, Clover saw the disapproving look Soleil was giving her. "Sorry."

Soleil turned back to the ground, scooping some of the dry dirt into a pouch at her side. The few braids in her long, flowing hair swayed with the same motions as the trees.

"If you don't see, then look. If you don't hear, make a sound. If you don't feel anything, then it's better to feel pain," said Soleil. "Old fae proverb. If you don't think he's dead, then find his body and figure it out."

"Van Doren says it doesn't concern me. He won't let me," said Clover. She could see that her friend was becoming increasingly annoyed. The world beyond the forest scared Soleil and she didn't like to focus on it for too long.

"You will never love again. I feel it in you." Her words were both comforting and not at all. "Though this was powerful, it was not the Breaking."

"What is the Breaking?" Clover looked up at the moon. "My mother said something about it."

"The Breaking is why she is the way she is," said Soleil. "When a fae loves, their two souls become connected. Were one of them to die—the connection is broken and with it goes much of one's self."

Clover pressed her fingertips hard into her forehead, trying to smooth away a forming headache. "Well, I'm still here... doesn't that mean he's alive?"

"Perhaps."

"Perhaps?" Clover resisted the urge to glare directly at her.

"You're still part human," Soleil said gently.

Clover closed her eyes hard, shaking her head. Grant was alive, Clover just had to find him—but if she was wrong, she was doomed to a life of loneliness.

Soleil came over and Clover stood and leaned forward so Soleil could press her forehead to Clover's. The fae believed that everything was connected, and physical touch was a large part of that: the connections between living things. In Clover's mind, this simple gesture was the best way Soleil knew how to tell Clover that she felt Clover's pain.

They pulled away from each other, but Soleil kept one hand on Clover's shoulder. "Find the body. Find the truth."

Clover put her hands on Soleil's shoulders and gave her a grateful smile. Dr. Van Doren would never let her see the body, but maybe that meant she would just have to do it without him. She wanted Grant to be alive, but even if he wasn't, she had to see his body for herself or she would never accept that he was gone. Clover could never move on, but at least she would be sure.

A horse shrieked in the distance and the two of them looked up. A cloud suddenly overshadowed the moon.

"What was that?" asked Clover, turning.

Soleil frowned. "There is danger close by."

"Is someone in trouble? A human? Maybe we could help them," said Clover. She didn't particularly want to help any human—but if more were taken like Marvin Hallows, then the Justice Riders would surely come.

Clover pressed silently through the forest without waiting

for Soleil's response. The forest moved aside as the two moved through it in the direction the sound had come from.

It wasn't that far away, but Soleil soon stopped Clover, preventing her from moving forward. "Wait. You don't know what's ahead."

The forest was darker now for the lack of moon, but through the trees ahead, Clover could see the flicker of fire. She smelled fear and hatred so strongly it made her eyes water. She was glad Soleil had stopped her. Horses whinnied and stomped around nervously as men's voices rose and fell.

"What do you suggest?" Clover spoke through the sleeved arm over her face.

Soleil looked around but a fluttering upward caught both their eyes. A white bird with feathers like leaves and flower petals flew from a high bough. Soleil scuttled upward and Clover followed her. Higher into the trees they went and closer to the flames, until they saw the whole area, a clearing of sorts.

"Veiled Ones." Soleil bared her teeth. Slowly, she moved the branches and their leaves closer around them, so they were completely hidden.

Clover frowned. "What are they doing?"

"Just watch."

So, Clover did. In the clearing below, she could see the Justice Riders moving about. Their silver horse-head badges winked in the firelight, their wide silver eyes watching the two hidden fae while the men remained oblivious to their presence. The Riders roamed around something in the middle of the clearing that Clover couldn't see. Each of the Riders held a crossbow and she knew they were iron-tipped. fae hunters, through and through.

Finally, the crowd of Riders parted enough for her to see what was in the middle of the clearing. It was another fae—

Clover could see her brilliant green eyes wide with fear, her hair in tight coils framing her face. She was bound in iron shackles around her wrists and ankles. A pulley of sorts had her strung up by her wrist shackles, her feet could not touch the ground.

"What are they doing to her?"

Soleil shuddered. "It depends on what she's done, if she's done anything at all."

A very official-looking man parted the Riders to stand before the captured fae. He grabbed her chin in his hand and forced her to look at him. She bore her sharp teeth in a rabid hiss, and he laughed.

"All you creatures are alike. We create peace only for you to undo it." He stalked around her. "We seek advancement, to make the world shine while your kind would drive us back to the earth, wallowing in mud huts, huddled around a pit fire."

"Your seeking will rid the earth of all life," said the captured fae.

"This was no argument," hissed the official man in her face. "I speak only truth, while you turn your falsehoods to your liking just so they can leave your mouth."

She tried to strike out at him with her bound feet but he easily stepped away. "Do what you will to me. I do not fear death."

"Good," said the official man. "Because your bounty said dead or alive." He waved one hand in the air, which seemed to be a signal to the other men, who lined up at the edge of the clearing while facing her. Each of them took up their crossbows.

Clover was breathing hard. "Can't we do something? Can't we save her?"

"There is nothing we could do for her that wouldn't end in

our own deaths."

"I can't watch."

"You must," said Soleil. "I want you to see what all humans are capable of."

The Rider in charge began to count down. Clover tried to look away but Soleil pushed her face back toward the captured fae. At the end of the countdown, all the Justice Riders fired their crossbows at once. The arrows flew with small sharp sounds but struck the fae girl with sickening wet thuds. She didn't even cry out as Clover's whole body tensed. The captured fae's body shuddered as she coughed up a mouthful of blood. She said nothing but all beings present watched until she let out one final slow breath.

The Justice Rider leader strode toward her and lifted her head by the crown of her hair. He seemed convinced she was dead, so they dropped her off the pulley and she landed on the forest floor in a heap. They dismantled the pulley that held her up and set the pieces of it on the back of a cart along with her chains but left their arrows in her body.

THE LAST OF THEIR HORSES' HOOFBEATS AND THE SAVAGE whooping of the Justice Riders faded into the distance. Neither Clover nor Soleil moved. The moon came out again and that seemed to be a signal to Soleil.

"Stay here," she said.

Clover frowned. "But what about—"

"Ah!" Soleil cut her off. "Stay, and keep watching."

So Clover stayed where she was and she watched Soleil slowly crept forward. Her head swiveled, listening for any sign that something was approaching. When she finally got to the body, she straightened it out and pulled out each and every one of the arrows. Clover wasn't sure what Soleil was doing exactly. She felt sick, but she also felt that whatever Soleil was doing must be right. The fae couldn't just be left there like that —surely the forest would do something.

When the last of the arrows were out, Soleil kept them clutched in her hand, dripping blood down her arm as she moved away. Soleil gestured for Clover, so she dropped out of the tree and brushed herself off.

A groaning turned her attention back toward the murdered fae. The sound came from an oak tree, its branches and roots reaching toward her. They wrapped themselves around the fae like a cocoon. Clover began to cry as the trunk of the tree pulled apart like a curtain and the fae was lovingly tucked inside. It looked like she was just sleeping now as the oak trunk closed around her. The roots and boughs of the trees went back to their natural resting positions and all was quiet, as though the Justice Riders never came at all.

"The forest takes care of its own," said Soleil. "But even it has learned not to fight back against the humans."

Clover thought about the marshlands, which were once as vibrant and beautiful as the scene before her.

"You must find the one you love. I understand. But don't waste your efforts on the rest of them. They've only ever proven themselves unworthy."

Clover wiped her eyes. "I have to get back."

"Just as well. I think I'd like to be alone," said Soleil, but still she turned and pulled Clover into a tight embrace. "Be careful. Please."

"I will," said Clover. "I'll find Grant and we'll leave that place forever." She let her friend go and a fresh wind blew through the forest.

Chapter Six

FINDING GRANT WAS FAR EASIER SAID than done. Clover knew Van Doren Manor like the back of her hand and Grant's body was nowhere to be found. She couldn't risk asking the doctor where he was. It would only end in her own pain.

"Perhaps he's not in the manor at all," said Clover as she ate dinner with her mother. The funeral was drawing close. Three more days and the coffin would be shut forever with iron nails—to prevent fae from stealing the dead. Why on earth humans thought that fae would want dead humans was beyond Clover. She had three more days to see Grant's body if he was truly dead.

"Not at all," said Torryn, and she kept repeating it until Clover put her hand over her mother's hand.

Clover took a deep breath, ready to be disappointed. "Mother, I need you to think back to the day Grant fell."

"Fell...fell like felled trees," said her mother. "Grant's gone."

"Did you see him fall?"

"Silence. Darkness." Torryn put her hands over her eyes. She wasn't in distress; it was more like she was showing something.

Clover tried again. "Did you see Grant's body?"

"Grant…such a playful boy. Playing hide and seek. Always wanting to play hide and seek," she said.

Clover rubbed her knuckles over her tired eyes. She remembered that about Grant, too. Hide and seek was his favorite game. When they were young, he would always hide because the punishment for being found was savage pinching. As they got older, it became tickling, then chasing, and it eventually turned to kissing.

Clover let a sniffling sob break from her before she pushed away her food and laid her head in her arms. She felt her mother's gentle hand on the back of her head, but Clover could no longer be comforted by her mother. She hadn't been for a long time.

She picked her head up, wiping her eyes. "Are you finished eating?"

Torryn closed her eyes and began humming a lilting melody, so Clover took their dishes and emptied the remains of their food into the waste bucket before washing the dishes and taking her mother to bed.

If Grant wasn't in Van Doren Manor, then that meant he was already in town at the undertaker's, being prepared for burial. She couldn't get inside. The townspeople were already distrusting of her with Marvin Hallows' disappearance, and their fear of body-snatching fae was only going to make that more intense. But even the undertaker's building had windows. This was her last chance. All she needed was an excuse to go into town.

"YOU WISH TO GO INTO TOWN FOR A SEWING NEEDLE?" DR.
Van Doren was sitting at the breakfast table after Clover made
her request.

Clover nodded. "All of mine have either broken or worn
through. Our clothes need mending to survive another
season."

"Well, don't be so foolish, get more than one," he said.
"And make it quick. It's laundry day."

"Yes, Master Van Doren," said Clover before stepping
back from the table.

When breakfast was finished and everything was cleaned,
Clover made sure her mother ate before gathering her own
things and walking into town. This was a dangerous plan. If
she was caught snooping, she had no doubt the punishment
would be severe. The sound of the Justice Riders' arrows
sinking into the body of the fae girl the night before echoed in
Clover's mind and her whole body flinched as a chill ran from
the crown of her head to the soles of her feet. Not only had a
boy disappeared, but now another boy was dead, both with
connections to her, if by nothing other than proximity. That
was enough.

As soon as she stepped through the gates, a hush seemed to
hang in the air. All the curtains in the houses were black and
there were few people along the dirt roads. Sprigs of sage were
hung over doorways and ash was sprinkled around the houses.
A mixture of mourning and warding off Death, the reaper
that was believed to take whoever crossed its path.

The smell of sage and ash was strong as Clover made directly
around the outer limits of the town so she could get to the eastern
side of Veritas, where Undertaker Hughes lived and worked. On

a normal day, peering out windows was a regular pastime in Veritas. Clover hoped that no one was bothering today.

Find the body. Find the truth.

Soleil's words echoed in Clover's mind, strengthening her resolve. She skirted around the edges of wooden fences and yards with small patches of dead grass and weak flowers and gardens. She made her way around the edge of the graveyard before arriving behind Undertaker Hughes' workplace. He had no fence, so it was easy for Clover to access his windows. She suddenly wished she'd gone at night, when she had the protection of darkness, but she'd never get through the closed gate, and she would have no light to see by. The curtains were drawn save for a sliver where she could see vague images that took some moments to decipher. This was some sort of kitchen scene, not what she was looking for.

Clover tiptoed to the next window, checking her surroundings thoroughly. The only way for someone to see her now would be for them to come around the back of the house. The next window was in a hallway. The one after that was finally a workspace.

Hughes himself was moving slowly about inside. He wasn't an old man, but he had an eerily slow way of moving that made him seem like he was ready for a grave himself. It disturbed Clover greatly. She turned the other direction whenever she saw him slowly walking toward her in town.

His back was to her. He hunched over a table where he pulled a sleeve onto a stiff and lifeless arm. A body! But was it Grant?

Clover stepped this way and that, but she couldn't see the body's face. The curtains were drawn too close. On the other side of the window, a summer-door's top half was open. She focused hard, calling on the wind to blow this object from her path, just to make it sway ever so slightly, but she might have been overzealous. The door slammed open, completely shocking Hughes—who Clover had never seen move so quickly—so that he jumped up to close it.

But in those few precious moments, the curtains moved aside, and she saw the lower half of the body on the table. Clearly male. He could be tall like Grant with a similar figure, but—

Loud voices came from around the side of the house.- Clover quickly stepped away from the window and rushed to the opposite corner of the house. With the smell of rotting metal and ash wafting constantly through the air of Veritas, she had no doubt that any punishment served could very well end in death.

❧

CLOVER RUSHED AROUND THE CORNER OF THE DARK STONE house just as Benjamin and the Vale twins came around the other side. They stopped in the middle of the lane behind Hughes' house.

"I'm telling you; Fanny Logan hardly leaves her house— there's no way she wasn't lured into the forest by some magic," said Gerard, and Clover slowed her breathing.

Another one missing? She scoured her mind for recognition of the name. Logan, Logan…yes! She was about two years younger than Clover, and she'd been lured into the forest? There must be a dark fae about. Clover was somewhat relieved that there was no obvious connection between her and another missing person.

Benjamin was looking around and his eyes landed on the edge of the house as Clover ducked out of sight.

Gerard went on. "Her house is close to the gate, and she's always got her window open. Those Justice Riders should have gutted that fae slave as soon as they got here, before it had a chance to—"

"Oi, shut up. Did you see that?" asked Benjamin.

There was a moment of silence before Walter replied, "See what?"

Slow steps came toward Clover.

"A little gray skirt rushing out of sight."

Didn't anything escape him? Clover was about to find out.

"Are you still on about that dirty-blooded waif?" asked Gerard.

Clover quietly slipped down the wide alley between Undertaker Hughes' and Mr. Holliday's houses. As she rounded in front of Holliday's house, she heard the footsteps of Benjamin moving faster and heavier. He was running, so she began running, too.

She ran around the side of Holliday's house until she saw a few bales of hay in the alley between his house and the Logans' house. Clover climbed onto them and slipped in through a high window before dropping into an empty horse stall.

The horse in the next stall turned her head and gave Clover a look that said, "Well, I didn't expect to see you here." The horse seemed to think Clover's business was her own and turned back to her feed while Clover sat very still.

Benjamin's steps came not long after, followed by the huffing and puffing of the Vale brothers.

"Where did she go?" asked Benjamin. "She couldn't have just vanished."

"Are you sure she couldn't?" asked Gerard.

There was a flesh-pounding sound followed by Benjamin's voice. "Don't be such an idiot. Only full fae can produce illusions."

"You sure do know a lot about those folks..." said Walter.

"In the bigger cities, they know everything there is to know about the fae. The scientists catch them. Young ones, old ones, and ask them questions. The fae can't lie...when you hurt them enough, they don't want to. Then when the scientists are done questioning them, they cut them open. Study what makes them so special. That's what I want to do."

"Have to catch her first," said Gerard.

Benjamin growled. "I know that, fool. She got away...this time."

Clover listened to the three of them leaving. They wanted to capture her, torture her, and cut her open. She always knew the people hated her, but this? This was something else. Her stomach turned with fear and hairs stood up all over her body, a chill she couldn't shake. She didn't want to move but she couldn't stay in this horse stall forever.

Her bones were weighed down with fear, but she forced herself to the door of the barn. The coast was clear as far as she could see. She skirted the edge of Veritas before deciding against Mulligan's Grocery altogether and leaving Veritas entirely. The main gates were open, letting a carriage through, and she rushed out with more questions than she came in with.

ON HER WAY HOME, SHE REHEARSED HER LIES UNTIL THEY felt natural and the itch and stiffness that came with them was gone. Grant could very well be that body on Hughes' table, but she still wasn't sure. She didn't know of anyone else dying recently, so that should be proof enough that it *was* Grant…but she couldn't shake the horrible feeling that he was still alive somewhere. Maybe, she thought, all this doubt was just part of the grieving process. She hoped it wouldn't end with the same fate that her mother suffered from.

Clover didn't bother going to Dr. Van Doren to see if he needed anything or to let him know she was back. She went about doing laundry, taking special care of Grant's clothing. One coat she set aside entirely; his scent still clung to it: a mixture of honey-scented soap and the spice of the substance Grant used to tame his curly hair.

When she was finished with the laundry, she took the coat back to Grant's room. It was the last room on the second floor on the eastern-facing side of the manor. Clover draped the coat over the back of his desk chair.

He hadn't made his bed that morning, and the book he'd probably fallen asleep reading was open, spine up, in his sheets. Clover picked it up, but she couldn't read many of the words. Her heart sank further. No more reading and writing lessons. Soon all of these things would be gone.

Humans believed that once a person was dead, their souls had moved on into the Grey, and that holding onto anything other than a single item that the person valued while alive was not only unholy but would cause the person to be punished in the afterlife. There was a greater chance that they would come back and haunt you, and that you would die shortly after they did. They called it the Cleansing.

Clover thought this was a terrible way to view the dead. She hated the nature of the Grey—it gave humans an excuse to devalue all life. In essence, it was the origin of their hate for the fae.

Her eyes welled. A single item. A fragment of Grant's life to be placed on a shelf. Everything else would be sold or burned, and for what? Ridiculous superstition. Clover felt sick. She slowly sank to the ground, keeping her head and arms draped over the side of Grant's bed. It still smelled of him too.

Not a minute later, she heard steps coming down the hall. Clover quickly got to her feet and pretended to be making the bed.

"What are you doing wasting time in here?" Dr. Van Doren demanded.

Clover turned. "I thought I would straighten up, make it easier to sort things for the Cleansing."

"There will be no Cleansing, you stupid girl. Out," he commanded.

Clover quickly left the room, but he grabbed her by the wrist while she was in the hall. "You are not to go into this room again. Understand?"

"Yes, Master Van Doren," she said looking at the ground.

He didn't let her go and she grimaced at the pain. "You think I didn't know what was going on? You seduced my son, turned his mind, and now he's gone."

Lies. They smelled bitter, like rotting fruit, and that scent filled the air now.

"You're lying." Clover turned her face up to look into his eyes. The ferocious anger she had felt before returned, but she regretted it instantly. Van Doren slapped her hard across the face, but it was strong enough to feel like a punch. She stumbled backward, her head bouncing painfully off the hardwood floor.

"You dare speak to me in such a manner!?" he shouted.

He reeled his foot back and kicked her hard. The blow landed on her right hip; she was glad it wasn't her ribs but it still stung.

"Continue to anger me and I'll make an example of you! The citizens of Veritas will do more than send you dirty looks if they find out how you bewitched my son—turned him against me. Your mother escaped judgement once. I doubt she'll be so lucky again. I'd have done it already. Unfortunately, I still find myself in need of you, but that won't last forever. When I'm through with you, my son can finally...final...I..."

Dr. Van Doren took a deep breath and calmed himself while Clover continued to lay on the floor. "Get back to work," he said through his teeth before kicking her out of his way as his shiny black boots stalked past her nose and down the hall.

Dr. Van Doren could have been about to say anything. *My son can finally rest. My son can finally be at peace. My son can finally be free of the fae.* But Clover knew that Dr. Van Doren was going to say: *My son can finally return.* Body or no body, Clover knew. If nothing else, Grant was his pride, and Van Doren would never kill his pride. And if he had wanted to say any number of other things, he would have just outright said them.

But his victorious speech hesitated because Dr. Van Doren had everything to hide. That he had—either by accident or on purpose—nearly killed his son, and tomorrow, Grant Van Doren's coffin would be buried empty. Clover didn't know where Grant was, but he was out there, and he was alive.

Chapter Seven

THE GATE SURROUNDING the town slammed in Clover's bruised face. On the other side, Dr. Van Doren pointed a finger at her.

"Stay back, creature. My son's life was tainted by your presence. I'll not have his death be the same," he said before walking away.

Once he was gone, Clover's anger boiled over and she slammed her hands against the iron gate, making the metal sing and her palms sting. Her mother, who stood behind her, pulled at the back of Clover's black cloak. Clover turned and took her mother's hands before getting an idea.

"Come on, Mother. Follow me," she said before walking around the outside of the town. It would be a long walk to the other side of Veritas, but worth it if she could see the funeral. They trudged across muddy marshland, staying close to the iron fence.

It was said that this land was once part of the forest, that the fae kingdom of Thea Serin once stretched as far as the eye could see. Human interference had shrunk the kingdom to a shadow of its former self. At least that's how Soleil described it. Now the land was marsh, all mud and dead trees and weeds. It was dangerous to venture too far out into them because there were sink-holes, but Clover was sure that if she and her mother stuck to the iron fence, they would be fine.

Clover had Torryn hold the bars to steady herself but it made their journey longer. By the time they arrived at the far side of Veritas, the funeral was nearly over. It looked as though the whole town was there in their mourning black. Wandering around the perimeter of the fence were men in black suits with a single row of silver buttons. Justice Riders. A silver upside-down triangle with a horse's head in the center adorned the upper arm of their coats.

The townsfolk began saying the final blessing over Grant's coffin before they lowered him down. It echoed over the flat-land and sounded as though they were right beside her.

FIND YOUR WAY
Into The Grey
May your path be true
May your feet never stray
No more speaking,
No more sound
As you lie
Beneath the ground
May your slumber be deep
May you never again weep
As you find your way
Into The Grey

. . .

CLOVER FELT HER STOMACH TURN OVER. AS THE PEOPLE chanted, she knew they lowered an empty coffin into Grant's grave. But it was the chant that made her sick. The idea of being buried in a box, cut off from the earth even in death and melding forever into some sort of gray void made her breathing come short and her throat clench. She turned and threw up into the marshes.

᠁

WHEN SHE WAS FINISHED RETCHING, SHE WENT OVER TO HER mother, who was sitting against the iron gate. Clover sat, putting her head in her mother's lap and wiping her mouth on her mother's apron. This was an unfathomable emptiness. Somewhere deep down, Clover knew this was the true cruelty: that she should lose Grant and have nothing but the hard earth to fall on, forced to rise, time and time again for her mother, who would never truly be there for her ever again.

"Empty, empty...do you still feel ill?" her mother asked.

Clover sighed. "I'm not ill. Just sickened. It's different, I suppose."

"A wedding. There's going to be a wedding," said Torryn.

Clover's face twisted in anguish at the mention of a wedding. She would have had one. It would have been private, secretive, even. But what did it matter if it was just them and the moon? Grant wasn't dead but he was still gone, and she had no idea how to get him back.

"Not anymore, Mother." Clover wiped her eyes on her mother. "No wedding."

Torryn shuddered. "That's what the doctor said."

"What?" Clover had been too busy trying to swallow the lump in her throat to comprehend her mother's words at first but now she sat up and faced her mother. "What did the doctor say?"

"No wedding," said Torryn.

Clover grabbed her mother's shoulders, struggling to be gentle. "You told Dr. Van Doren Grant and I were going to be married?"

Torryn put her hands over her mouth. It was a childish gesture, but that's exactly what her mother was. A child.

Clover gripped hard at her mother's dress. A wave of despair washed over her, dark as night. This was the person who was supposed to protect her, to shield her from the evil— from Dr. Van Doren. Instead, it was Clover who stood in the fray between her mother and the evil, and now this? Not only was her mother a danger to herself but now to Clover as well. Clover wanted it to stop. She just wanted everything to stop but it wouldn't. The darkness would keep crashing against her. It didn't matter if she was on her feet, or flat on the ground.

Clover closed her eyes and leaned her head forward until it rested against her mother's shoulder. Torryn leaned her head against Clover's, but otherwise made no motion to comfort her. Clover sobbed, waiting for a comfort that might never come.

THAT NIGHT, CLOVER STEPPED CAREFULLY INTO THE FOREST. Pale blue dragonflies fluttered around her as she walked. As it got colder, they would curl up along with the flowers when they made their way underground. She was able to walk without trying too hard to find her way. The place she was visiting was a place she'd been hundreds of times before, but the first time she'd gone there was the most important.

In the middle of a small pond rested a slanted hill steeper on one side than the other. In order to get to it, there was a single steppingstone. She hopped to it with ease before springing onto the small hill.

The night was clear, so she could see all the stars, just like the night she and Grant first came here, when he kissed her for the first time. It was a strange memory, having been kissed, then shaking it off as though nothing happened. It wasn't until much later that she realized Grant held affections for her. The idea made her want to laugh now, but she didn't. She could hardly cry anymore after what she found out at Grant's funeral.

Clover took a deep breath and ran her hands through the grass under her. The air was getting colder as the night went on, but she barely felt it. Here she somehow felt closer to Grant than she had since he'd gone. She never wanted to leave this place…but what would happen to her mother? And if Dr. Van Doren sent the Justice Riders after her, she'd either be taken back alive and clinging to life or heinously murdered. This left her only with the option of returning to Van Doren, but he wouldn't need her until morning. She had all night to stay here and wish that she could go back in time. She would rather hide for the rest of her life than for this—for Grant to be gone and for her to be alone for the rest of her life.

Movement to her left caught her eye, and when she turned, there was a midnight-black stag drinking from the small pond, making glowing ripples across the water that distorted the reflected stars.

The stag looked up at her, and with every blink, its eyes seemed to change colors. It was…beautiful. Clover blinked a few remaining tears out of her eyes before looking back at the stars.

IN THE MORNING, CLOVER SCRUBBED THE FLOOR OF A PATIENT room until her hands were raw. Just how far would Dr. Van Doren go to keep his son from marrying a girl with tainted blood? Days had passed since the false funeral. Clover had been over the manor a hundred times and found no place where he could be hidden. Soleil said she would know if Grant's body was somewhere in the woods. The fae were aware of all things living, and the fae were everywhere. If there was a human boy in the woods, they would have come across him by now.

As Clover scrubbed, she heard breaking glass in another one of the rooms. The season of Grey Fever was starting. The patient who recently left Clover's room had nearly died, though Clover couldn't remember her name. She was a young woman whose fever had run hot enough to heat the room itself. Clover could feel her pain from across the house and was glad once the girl was gone.

In the other room, there came a few barking words from Dr. Van Doren but no other sounds. He never beat Clover or her mother in front of his patients. Not that it would matter, since the patients of Veritas would have considered it an entertaining show—but the doctor wanted to give his patients the idea that he was not a rough man. That's what he'd said to Grant.

"Your assistants are ignorant creatures. They're bound to mess things up in one way or another. If you must beat them, don't do it in front of a patient. They don't like it when the hands that heal are also the hands that hurt."

Then why do it at all? Clover had wondered.

Now she stood to see if the doctor required any help.

Instead, she found her mother outside the room. Her hands were up like she was holding something, fingers clenched and shaking. Torryn herself showed no signs of pain in her blank stare. Clover tried to get her mother's hands to relax but they wouldn't. They were like stone.

"Mother, unclench your hands," said Clover.

Torryn's face twisted and her eyes closed hard. Her hands shook but still they didn't open. Clover held her mother under the elbows and guided her into the kitchen before rushing back to the room where the doctor was working.

She knocked. "Dr. Van Doren, my mother is unwell. Do you need any assistance?"

"Go away," he barked, and Clover shook her head before going back to her floor scrubbing.

Angela Hallows. That was the name of the girl who'd been in this room. Clover suddenly recognized the name from one of the doctor's endless list of names. Angela was Marvin Hallows' older sister. She had coughed up blood for three whole days and Clover could hardly clean the linens fast enough. Usually when that happened, the patient didn't recover. But Angela miraculously had. She was a pretty girl with straw-colored hair, bluebell eyes, and...shapely. She had even smiled at Clover. Smiled. It had frozen Clover in place like a statue of confusion and uncertainty. People in Veritas didn't smile at Clover—she wondered if they smiled at all. Soleil was thoughtful and her smiles were reserved for the purity of the forest. Torryn's smiles were echoes of memories long past, indirect and vague in nature. No one except Grant had ever smiled directly at Clover in years.

Clover chalked it up to some lingering fever daze. Now all she could think about was Grant's smile and she swallowed the lump in her throat until her throat was raw as she washed the single window.

❦

THE CLOTHS CAME OUT OF THE POT STEAMING ON THE END OF Clover's wooden spoon. She set them in a bowl and let them cool before picking them up and rinsing them out. When they were damp instead of sopping wet, she placed them around her mother's hands. Torryn sat at the wooden table in the kitchen, hands still clenched, tears streaming. The cloths seemed to bring instant relief and between dinner cooking activities, Clover continued replacing the cloths and massaging her mother's stiff joints.

Clover had never seen anything like this, and she'd never seen her mother with a physical ailment of this kind. Of course, she was occasionally beaten by the doctor and hurt in her wanderings, but this was different. Something had gone wrong on the inside that Clover couldn't see.

Finally, just before dinner, Torryn's hands came out of their locked position and she let out a breath, laying her head on the table.

If Grant were here, he could explain what this was. Clover could sneak into the library to try to read one of the hundreds of medical books but what would be the use? She didn't know half the words. Clover brought the fresh bread out of the ovens and a thought ran through her mind.

Medical books. Medical books? Is that why Grant was in the library? Clover couldn't recall what was on the shelves in the library where Grant had supposedly fallen. Perhaps something there could shed a little more light on the situation.

She placed the bread on a tray and brought it out to the

table right as Dr. Van Doren came into the room. Clover stepped away to stand with her hands behind her back. When was the last time Grant had gone to the library for medical books? His rooms were absolutely full of them. Was he looking for something new? And what was wrong with her mother? She couldn't keep helping Dr. Van Doren if her hands were damaged somehow.

Questions kept running through Clover's head as the dinner dragged on through the night.

　　　　　　　　　　　　🙢

IN THE MIDDLE OF DINNER, DR. VAN DOREN PUT DOWN HIS spoon and knife and sat with his hands folded on the edge of the table. Clover went forward to serve him in some way, but he held up a hand.

"I have an announcement to make. It does not require conversation, so I expect you to keep your tongue between your teeth."

Clover said nothing and stepped back. A ripple of fear radiated from her stomach to the tips of her fingers, sending pins and needles across her skin.

"Tomorrow morning, my nephew from Hirane will be arriving to take up Grant's training. He will be my apprentice, and as my son in his absence, you are to treat him as such. I will not let you seduce him as you did to Grant. Do you understand?"

"Yes, Master Van Doren," said Clover, but she was seething. As though she could ever love another! She didn't want this nephew to come, another Van Doren on her back.

A memory came to her of a time when she was serving a patient of the doctor's. She was a young girl, maybe twelve or thirteen. Moments before, Clover had been slapped out in the hallway. So, when she brought the girl her food, the patient took it upon herself to give Clover a slap as well.

Clover remembered stumbling back and looking at the girl in shock. There was a cruel sneer on her young face. It was the face of a person who tasted another's pain and liked it. Humans were all the same. Clover had wanted to grab the girl, to scold her, to demand why the child thought that was acceptable, or good, or right—but Clover hadn't. She already knew the answers to those questions. Once a person of reverence committed an act of good or bad, weren't all those under them permitted to do the same? So, the girl had tested her newfound ability on Clover and found it powerful indeed. And Clover did nothing, not even scowl. Now in the present, she could already see this new Van Doren doing the same, and she was less than pleased.

THE NEXT DAY, WALTER VALE WAS WAITING FOR CLOVER AT the entrance to Veritas. He stood on the other side of the gate, smirking with his arms crossed. Clover sighed before turning and walking straight into the forest. Walter's smile vanished.

"Hey!" he shouted, and Clover nearly laughed aloud. What was he going to do? Follow her inside? Only a fool would, even if there weren't already two people missing.

Once within the trees, the air seemed to push around Clover like a gentle hug before letting her go. She allowed herself a smile then. The forest was a friend to those who respected it, a benevolent giver to those who were loving and kind in return. Disrespect it? It called to the fae, its protectors.

The forest wouldn't punish you unless the fae called on it. Besides, the fae would do that work for it.

Clover was lucky to travel through the forest today. She wished she didn't have to go into town at all. This new Van Doren would never go into the forest, which unfortunately meant passing back through the town in order to get back to the manor. Would he deign to go into the forest, or would he be too afraid? She could take him through the marshes, but again he might not stand for it.

Her skin crawled at the thought of going through town and encountering Benjamin. She tried to think of something else. This new Van Doren, would he be like his uncle? Or would he be more like Grant? No. No one could be like Grant. He was one of a kind, he had loved her. Clover wondered if other humans had any love in them at all. If they did, she had certainly never seen it.

"There are good people in this world, Clover. You just haven't met them yet."

Grant's words stopped her cold and she felt out of breath. Clover bent over and leaned against a nearby tree. Her eyes burned and fogged, not just because his words had come back to her, but because she'd heard them. Spoken. Out loud, from somewhere right behind her. She didn't want to turn—afraid of what she might see.

"I feel strange. As though in a dream," he said.

Clover whipped around and there he was. "Grant?"

He was a lesser version of himself. There, but flickering as though the wind could blow him away. She could see through him like colored glass.

"Why do you look so surprised?" he asked with a grin.

Clover stood and stepped toward him, one hand outstretched.

"What are you doing?"

She said nothing but continued her path forward. When she was finally close enough to touch, her hand went right through him, and he watched it with a look of horror, taking a step back.

He reached up to touch his own chest. "Well, that's not normal."

"Oh Grant, please tell me you're not dead." Clover hovered her hands over his visage. "I know in my heart you're not but if I could hear it from you..."

He shook his head. "Why would I be dead?"

"Where are you then?" she asked, struggling to control her breathing as her throat closed with the growing urge to sob. "I can't find you."

"Can't find me?" He smiled. "But I'm right here." He reached for her hands, but they passed right through. "Albeit in some kind of incorporeal state." He looked at his hands but as he did, the vision of him began to flicker. "Clover?" he asked, and she reached for him before he faded entirely.

She took several deep, strained breaths. She must have been imagining the whole thing. This worried her, though she wished it had been real. It was so good to see his smile again—to hear his voice. Clover lowered herself to her knees and closed her eyes to savor the memory.

Grant had been wrong about humans, but so optimistic, so sure. Where was he? Was he hurt? Was he safe? Was he in another town? Was he trying to get back to her? Clover didn't know, but she knew he wasn't dead. In her heart, she knew he was alive, and she had to trust that feeling, or she would crack and crumble like the dirt under an unforgiving sun.

Gritting her teeth, she wiped her eyes and gathered herself. Just get Warner Van Doren and bring him back to the manor.

Moving through the forest bolstered her strength, and everything became more alive around her. The grass grew thicker, the trees groaned as they swayed, their roots snaking through the earth, connecting to each other in an eternal web. Once out of the forest, the world looked dull and gray in comparison.

A YOUNG MAN WAS LEANING AGAINST THE OUTSIDE OF THE gate, waiting. He was tall and looked strong with broad shoulders, his large hands busy flipping through what looked like papers. Unlike the traditional black, he was wearing city clothes, a fancy blue suit. Clover approached cautiously but his eyes flicked to her while she was still a way off. Before she turned her gaze to the ground, she noted Warner Van Doren's brown eyes, just like Grant's.

"Are you…Clover Grimaldi?" he asked, looking down at one of the papers.

Clover nodded. "Yes, Master Van Doren. I've come to accompany you back to the manor." There was silence and suddenly Warner was leaning down to try to be in her vision. She looked away again. Was he gawking at her?

"You got eyesight problems or something? What's with the master stuff?"

"Dr. Van Doren…" Clover's chest got tight, and her nostrils flared. "…owns me. I serve him. You're his family. I serve you, too."

Warner snorted. "I heard things were different out here, but jeez, I didn't think it would be this bad. Listen, none of that master stuff, I don't like it."

"Well, what would you have me call you?" she asked, a

little annoyed. Where were the iron hands? The harsh words? The cutting gazes?

Warner stuck out his hand. "People call me Knox."

"Knox?" Clover's gaze drifted upward to look into his brown eyes. The color was where the similarities stopped between Grant and Warner. There was a painting in Dr. Van Doren's room of some old, distant relative who Clover had forgotten the name of. But this distant relative had been a soldier in a war she'd also not remembered the purpose of. Point being, Warner had eyes like the soldier in the painting, like he'd seen terrible things, weary eyes that belonged to someone much older than the young man before her. Grant's eyes, though hardened by his father's abuse, still held some of the bashful innocence of youth. She so wanted to see them again, like she had in the forest moments before. Perhaps losing her mind would be worth it if she got to see Grant again.

"It's just a nickname," said Warner, or Knox rather, before running his hand through his blond hair. "Guess you don't shake hands around here, either."

Clover folded her hands in front of her. "Best if we don't touch, Master...Knox," she corrected herself. "It's considered unclean. And I will be referring to you as Master when the doctor is around, regardless of your feelings about it."

"I have a hard time believing Grant had you calling him Master," he said.

Clover looked back down at her shoes.

"My condolences."

Clover swallowed the lump in her throat. This man was not to be her friend. He was not to be anything except someone to serve. He was kind, but kindness could be worn out with time, and if she even considered him a friend, Dr.

Van Doren would hand both Torryn and herself readily to the people of Veritas. She wasn't about to let that happen.

"Save your condolences for the doctor. As a servant, my allotment of mourning time is long over."

"Right...shall we?" he asked, gesturing to the gate.

"We should go through the forest, it's safer," said Clover, scanning the streets of the town to see if the other Vale twin or Benjamin were waiting for her. She knew the chances of Knox saying yes were small, but it was worth a try.

Knox laughed, heading for the gate. "Please, I've lived in Hirane my whole life. You're either getting beat up or you're beating someone else up. I think I can handle some country folk." He opened it and stepped through without her.

She wanted to call out for him to come back, but she doubted he would listen. Instead, she frowned before catching up to him.

She could already tell Knox's ignorance was only going to end in her suffering.

Chapter Eight

Dr. Van Doren's fist came faster than Clover was ready for, and she didn't tense up in time. His blow connected powerfully with her midsection and the breath rushed out of her so quickly that she wasn't sure she'd be able to pull it back in. The ground rushed toward her as the world spun. The stone floor outside the room of the doctor's most recent patient connected painfully with Clover's head.

Breathe in! Breathe in! Clover's mind screamed at her lungs, but they refused to obey. Her body writhed on the ground, straightened out, hands grasping for some unseen force that would allow her to survive this moment.

Finally, Clover's lungs responded. She sucked in a breath but the pain that followed was enough to make it rush out again. At least she was breathing, horrible, ragged breaths, but at least she was alive.

"Don't ever question me in front of a patient," said Dr. Van Doren, standing over her. "Now get up and gather my instruments. I will not let your incompetence stop me from healing this child."

He walked away and every muscle in Clover's midsection tensed under the pain of moving, but she managed to get to her feet. Her lungs wheezed horribly as she moved, gathering a tray of instruments. Clover was spending more and more of her time as Dr. Van Doren's assistant. Today, Torryn's spine was stiff as a board and the woman walked nearly completely bent over. That simply wouldn't do for the doctor, so he'd locked her in her room. Now Clover was his assistant while her other duties went undone.

And of course, they were expected to be done.

Clover went into the room with the instruments, her breathing back to normal. The young man inside watched her every move as he coughed up bright-red blood. They were all coming in so sick. Clover wondered what made them this way.

Some harsh darkness invaded Clover's mind suddenly and she turned to find the source but there was nothing in the room. It was sharp, like a knife cutting down the center of her head. She turned away from the boy and gently touched her temple, trying not to cry out.

Dr. Van Doren came in, his expression calm. "All right, Theodore. Open up wide, I'm going to take a look into the back of your throat."

Clover stood still and tried not to show that the pain was making her vision go as red as the blood staining the cloth of Theodore's towel.

"Ah yes, I see. This is perfectly treatable. I'll have you out of here and back to Veritas in the next day or so," said Dr. Van Doren.

Clover was suddenly released from the pain, and she let out a long breath of relief. The darkness faded and she felt exhausted. Dr. Van Doren set his tongue compressor on Clover's tray and she straightened out of the leaning position she'd been in.

"You are dismissed to attend to your other duties," said the doctor.

Clover bowed. "Yes, Master Van Doren."

Clover set down the tray and left the room, rubbing exhaustion from her eyes with the heels of her hands. She had work to do, and she wasn't thinking about her household chores.

DUST FLEW THROUGH UNUSED ROOMS, DOOMED TO SETTLE back down again after Clover left. Her hands were rubbed raw before she even got around to hanging the damp pieces of laundry on their lines. Her hands were made even worse when she washed the windows, specifically the ones for Knox's room. She had never washed them before because it was a guest bedroom and they never had guests.

When she was finished cleaning, Clover cooked lunch, a simple soup with bread. With lunch out of the way, this was her chance to focus on what really needed her attention. Grant.

Clover took the doctor's lunch to his office, and he accepted it with a wave of his hand. Next, she took Knox his lunch. He was conveniently in the library today. He was supposed to be studying anatomy to become a doctor, but he was lying on the couch with his boots up on its arm.

He groaned when he saw her. "Thank the Grey, I was about to wander into your precious kitchen."

"Stay out of—"

Knox nodded. "I know, I know, stay out of the blasted kitchen." He laughed. "It's no trouble, I can get my own food."

"Of course you can, but this is my job." Clover took out a rag and began to wipe the tabletops and numerous busts and glass cases of books too old to be read unless you had the most gentle of hands.

"Your job? Are you getting paid?" he asked.

Clover scoffed. "Of course not, I'm a servant."

"No, you're a slave," said Knox. "Even servants get paid."

"Play with words all you like. It doesn't change the fact that I have work to do," she said, mostly ignoring him. She was eyeing the spot where Grant had supposedly died.

Knox went on. "Playing with words is my job. I'm a journalist, not a doctor. I shouldn't even be here. I was so close to getting inside that fae experiment laboratory in Hirane. At least that's what I believe it is. Do you know what a 'front' is?"

Clover didn't respond. She wasn't supposed to be speaking to Knox at all and she had to tread carefully. She did her best to be short with him, but she didn't see what the harm was in talking. She moved the rolling ladder over to where it had been when Grant fell. She climbed up and looked at each shelf. Plant biology books. Histories of medicines. Histories of illnesses. Infections caused by animals. Infections caused by magic. Infections caused by humans.

Maybe Grant would read some of these for whatever reason, but that's not what stood out to her most.

"What are you doing?" asked Knox as he came over to her. "Studying to be a doctor?"

Clover gripped the ladder tightly. "No. I can't read. This is where Grant fell to his death. He landed down there."

Knox leapt away from that area of the floor like it was

cursed. "By the Grey. What would you want to go up there for?"

"Nothing." She climbed down. "Nothing at all. Call me when you're finished eating, I'll be tending to my mother."

"A-all right. I will. Thank you," he said, still looking shaken.

Grant could have wanted to read any number of those books and he would have, but none of those books or their shelves had been touched. Her breathing had been the only thing to disturb their dust layers in years. Grant couldn't have been anywhere near that bookshelf.

Dr. Van Doren was lying.

CLOVER SNAPPED OUT OF HER HALF SLEEP. STRANDS OF HER hair had fallen from her bun and were dripping from being in the sink full of suds. She'd fallen asleep into the dishes, so she straightened her aching spine and washed more vigorously, finishing her chores for the day before she could fall asleep again.

Her head constantly throbbed, and she had been worked to the bone every night. Finding little clues like a lack of dust disturbances was less than encouraging. When she was finished with the dishes, she went into her room and began filling her washtub. She undid her hair and let it hang around her shoulders.

Clover could always tell the difference between when Grant was in a room and when he wasn't, even when she couldn't see him. It was like a sort of invisible tether connected them. She could pull on it and feel the tension of him pulling back—and though it was still taut, his ended in darkness that she couldn't see through. Grant was alive, but missing, and she had nothing to go on but mysterious circumstances, lies, and the tether with Grant's end shrouded in darkness. It wasn't enough. She wanted him back.

After washing, she changed into her nightgown and peered into her mother's room. She made sure her mother was sleeping peacefully before going into her own room. What she needed was time to search for him. He must be close by. She would start with the house, then work her way around Veritas. Perhaps someone in town was hiding him.

But first, she needed sleep. The pain that had exhausted her earlier made her more tired than usual. She didn't know where it had come from, but fortunately, it was gone now. Clover fell asleep before she was completely lying down.

She was no longer in her bed. She was in the forest, lying on the soft earth, but she didn't care because she was too tired to care. She was too tired to do anything...

"Too tired for a writing lesson?"

Clover's eyes flashed open at the sound of Grant's voice. He smiled down at her, holding the pen and the book. Her heart skipped a beat and her eyes misted. He was here, alive as though he'd never left. It must have all been some horrible dream: his death, and Benjamin, and her mother's failing health. A dream, all of it.

"Come on, Clover. I know you've been slacking, but you've got to learn this stuff. It's important." Grant stood and nodded for her to follow. He walked away and Clover struggled with a blanket of roots that had settled over her. They wrapped around her, trying to strangle her, and she fought to get them off. Her panic grew. Grant was leaving.

Finally, she kicked the roots off, but Grant was already far ahead.

"Grant?" she called once she was free. He became shrouded by a forest filled with life and she ran after him. Why was he going further into the forest? Shouldn't he be going to the tower?

"Grant, wait!"

She chased after his retreating form. She was already out of breath, as though she were running a great distance. Her mouth felt dry, her voice muffled. Why wasn't he hearing her?

As Clover hurried across the forest floor toward him, she almost grabbed his shoulder, but her feet stuck into the ground. She lifted her foot and heard the ripping of dead grass that trapped her. Grant slipped out of her grasp. Clover shouted with frustration.

"Let go of me!" She ripped her feet away from the grass, each step more arduous than the last, though Grant was always two steps ahead. "Grant, stop!"

But he didn't stop, and it became even worse. Branches pulled at her clothes, while their leaves cut her skin. Vines wrapped around her wrists and ankles and neck, slowing her down. Her breath came in short bursts as her heart raced. She couldn't let Grant get away again. He must be under some kind of spell.

The tiny tinkling of glass breaking sounded in her ears as the forest closed in farther around her and she couldn't move anymore. Grant walked out of sight into the forest, but she couldn't cry out. When she opened her mouth, dirt and dead leaves rushed in, choking her. Everything was dark. Her hands came up to push back against the nature trying to kill her, but she found the walls of her prison to be smooth dead wood. At the edges, iron nails burned her skin.

Clover was in a coffin. Grant's coffin. She screamed, the

same sort of scream that she had when she thought Grant was dead.

Burning, her whole body was burning. Clover scrambled out from under the thin blanket on her bed and onto the cold stone of the floor. She let it cool her skin as she tried to catch her breath and slow her pounding heart. It was just a dream but that didn't stop her from crying.

GULP AFTER GULP OF WATER, SOMETIMES ACCIDENTALLY TAKING in air, helped settle her nerves, like watering a plant that clearly hadn't been helped in days. Clover caught her breath, cooled off, and let the last of the dream wear off her skin before she felt something new. Sometimes, when she was a child, she would wander into the forest at random times. Soleil said the forest called to her, as it called to all fae. Full fae couldn't ignore it, and Clover felt it now and then, but it was often overwhelmed by other feelings, like fear or pain.

There was no ignoring it now. The forest wanted her to see something, and a restlessness burrowed into her skin, a painful pressure in her knees and spine. Clover didn't bother to put on a jacket or shoes or worry about being seen. The coolness of the grass brushing the bottom of her feet and the forest holding her like a loving embrace was a comfort after the nightmare of a forest that had turned on her.

Is that why the forest called her? Just to let her know it was still on her side? No, that wasn't it. And she was not alone.

"Soleil?" Clover peered through the darkness of the forest. Her legs were tickled by a small bush reaching out to touch her. The darkness seemed to shift, and Clover felt that presence, the one that had exhausted her. Her head throbbed with every beat of her heart, starting at the crown of her head, and driving downward. She shouted, holding the top of her head.

A laugh came and a figure stepped into the partial light provided by the moon. "Soleil, what a pretty name—though I don't belong to it."

"Clearly," said Clover, still wincing. "Who are you? What are you?"

"What am I? Don't be so rude. You and I are the same." He stepped closer. A set of lavender-colored eyes peered out from under a tattered black hood. "And we both want the same thing."

"I doubt that. You're a dark fae, aren't you? I can tell by your eyes." Clover let her hands down from holding the top of her head. The pain had faded to something more bearable. "We are not the same."

His hood came off, revealing a gaunt face. His skin was even darker than Soleil's, making his eyes stand out like purple stars.

"Oh yes we are." He grinned with sharp teeth. "We are exactly the same, both scorned by those who would claim to share our blood. Bitter over the death of a loved one. But that can all change…for you, at least."

"I'll tell you my name if you tell me yours," said Clover. She was afraid, her hands shook, and she wanted to run—but unsuspecting humans fell prey to dark fae and she could suffer the same fate if she wasn't clever. So, she would play his game…for now.

The dark fae smiled. "I am Cypress." He bowed low. Fae couldn't lie, but could dark fae?

"Clover."

"Got a last name?" He grinned again, sharp teeth glinting.

Clover forced a convincing smile. "Not one I want to give to you."

"Smart girl…so I take it you're interested?"

Clover was. She could lie but it would take a minute. There was no need, however, because Cypress took her silence as a yes.

"Good, smart again." Cypress circled her. "Here's the deal. I hear you lost your man. I can feel his body deep, deep down in the ground—but he doesn't have to stay there."

"He's not dead." Clover's hands clenched. "He's alive, I just can't find him."

Cypress sighed. "You poor thing. You know, light fae will say just about anything to ease the pain of the Breaking."

"And dark fae will say just about anything to strike a deal and trap innocent people with their evil magic."

"Innocent? Aren't you the optimist."

"He's not dead. You have nothing to offer me." Clover didn't want to hear any more. She didn't want to be trapped by his words. That's all they were, she tried to convince herself. They were just words. She turned to leave but Cypress appeared suddenly before her, making her step back.

"Do you really want to take that chance? You haven't even heard the good part yet."

Clover crossed her arms and waited. If he wasn't going to let her leave, trying might end in him attacking her, and she wasn't sure she could fight him.

His hands came up, pressed together before he spread them apart. Out of them came a blood-colored light show. She didn't want to look but she also couldn't pull her eyes away. She saw herself and her mother depicted by green silhouettes and a red one beating them and shoving them in a cage.

Clearly, this was the doctor. Another silhouette, a blue one, stepped between her mother and stopped the doctor.

"You want to be free, free and in love. The only thing standing in your way is a wicked man and our good friend death. Here's the deal..."

Clover watched one of the green figures approach the red figure who wasn't looking. The green figure took out a dagger and killed the red one. Blood splattered across the vision. She didn't mean to flinch, but she did anyway.

"Kill the doctor and bring me his heart."

The green figure brought a beating red heart to a black figure, who produced the blue figure from the first vision, who took the green one's hands.

"In return, I'll give you your man. We all live happily ever after."

Cypress finished and the vision faded. Clover shook herself out of the illusion magic that he'd held her in.

"What do you want with the doctor's heart?" She knew that eating the hearts of their victims was a trademark of the dark fae, but she didn't know why they did it, and she knew she'd get Soleil's disapproving silence at her asking.

"You don't know?" He smirked. "Well, you see, light fae, they live long and wonderful lives if they want to. Some of them choose to age—mostly if they happen to be close to a human. But dark fae, see, they get that option stripped away from them. They age fast." He snapped his fingers. "Unless they consume the hearts of humans—it's a nasty business, but I'm not quite ready to pass. Revenge to enact, deals to make, you understand. Our deal is as good as it gets. You kill him, I get his heart, everyone wins."

"It would make me a murderer."

Cypress shrugged. "Them that kills a killer is a hero."

Clover had no reply to that. That couldn't be true, and yet she couldn't help but think the world would be a better place without Dr. Van Doren in it.

"No." Clover stepped back. "No. I won't do it because he's not dead. Grant is still alive; I just have to find him."

"I can see that you'll need some time to decide. So listen." Cypress stepped forward and grabbed one of her hands. She flinched and pulled away when he took out a dagger, but he simply placed it in her hand. It was small, no longer than her forearm—hilt and all.

"Keep this with you. When that special moment comes when you just can't take it anymore, kill him. Carve out his heart. I'll be waiting for you."

"I won't do it."

Cypress chuckled. "Then consider this a gift of condolences for your lost lover." He shoved her away from him and she cried out as she fell backward.

Clover sat up in her bed with a gasp and looked around her room. She couldn't believe it. It had all been another horrible dream? Her cold hand met her hot forehead as she rubbed off the last of the shock. It was growing lighter outside. She needed to get up and get a head start on her chores.

Clover pushed off her blankets and got out of bed, but a metallic clattering followed her. She jumped away from her bed before slowly getting on her hands and knees. Her breath shuddered out of her as a glint caught her eye from the darkness beneath. Unseeing, she reached into the darkness and grabbed the object, bringing it into the light.

Cypress's dagger shone evilly at her, winking like they were in on a secret. Clover's teeth chattered, but not from the cold. Her hands shook. She shouldn't even be considering this. She wasn't a killer. She could not kill. Grant was alive somewhere.

She felt like she was trying to convince herself, which only scared her further. Where was she supposed to hide this wretched thing? Clover saw her red dress hanging in the closet, the one worn only on the Blood Solstice. There she slipped the dagger into the pocket and tried to forget all about it.

Chapter Nine

Knox opened the gate into Veritas for her and Clover walked through, scanning every building and street in sight. Knox pushed her forward a little as he came in behind her and closed the gate. Her fears about the Justice Riders still being in town were confirmed as she scanned her environment. The Justice Riders had hard faces with eyes like coals, flickering and burning. They dragged with them the rotting-corpse scent of hatred.

"So, what's the trouble? Why am I pretending to yearn for my mother's letters?"

Clover glanced at him. Asking him to pretend to want to go into town was a necessary evil. If there was even a chance that Knox's presence would protect her, then she had to take it. But tell him the truth? If she didn't, would he leave? She couldn't risk it.

Clover cleared her throat. "There's a gang of boys who want to cut me open and experiment on me, and bounty hunters who would love nothing more than their iron-tipped arrows in my corpse."

"Oh, is that all?" he asked. He looked a little green, and Clover wondered if he was really as capable of protecting her as he claimed.

"Stop right there," said a rough voice. They both turned to face a Justice Rider, though this one had a cap on with the same horse's head insignia that was across his upper arm. "And just who might you be?"

"Warner Van Doren, Mr.?"

"Captain Dawson." He was the exact opposite of Officer Gennady. He reminded Clover of a statue having come to life: cold and stone-like.

Knox put on a charming smile. "Of course. My apologies, captain."

"And does this half-breed have a name?" When the captain looked at her, Clover averted her eyes to the ground. She might want to push the boundaries with the doctor, but this man would kill her just for looking at him too long. That and the disgust on her face wouldn't help.

"This is Dr. Van Doren's servant, Clover Grimaldi."

Captain Dawson leaned closer to her. "Can you smell my hatred? Is there an ice-cold fire between those narrow shoulders?" He grabbed her jaw hard and turned her face toward his. Clover let out a shuddering breath, fear had tightened her chest. "Light fae." He let go of her jaw and shoved her away. Knox grabbed her by the sleeve, so she didn't fall over.

"Lovely meeting you, Captain Dawson. May the Grey bless your day," said Knox before pulling her away by the same sleeve he'd used to hold her up.

"You all right?" he asked quietly once they were well away from the Justice Riders.

Clover shook her head. She could not answer, she feared what might come out of her mouth. As they walked through Veritas, she took deep, even breaths until she was calmed. She just had to focus and remind herself why she was here.

🐚

Today's errand into town was to pick up packages from Hirane. The doctor said they were books, and they were urgent. Clover didn't know what could be so urgent about a book, but she asked no questions. Her stomach was still recovering from the other day when Van Doren punched her. She couldn't keep down much. And last night…Cypress's words and the whispering dagger were ever present at the back of her mind. They were barely outweighed by the continual throbbing

They were about to step into the post office when the door opened. Clover stepped aside to let the young woman out.

"Oh hello, you're Dr. Van Doren's fae assistant, aren't you?" said the girl. There was no malice in her voice and when Clover looked up, she recognized Angela Hallows, the patient who'd smiled at her.

Angela's smile brought with it the smell of flowers in their fullest bloom. Clover wanted to smile back…but she wasn't sure if she should.

Clover nodded in response to Angela's question. "Yes, Miss Hallows. I'm glad to see you in good health. This is Warner Van Doren, the doctor's nephew."

"W-warner—Knox?" Angela's smile stayed but her eyes conveyed shock.

Knox was staring at her, and even though his face mirrored

Angela's shock, Clover took in the delicate smell of love. Then she was the one to be shocked.

"Hi," Knox said finally.

Angela waited for him to say more but he didn't, so she continued. "It's so good to see you, and I hope you don't mind me asking but what are you doing here?"

"I..." He closed his eyes and shook his head as though to clear his mind. "Grant."

Clover frowned, confused.

"Grant?" asked Angela. "He's your cousin, isn't he?"

"Yes, Grant," Knox said once more, and Clover wondered if he was ill or poisoned or bewitched somehow. Knox cleared his throat. "Grant is my cousin and I've taken up his apprenticeship temporarily."

"Oh." Her smile fell slightly. "You're not going to be a reporter anymore? But you're so good at it."

A blush colored his cheeks and Clover politely looked away.

"Only temporarily. Then it's back to Hirane...where we met."

"I remember." Angela smiled, blushing as well.

Clover wanted to leave them alone, but the sudden arrival of Benjamin made the hairs on the back of her neck rise. She reached out and tugged Knox's sleeve, but he didn't tear his loving gaze away from Angela.

"Angela!" snapped Benjamin, his tone seething. The scent of love was overwhelmed by the rotting smell of hatred.

Angela's expression fell considerably. Benjamin Freeman's face was red, and his clenched hands trembled. Angela put on a big, empty smile before she went to him and took his hand, guiding him away while Benjamin stared right at Clover.

Clover thought about looking away, but why? Why should

she submit to such a terror? This only seemed to make Benjamin angrier before he was led away by the pulling of Angela.

"Charming," said Knox. His hands were in the pockets of his coat, and he watched Angela and Benjamin's retreating forms with a look that she'd sometimes seen on Grant. Eyes narrowed, posture rigid, head tilted forward. As though he were challenging new information to elude his sharp mind. Knox nodded finally, posture relaxing. "Knowledge doesn't necessarily breed intelligence—and that young man has only knowledge."

Clover frowned, but she believed him. "They must be courting, which is curious, since you're clearly in love with her..." She in turn studied his look of longing. "Don't go getting yourself in trouble, too."

"How did you get *yourself* in trouble?" asked Knox.

"They think I lured Marvin Hallows and Fanny Logan into the forest to be taken by the fae," said Clover, heading for the door to the post office.

"Did you?"

Clover gave him a look.

He nodded once. "Right."

CLOVER PASSED THE IRON KEY FORWARD TO RECEIVE DR. VAN Doren's books. This time, Mr. Winetrout wouldn't even look at her, and when he spoke, he clearly spoke to Knox.

"You best be careful on the road to Veritas, son," he said. "There's fae going about snatching up young folk like yourself."

Knox didn't even glance at Clover and her stomach

untwisted ever so slightly. "So I've heard. My condolences about the missing two."

"Three," said Mr. Winetrout, and Clover's head snapped up. "Just the other day, Mr. Freeman said he saw Gillian Holliday run out the fence and straight into the forest."

Knox frowned. "He didn't try to stop her or go after her?"

Mr. Winetrout put the packages down on the counter a little too hard. "You know, you city folk are all the same, living with the fae under the protection of the Justice Riders—out here, us honest country people got no one but ourselves. You run after an enchanted person into the woods, your bones will end up under the same sun as theirs. You remember that!"

"Forgive me, sir. I had no idea. And thank you for the advice," said Knox. His faux shock and sincerity were not lost on Clover or Mr. Winetrout.

Clover held her hand out to Mr. Winetrout for the key back. He forced it hard into her hand and held it there, causing it to singe her skin before she yanked her hand away. Clover grabbed the books before she and Knox left the post office.

Knox tried to carry the books for her, but she shook her head, pulling them away. He gave her a look. She gave him one back.

At the western gate, they were met by Benjamin and the Vale twins, smiling kindly rather than scowling. She took a sharp breath through her nose and held it. Clover had no idea what was going to happen now. Could Knox protect her? *Would* he, if he felt he were outnumbered or if he began to lose this fight?

Knox and Clover stopped, making no greeting toward them.

Benjamin's smile fell a little, but he quickly picked it up.

"It's come to my attention that you're the new Van Doren. Welcome to Veritas."

"Thank you," said Knox, not moving.

Clover looked warily between the two of them. If Knox gave her up, she could run with the books. But could she run all the way to the other side of Veritas without being caught? Doubtful. Her fingertips buzzed with numb fear.

"Things are probably a little different here than they are in fancy ol' Hirane."

Knox laughed. "Undoubtedly."

This nearly knocked Benjamin's smile off entirely. "Well, I understand some of you boys in Hirane are all close and cuddly with the fae, but we don't stoop that way around here. We keep the faith."

The Vale boys were drawing closer. Clover wanted to step back but Knox made no motion of moving, so she stood her ground. A fierce cold began to grow in her chest and the wind howled. Why were her powers acting up now?

"Your faith tells you to beat up innocent girls? How primitive," said Knox with a smirk. He stood tall, feet squared, hands clenched into fists—so confident, but it was one against three. "I'd love to stay and continue this little debate. But these books for my uncle are urgent, so if you'd kindly step out of the way." Knox stepped forward and the Vale twins moved aside, but Benjamin wasn't so easily swayed.

"I'm sorry for the hold up, but the abomination and I have unfinished business." Benjamin held up his hands apologetically.

Knox smiled. "Of course, you're welcome to any abomination you come across."

For a moment, Clover wondered if Knox was giving her

up, but he merely moved her past Benjamin and toward the gate.

Benjamin reached out and grabbed Clover's upper arm hard enough to make her cry out.

There was movement behind her and then Benjamin was the one crying out. Benjamin let her go and she turned to see Knox holding Benjamin by the back of the neck like a mother wolf holding one of her pups.

"That wasn't very nice. Didn't you ever learn any manners?" asked Knox.

Walter Vale ran at Knox with a clenched fist, ready to punch, but Knox simply grabbed Walter's fist and twisted it, making Walter shout with pain. Knox now had both boys easily in his grasp. Gerard had his fists up, but he was hesitant to attack the man who had taken out his leader and his brother.

Knox laughed. "Come on, lad. Let's go three-for-three."

Gerard gritted his teeth and ran at Knox, who twisted Walter's arm harder before chucking him at his brother. Walter fell hard on Gerard, knocking them both to the ground. Knox then added Benjamin to the pile and the boys groaned, trying to get off each other.

"We better get lost." Knox moved past Clover to the gate. He opened it for her, and she rushed through before he closed it behind her and they walked on. They turned when they heard shouting.

"You're lucky your uncle is the doctor, Van Doren!" shouted Benjamin. "You won't always be around to protect that creature!"

"Guess I better teach you some moves," said Knox to Clover.

She assessed the amount of damage he had done. He had

taken on three other boys equal to him in strength, if not in height or skill, and he'd won! He didn't even look tired! Clover was impressed, not only by the fighting but because it was in protection of her. She was confused but her gratitude was more important.

Clover let a smile pull at the corners of her mouth. "A kind thought. But if I even thought about raising a hand against a human, they'd kill me and leave my body to the marsh crows."

Knox shuddered.

They were halfway back to the manor when Clover looked at the books and worked out one of the words.

"Fae?" she said. That didn't make sense. Dr. Van Doren hated the fae as much as everyone else. Why would he be reading books about them?

Knox looked at the books. "I thought you said you couldn't read."

"Grant was teaching me; I can read a little. What do these books say? What are they about?" asked Clover.

What if Dr. Van Doren was getting the same ideas as Benjamin? To cut her open and study her? Her mouth felt dry, and she tried swallowing a few times, but it wasn't helping, and she coughed.

Knox took the books. "*The Fae Treaty,* and *Magic in Our Time, Science on a Magic Scale,* and *The Roots and Causes of Grey Fever.*"

"What's a treaty?" she asked.

"It's sort of like an agreement. Have you never heard of the Fae Treaty?"

Clover shook her head.

"What do they teach out here?" Knox let out an exasperated sigh. "The Fae Treaty is the only thing keeping the humans from burning down that very forest."

Clover looked at it and heard the trees groaning in protest at the mention of fire.

"The humans agreed to stay out of the forest, and anyone who wanders in does so at their own peril. The fae agreed to let a road pass through their lands and leave be anyone who travels it. They also agreed to keep their borders, no expanding."

"I had no idea," said Clover. She had never wondered why the humans didn't take out their hate for the fae on the forest anymore. They had only done so once that she knew about. Clover looked out at the marshlands stretching into the distance.

Knox followed her gaze. "Hard to believe that was all forest once. Its destruction was the very reason the treaty was created."

"It doesn't seem fair," said Clover. "This all belonged to the fae before."

"It wasn't a perfect trade, but it stopped the violence. fae are forbidden from reclaiming their destroyed lands—humans are forbidden to destroy any part of the remaining forest. The Justice Riders take care of anyone trying to break those laws."

"What about dark fae?" asked Clover.

Knox shrugged. "It depends. The fae usually take care of their own criminals—but every now and then, the Justice Riders will beat them to it and there'll be some uproar. Nothing that gets out of hand, though."

Clover's pace slowed as the whisperings flowed through her mind again and she gritted her teeth to block them out. She had just forgotten about Cypress and his offer. She was not going to commit murder. She was not capable of murder. The resolution sounded hollow, and the whispering continued.

&

KNOX WENT THROUGH THE SERVICE ENTRANCE WITH HER AND while he went to the library for more "studying," Clover took the books up to Dr. Van Doren's office.

"Put those down and get to work on lunch already. A new patient has come. You will help me after lunch is served."

"Yes, Master Van Doren. Anything else?" she asked.

He waved her off, going back to whatever he was writing. Back to work then.

Torryn was about in the main hallway, wiping the bannister with a rag. She had recovered somewhat, though her hands still shook quite violently.

"Mother, are you hungry?"

Torryn went about her task as though she hadn't heard her. Clover's eyes stung.

She went over and gently took Torryn by the shoulders. "Mother?"

No response. Torryn turned away and began working as though nothing had happened.

Clover's head pounded and she held the top of her head with one hand before forcing herself to work. In the kitchen, she chopped vegetables with a vengeance. Clover carved up chicken and felt the cold returning to her chest. Dr. Van Doren had destroyed her mother, he had taken her mind, he had taken her body, and Torryn knew nothing now except work. She was a shell.

Clover funneled her hate so violently that the vegetables on the counter began to rot and the water in the iveen cooking-pot began not only boiling on its own but also turned a dark shade of red.

She brought a finger of the red liquid to her lips and tasted the metallic tang of blood. Quickly, she dumped the pot into the sink and washed the rest of it away with fresh water before cleaning the pot and starting over.

Even on her second try, the soup came out tinged with red, so she added tomatoes and decided nothing else could be done to salvage it in time for lunch.

CLOVER SLAMMED A BOWL ON THE DESK NEXT TO KNOX, waking him from a nap he was taking.

"Here's lunch. Don't eat it, you'll be sick," she said before plopping down on the couch and running her hands over her face, trying hard not to cry. All of this anger, all of this *hate* was getting out of control. Cypress said they were the same. What if he was right? If she couldn't control these emotions, then it would only get harder to stop herself from becoming a dark fae—but she didn't know how to stop feeling all these terrible things.

"What's the matter?" Knox yawned.

Clover shook her head, swallowing her tears several times before answering. "Nothing." She stood, smoothing the front of her apron. Her throat was beginning to close. "I'll get you something you can actually eat."

"Do you still want to learn to read?" he asked.

Her footsteps stopped as she got to the door. Learn to read? Without Grant? Knox was being thoughtful, but the question stung as though he had dragged a blade across her skin. She thought about snapping back, but he had protected her. She couldn't risk being his friend, but she couldn't risk him becoming her enemy, either.

"No...I don't care to anymore." She thought she would

feel the strain, the pressure of lying, the truth trying to force itself out of her mouth. But she felt nothing. Maybe the truth was simply too complicated. She wanted to know how to read...but she wanted it to be with Grant. Knox's offer was kind, but it just wasn't the same.

She made her way out into the main hall and stopped at the base of the stairs to collect her thoughts. Clover was sure she could make a sandwich before the doctor would call on her for assistance. But the stomping of feet down the stairs told her otherwise.

THE BOWL FLEW RIGHT PAST CLOVER'S NOSE AND SMASHED against the stairs. She turned and saw Van Doren storming toward her.

"You wretch!" he bellowed. His face was pale, highly contrasted by the red stain of blood on his lips. The tomatoes hadn't masked the blood as well as she'd hoped. His fists were clenched and ready to come down on her.

Clover backed up until the soles of her boots hit the first step, but then he was on her with a hand around her throat, instantly cutting off her air so she couldn't scream. He pushed her back and she hit the steps painfully, but the pain was pushed aside as she gasped for air and found none. Clover wasn't one to fight back, but now was not the time to lie down and take it. Her hands came up and wrapped around his wrist. She tried to take another breath—nothing. Her legs flailed, but found no purchase. She dug her nails into Van Doren's skin.

"You try to poison me? I have given you everything! I'm the only reason you're alive! You and your mother both!"

Clover tried to push him off, but she wasn't strong enough.

She tried to summon her magic, but it was flickering and fading, fading, turning inward and making her feel numb and hollow. Her sight grew dark around the edges, and her heartbeat slowed.

There was a shriek, a woman shrieking as Dr. Van Doren suddenly let her go. He tumbled off Clover and she took in rasping breaths of burning, blessed air before sitting up. Her mother had jumped on the doctor, and they had landed at the bottom of the stairs, stunned. Dr. Van Doren got his senses back first and stood, grabbing Torryn by her hair. He brought his hand up to strike her. Clover tried to stand but her legs failed her, and she toppled back to the stairs.

"What are you doing?" shouted another voice. Knox had come out of the library sometime during the fight and now he had Van Doren's arm locked in a death grip, keeping the doctor from striking Torryn. He'd defended her from Benjamin and his gang, but the doctor was strong, and Knox was overpowering him. The veins in Knox's neck stood out, like he was straining, but he was still doing it. Unflaggingly.

"Let her go."

"You do not tell me how to keep my house," said Dr. Van Doren. He grunted and tried pushing back against Knox, but Knox wasn't having it and he pushed back as well. They were matched and the glare-off continued.

Knox gritted his teeth. "You let her go right now. You might be above the law around here, but you have no right to treat people this way."

"You're mistaken," said Dr. Van Doren, almost gently. "They aren't people. Your mind has been tainted with big city ideas. You think they don't pose a threat to us? You think they don't still steal children and lure men to their deaths? What do you think happened to my son? Seduced by that witch."

Dr. Van Doren turned and lunged at Clover. Knox stepped between them while she skittered away, dragging her dress through the blood soup and over to where her mother was lying, sobbing quietly on the floor.

Knox turned and shot Clover a raised eyebrow. She'd never told him of her relationship with Grant. Perhaps she should have.

Knox turned back to the doctor. "Your son is dead, and you're still in mourning. Clover, why don't you try again at lunch—"

"She is to assist me—"

"I'm going to assist you today," said Knox, cutting off the doctor. "That's what you want, isn't it? For me to be a doctor. Well, I'm ready for lesson one."

Behind his back, Knox was motioning for her to leave. Clover picked up her sobbing mother and pushed her out of the room, through the dining room, the kitchen, and into the servants' quarters. Clover wanted to tell her mother to lie down, but no noise would come—hardly any air would. Her entire neck ached and throbbed, and Clover worried she would suffocate anyway, but gradually, her airways opened and she could breathe normally. But still, her voice wouldn't work.

Her mother was whimpering as Clover tried to recover. She looked at her mother thoughtfully. Torryn had attacked the doctor, to protect her, for the first time in years. It wasn't entirely effective, but it was something, and Clover squeezed her mother's hand in thanks. Perhaps there was something still alive deep within her, something that could be salvaged with enough time.

Torryn laid down and fell into a fitful sleep before Clover left to make the lunches, thinking about everything that had happened. Knox barely knew her, barely knew her mother, and he had protected them from Dr. Van Doren. Perhaps he could be trusted with more information. Perhaps he could be called "friend."

❧

AFTER DINNER, KNOX SNUCK INTO THE KITCHEN WHILE Clover scrubbed at bowls and plates, looking for more signs of blood.

"That was exciting," he said with a grin.

"We need to talk." Clover cut him off and his grin fell. Her voice was a raspy whisper, which suited the secrecy. If Knox was going to know everything, he needed to know it quickly. No long planning, nothing that could be picked up by Dr. Van Doren. Her neck ached at the thought of Van Doren thinking she and Knox had any relationship other than master-servant.

He looked around. "Is this not talking?"

"Meet me in the tower," she said.

"Where's that?"

Clover sighed. "Shall I draw you a map or..." She coughed gently, clearing her throat. "...would you like more hints at where to find this place?"

"You're spicy, you know that?"

Clover waved a wooden spoon at him. "Out."

He left and Clover watched him go before returning to her dishes. She would tell Knox everything and maybe he could shed a new point of view on her current dilemma. Grant was alive. She just needed to find him. Sometimes the best way to find something was to have the help of another set of eyes.

Chapter Ten

CLOVER PUSHED OPEN the hatch leading to the tower. In the moonlight shining through the stained-glass windows, she saw Knox sitting in Grant's place. He shifted around. He was bigger than Grant, after all, and didn't quite fit in the space. But he shouldn't have been in that spot, Grant's spot. Clover's eyes misted.

"Isn't this cozy," he said.

Clover climbed in and sat on the edge of the opening. She hadn't been in the tower since the night with Grant before she'd decided to run away, before he'd stopped her and asked her to marry him. Clover's tears fell freely. She couldn't stop herself from feeling this pain.

"Oh, I didn't mean anything by it. It's a nice place, really," said Knox.

She wiped her eyes. "You sit over there." She gestured to her former spot. There were only so many places to sit, and if anyone was going to sit in Grant's spot, it was going to be her.

He sighed but moved over so she could sit where Grant once did.

Once they were settled, he held out his hands. "So you wanted to talk. This wouldn't happen to be about Grant, would it?"

"I didn't seduce him," said Clover defensively.

Knox laughed. "I figured as much. You're no charmer, but Grant certainly was." He smirked but he looked ridiculous crammed into the small space, so his attitude was dimmed by the fact that his knees were nearly in his mouth.

"Funny." Clover looked down at her hands. "We were going to get married."

"I'm sorry. I didn't know."

"Dr. Van Doren did," said Clover. "My mother told him… when she was still capable of speaking. She told him, and then while I was in town, Grant—a young man of nearly twenty years—suddenly falls from a ladder and dies, searching through books covered in dust that have remained undisturbed for years by even the faintest breath."

"So you think he was murdered."

"No, I think he's still alive. The doctor has taken him away somewhere I haven't been able to find him." Clover wanted to tell him that she'd had a visit from Grant, but she hesitated. She and Grant shared that invisible tether, but that was just the thing. It was invisible. She couldn't prove it and Knox would need something more real to convince him.

Knox squinted. "But there was a funeral."

"I never saw his body, no one but the doctor and the mortician did."

"Clover." Knox sighed. "It's been over a month—"

"You think I don't know how long it's been?" she snapped before closing her eyes tightly. Her throat tightened into a fist.

"All fae may love once and never again. We are connected to the other person. When the connection is severed, they call it the Breaking. Something inside them dies. The same goes for humans who love fae."

"Your mother," said Knox. "That's the reason she's…"

"Yes," said Clover. "I know Grant's alive. I can still feel the connection, and clearly, I'm nothing like my mother. But I don't know where he is. I want to go, to get my mother away from here somewhere safe, but I can't leave without him. I won't."

Knox nodded thoughtfully. "Back in Hirane, I would write up reports on murders. Use facts to inform the public. What we need are facts. Grant was strong and a sudden fall to his death is strange. The dust is good, too, but there has to be more than that. You say no one saw his body?"

"The mortician," said Clover. "But if the doctor asked him to keep quiet, there would be no use trying to reason with him."

"So, the doctor sews up his loose ends tightly. I'm going to need some time to think about this. Try to remember everything you can about the day of Grant's death and let me know if you get any ideas. I'll be writing everything down."

Clover let out a breath of relief. He understood. He believed her. It felt good to have someone she could talk to, someone who would be on her side who had resources and knowledge to help her.

"All right," she said. "We should get some sleep."

"You go ahead, I'm a bit of a night owl," he said.

Clover went to the opening. As she was halfway out, she paused and looked back at the serious-faced Knox Van Doren.

"Thank you for helping us," she said.

He smiled at her. "Hey, if I'm out here, might as well do

something I'm actually good at. If there's any chance that Grant is alive, I want to help, and if you two were going to get married, then you're family, too."

Clover hadn't thought of that, but she liked the idea. She remembered the doctor and her good feelings toward the thought dimmed slightly, but Knox was clearly the same kind of Van Doren, the same kind of human, that Grant was. Someone she wouldn't mind considering family. Grant would just love shoving this in her face, her admitting that there might be one—*one*—other good human out there.

"Goodnight, Knox."

"Night, Clover."

Clover polished the steps of the grand staircase. In her initial washing, she'd picked up the last remnants of the blood soup. What had she been thinking, serving it to him like that? She should have given up on the soup and made something else. But would it have ended the same way?

It didn't matter what she did. She would always want the doctor to just die. Couldn't he just die already?

Them that kills a killer is a hero.

Clover banished Cypress's words. She was not a killer and killing Dr. Van Doren wouldn't make her a hero. It would make her a murderer. Besides, Grant wasn't dead.

Clover's movements halted and she checked the bond tying her to Grant. Still alive and as shrouded in darkness as ever— but there and intact. That was all that mattered. Her head began to pound, and she pressed both hands, gripped into fists, at the crown of her head. The knife-like pain kept digging in and she grunted, closing her eyes.

The gentle clicking and stomping of shoes coming down the stairs stole her out of her pain, though her vision was blurred with tears when she opened her eyes.

She looked up to greet Knox only to see Grant. Clover gasped and stumbled back, nearly losing her footing. She had to grab onto the bannister to keep from tumbling down the stairs completely.

He was in his work clothes without his jacket. Clover shrank back as he walked right past her and down the stairs. Another vision?

"Grant," she said quietly, but he made no notice of her.

Grant continued into the dining room. Perhaps this was something different. Clover stood, teeth chattering, and moved with surprising speed, considering her heart was pounding so hard that it was causing her hands to shake.

He seemed to be sneaking even though it was the middle of the day. Clover wanted to call out his name, but she didn't want the doctor to hear her. So, she simply hurried behind him. When she got to the kitchen, he wasn't in there. Clover let out a slow breath, relieved for whatever that was to be over.

Only it wasn't over. Grant came back into the kitchen, followed by her, only…she was younger, and she noticed for the first time that he was, too.

"Grant, stop," said the younger Clover. "We shouldn't be out. I already took you into the forest, and that was dangerous."

Grant turned. "We're not going to leave the house." He took the young Clover's hand and pulled her along. They left the kitchen and Clover followed.

The two of them went back up the stairs, moving slowly, like they were sneaking. Clover watched them closely and remembered. This moment had happened before. She continued to follow the two out of the kitchen. They stopped on the stairs.

"Shh," said Clover. The two of them hunkered down.

Grant frowned. "What? He's been asleep for hours."

"I'm too scared, I'm going back to bed."

"No, please." Grant held her hand harder, pulling to go up the stairs while the younger Clover pulled to go back down. "Be brave."

Clover's past self looked behind her once more toward what might have been safety but instead, she followed Grant up the stairs. Clover in the present smiled. Isn't that how it had always been? Grant was the brave one, she was the cautious one.

Clover followed her memories up the stairs, too wrapped up in the ease they brought for the aching in her chest, the yearning for these moments that shadowed her through the day.

They went up to the attic, Grant moving through the maze of chests, of furniture owned by the long-dead, to finally get to the ladder that led to the tower.

"What's up there?"

"I call it the tower," said Grant. "I found it the other day when I was..."

Clover's past self raised an eyebrow. "Excusing yourself early from your lessons?"

"I already finished them. Besides, it's the same old stuff. I want to learn new stuff but that's beside the point." Grant went up the ladder and Clover followed.

Presently, she stayed at the bottom of the ladder. Her legs grew weak from the melancholy that hollowed out her bones and she leaned her head against the ladder. The conversation could still be heard.

"A secret place, just for us," said Grant.

"Us?"

"Yes. We can come up here at night, just like this. I can tend your wounds and teach you how to read and write."

"What would I use those things for?"

"They're useful skills. Useful for everyone, you never know when you'll need them."

"So you'll just do all this for me? What do you want in return?"

"Will you be my friend?"

Clover began to cry, her head aching from where she'd leaned it against the wooden ladder. What had started as a gentle and comforting retelling of the past had ended in a misery similar to her initial pain at Grant's passing.

She wanted this to stop. Stop!

"Stop! Stop this! Please!" The real Clover pressed her hands over her ears. The pain returned and she shouted. All she could hear now was her pounding heart and her own panicked breathing. After a moment, the pain lessened until it dulled to its usual tolerable throb.

Clover caught her breath. There was only silence, and after a moment, Clover dared to open her eyes. The memory was gone, and she could think clearly.

Her first thought was that this could only be the Breaking, but the bond was still intact, and the connection was strong. Grant was alive, so what was happening to her? Was this some kind of spell cast on her by Cypress? Some dark magic, like the kind that had come over her that day as Dr. Van Doren's assistant—no doubt Cypress's work too. Why was he doing this to her?

There was only one person who could help her, who might have answers to all her questions.

SOLEIL HELD CLOVER'S FACE IN HER HANDS, AND SHE TURNED it this way and that before picking up one of Clover's hands and holding it to the light, even though it was nighttime. Soleil had made a hot drink with lots of strange ingredients that restored Clover's voice and even brought a little relief to her pounding head.

"I see a knife," said Soleil. "A knife-like darkness siphoning out your life force." Soleil let go of her hand.

Clover rubbed her eyes. Siphoning her life force? Was this Cypress's doing? She couldn't think of anyone else.

"It's digging into the top of your head."

That's what it felt like. "Can you tell me who's doing it and how I get rid of it?"

Soleil reached forward, took Clover's face in her hands, and pulled her head down so she was looking at the top of her head. Clover let out a cry of protest, but Soleil ignored her.

"I don't know who's doing it. It's hard to trace magic this amorphous back to its caster. You're not strong enough to get rid of it," said Soleil. "No, that's not right. You're not experienced enough to get rid of it. I thought, as time went on, you would learn to practice your magic on your own, learn to control it—but the humans have forced it down inside of you. I see now. I'll train you."

"What? I don't have time for magic lessons. I've got other work to do."

"Unimportant work. Useless work. Slavery," said Soleil. "I will show you what's important."

Clover gave her friend a look. "I'm still trying to find Grant."

"Perhaps the magic can help," said Soleil with a shrug.

"You will meet me at night. Do you want to be bested by the darkness? Like your mother?"

Clover thought of her mother, wandering aimlessly through memory and time until her life eventually ended. No true identity, no true connection to her daughter. Clover's fingers ached with anxiety.

"Of course not," said Clover.

Soleil smiled. "Good. Then we will train, and you will finally learn what you're truly capable of."

"We'll start tomorrow, I've been out long enough as it is." Clover rubbed her eyes. "I need to get some sleep."

Soleil nodded as she took Clover's hands. "Tomorrow then, but before you go, I have to ask if you have seen any..." Her green eyes flitted away. "Dark fae around?"

"Yes, I met with one last night, or was it two nights ago? I can't remember, but his name was Cypress."

"Tell me you didn't make a deal with him. Tell me you weren't that foolish," said Soleil. As she spoke, she looked Clover directly in the eyes. Her whole body tensed, ready to pounce, as though the dark fae was directly behind Clover.

Clover arched an eyebrow at her friend, which was answer enough for the anxious fae. Soleil's body relaxed, the tension unwinding, but not completely.

She let out a slow breath. "Good. Dark fae still follow the old ways. Other fae said there's been one lurking about near Veritas."

"Maybe he's the one who took Marvin Hallows. If so, he's been taking others, too," said Clover. She pictured Marvin Hallows, Fanny Logan, and Gillian Holliday lying in the woods with their hearts missing from their chests. Clover shuddered before rubbing her hands over her arms.

Soleil nodded. "The two girls, but no boy. The forest already claimed him, perhaps?"

"What is it that dark fae do, exactly?" asked Clover. "How did they even get that way to begin with?"

"All fae are born light. We follow the path, we listen to the earth and the sky. We give life unless circumstance calls for other action. If that happens, then we are judged by the earth. Dark fae have their light stripped from them because they took life with vengeance, with pleasure, and without remorse."

Clover frowned. This was new information. She thought killing alone made you a dark fae. She was only half-fae to begin with, but it was still part of her, it could still be turned dark if she killed Van Doren.

"Can they do nothing to earn their light back? Is there no forgiveness?" Maybe there was some hope for her if she decided to risk it all and make a deal with Cypress.

"Of course there is, but it's a difficult path, and most dark fae are too consumed by their evil deeds to take it. So they remain, in pain—but less pain than trying to get back to what they once were." Soleil leaned in to whisper, "It is the aim of many in the dark to turn others like them. No matter what deals they make, they can never give you what you truly want. Promise me you will never go through with whatever Cypress offered you."

Clover took her friend's hands. "I promise."

Even as she said it, she wondered if she meant it. Clover wanted to find Grant, but if she lost all hope, would she resort to such dark measures and risk the struggle back to the light? She wasn't sure, she wasn't that desperate. Not yet, anyway.

"What did he offer you?" asked Soleil.

"Grant," said Clover. "But I know Grant's alive and I'm

going to find him with help from you, and maybe even from Knox."

"Knox? That's a strong name. Another fae?"

Clover shook her head. "No, I forgot. Knox is Grant's cousin come from Hirane."

"I hear good and bad about the city. Keep your friends close—"

"And your enemies far enough away that you can see them coming," said Clover, finishing the old saying. She and Soleil embraced.

Clover knew deep down that if she lost everything tomorrow and the whole world turned against her, she would still have Soleil. They had grown up together. Soleil taught her everything about the forest, about the fae, about magic. She had comforted Clover in her times of despair.

But Soleil had her limitations. She would never truly understand Clover's life, why she loved who she did, and why she would choose them over the forest. Clover knew it made no sense to her friend and so she didn't bother trying to explain it. It was a small barrier between them—but it was still something she could trip over.

"I'll let you know if I find anything else," said Clover.

Soleil leaned forward like she wanted to say more but she didn't. "Blessings upon your search," said Soleil. They separated and she frowned, looking at Clover's neck and the dark bruises there. "The depth of human cruelty truly knows no bounds."

"They're not all bad," said Clover, which shocked her. When she'd told Grant in the tower that he was the only good in all of humankind, she'd been so sure. Now that Grant was gone, other humans were popping up to prove her wrong. She didn't know if that made her wrong, or if she was simply being too trusting, grasping at kindness and assistance wherever she could find it to get Grant back. Even if Clover was wrong, Soleil would be safer remaining in the forest than if she struck out and tried to find the goodness in humans, at least from the ones in Veritas.

⸎

CLOVER HAD ONLY LAID HER HEAD ON HER ARM FOR A MOMENT, but realized it had apparently been longer when she felt Knox put a hand on her shoulder.

"Clover? Are you asleep?"

She shook her head and went back to what she'd been doing before, which was scrubbing the second story floor. Assisting the doctor with more of his Grey Fever patients had left her tired and with a new sharp pain in her skull. But in addition to that, she had scrubbed the entirety of the first floor, washed the bloody linens, cleaned Van Doren's room, laundered everyone's clothing, cooked all the meals, kept the fires going in every hospital room, and shined the shoes of a particularly idiotic patient visitor from Veritas.

Clover felt wrung out like a wet rag. She wished she had more of that drink Soleil had given her the night before. She should have asked for the recipe—maybe it would help her mother somehow, too.

"Maybe you should take a break."

Clover laughed, but not too loudly before whispering, "And do what? I can't read, I can't write, I can't do needlepoint, or paint. What could I possibly do with a *break*?" Her voice dropped to a grumble. "Other than be brutally punished afterward?"

"Oh, I don't know, you could try doing nothing," he said. "I do nothing all the time."

"Am I supposed to think that's admirable?"

Knox rolled his eyes. "Don't be so sour. I came up to ask you something."

"Where's the doctor?"

"I left him in his study after a thorough tongue lashing from him about my views on fae and being a reporter, and where I grew up, and everything about me, really," said Knox. "Anyway, about my question."

"Go on," she said, still scrubbing the floor and rinsing the gray water out into the bucket beside her.

"You are half-fae, but what exactly does that mean? I know fae typically have three schools of magic. What are you capable of?"

"Why?"

"No respectable journalist doesn't know the entirety of the person they choose to take on as a partner. You may ask me anything you like too, you know."

Clover sighed, shifting her weight to her feet and giving her hands a break. Her spine crackled and so did her fingers. Her eyelids were so heavy she wanted to pass out right there, but she held it together. "Knox, I don't even know what the three schools of magic are."

"Natural, emotional, and mental."

"Hmm…"

Clover had always struggled with the elements. They fought against her, pulling back like there was only so much they were willing to obey. Air was the easiest, she barely had to try. Earth was a little more difficult but responded when she pushed. Fire and water were hopeless, not even a spark or a ripple would they give her. Plants were a different story; nearly all of them warmed to her instantly, did as she asked and waited for her to command, but she knew all fae had an easy connection with plants and she wasn't sure that counted.

Emotionally, Clover considered herself only slightly more experienced. She could sniff out a range of emotions, but she knew no magic to change emotions and according to Soleil, only true masters could accomplish that.

As far as Clover knew, she had no magic in the mental category. She could make no illusions or manipulate people's thoughts or dreams. Light fae could do it, but it was more in the nature of a dark fae to do those things. She thought back to the night Cypress had slipped into her dreams. The whispering started up and her teeth chattered, but she realized Knox was still waiting for an answer.

"I have a little ability with nature and emotions, but not enough to be of any consequence," she said. She looked around and went back to scrubbing the floor, just in case Dr. Van Doren snuck up on them—she could at least try to look innocent.

"Iron hurts you, but can you lie?" asked Knox.

"It depends on the lie."

Knox frowned.

Clover looked around again before whispering even more quietly, "Yes, I can. But if I don't practice it beforehand, I can't lie for very long. Try it."

"Oh, uh, did you love Grant Van Doren?"

"No," she said. Immediately her chest began to itch and her throat began to tighten painfully. The fingers in her hands began to stiffen and she gripped them into fists. The longer the lie went on, the more it began to eat its way up her throat.

"Yes!" she finally gasped. The pain faded and she flexed

her fingers. She leaned forward to catch her breath before looking up at Knox, who seemed thoughtful.

"That's everything, though Soleil thinks I'm capable of much more. I doubt it." Clover picked up the scrubbing brush and went back to the floor.

"Soleil?" Knox's eyebrows shot up and he smiled. "Who's that?"

Clover froze mid scrub and gritted her teeth before closing her eyes. She wasn't usually so careless. She trusted Knox, but this somehow felt like a betrayal. Clover resisted the truth building inside her. There was a lot of harm in this information.

"It's all right, you don't have to tell me. Your sources can remain your own," he said.

She looked up at him and saw a knowing glint in his brown eyes and he gave her an understanding smile.

"Thank you, Knox," she said, going back to the floor.

Knox sat a little ways from her, cross-legged like a child. "Is there anything you'd like to know about me?"

"Not really—well actually, yes." Clover suddenly had a thought. "Why the nickname? Why Knox?"

"Well, you remember in Hirane how I told you the strong survive?" he asked and she nodded. "Knox is the street where I showed the boys of Hirane that I was a survivor, and ever since, that's what my friends have called me. A lot easier than Warner, which doesn't have a shorter version."

"Why do names need a shorter version?" she asked.

He shrugged. "It shows familiarity…I could shorten your name to Clove, but I think I'm going to call you Grim." He pointed at her frowning face. "And that is exactly why."

She turned away from him and looked around on the

ground floor and at the doctor's bedroom door before turning back to her friend.

"Have you been thinking about where Grant might be and what happened to him?" she asked.

"Yes, I've got a process of elimination going," said Knox. "You're sure he's not here in this house?"

Clover glowered. "I have cleaned every inch of this house since Grant disappeared. If he were here, I would have found him."

"Do you think he could be in Veritas? Lots of places to hide someone."

"You think he's just locked in someone's basement?" she asked.

Knox turned away; eyebrows furrowed. "Can you think of anyone who would do that for Dr. Van Doren?"

"He would have to pay them, and the people are loyal to him...but who?" she wondered, mostly to herself. There weren't many people in Veritas who would do such a thing. But with loyalty to the "good" doctor? Money? And to keep Grant away from fae seduction? The answer came to her immediately.

"Taverty," she said aloud.

Knox squinted, thinking. "The horrid church couple?"

"Reverend Taverty and his wife live in a small corner of the church. They are definitely the sort of people to keep someone locked in their basement. They'd see it as holy, and it wouldn't hurt if they were also being paid."

"I don't like Grey Services; I avoid them whenever possible," Knox said.

Clover stared at the brush in her hand. "Well, I'm not allowed in the church except on the Blood Solstice, and that's not for another two weeks."

"It's a start," said Knox. "But we should still plan for him not being in the church. There are only a few more places he could be." Knox rubbed his jaw. "Laewaes and Northburry aren't far from here. I've called in a favor from a friend in Hirane. If Grant's not in those other towns, that leaves the forest."

"Dr. Van Doren would never go into the forest. He hates it, that's why there's a wall between them and us." It was one of Clover's responsibilities in the summer to test every brick to make sure they weren't loose or crumbling, and if they were, to replace them. It was the only wall that was relatively new-looking. Dr. Van Doren only ever asked her to check that one, the one separating them from the forest.

Knox tilted his head. "I don't know, I've seen desperate men do some things they never would have done in other situations. I'm not ruling it out quite yet."

Clover felt some of her anxiety melting away. With Knox's resources and thinking, she wondered if finding Grant would be as hard as she thought. There were only so many places Grant could be. They would find him. They had to, for all their sakes.

Chapter Eleven

AN ICY BREEZE swept across her back, and she shivered. It made it hard for her to distinguish between the weather and her magic. The swelling chill built in her chest and Clover pushed it hard, forcing it to grow, to envelop her like the breeze. The forest around her groaned and she felt a sharp sting against her shoulder. The cold imploded and disappeared. At least the cold in her chest did.

"Ow!" Clover opened her eyes. She was kneeling on the forest floor while Soleil stood over her, holding a small green switch in her hand and smirking. Clover rubbed the spot on her shoulder where she'd been whipped. "What was that for?"

"You're using the magic of the forest as a crutch. The magic isn't coming from you."

"What are you talking about?" Clover was confused and a little irritated at the whipping. How could her magic not come from her? Where else would it come from?

Soleil sighed. "You let the forest coddle you, hold you up. You need to be able to perform magic without the forest. All fae must learn this." She turned and held up her hands. The wind picked up and a blistering heat seemed to shoot down from the starry sky and focus itself on Soleil. The leafless trees began to inch away. The shrubs and small grasses followed, leaving dry, cracked earth in their retreat.

Soleil did this until they were in a clearing completely devoid of all life. She turned to Clover. "There, a proper space. I'll fix it when you've learned this lesson."

"Now what?"

"Now do as I said and make fire."

Clover looked around at the clearing, which held nothing but dirt and rocks. "There's nothing to catch."

"You see? Your crutch. The entire forest would catch fire if you wanted it to, but it wouldn't be *you* creating the burn. Focus." Soleil whipped her again.

"Stop that!"

"Make fire."

Clover shook her head. "*Make fire.* Fine!"

She closed her eyes hard; the cold feeling came back but it was small and weak, weaker than she had ever felt it. Soleil was right, Clover really had been using the power of the forest. Fire. What she needed was a fire.

She took a deep breath and imagined a fire. It was small, so she made it bigger, and in her ears there was a clicking noise, like a spark trying to come alive. Clover let out her deep breath and imagined the spark, the fire and the heat it would create, but then she heard a fizzle like water being dropped onto a burning pan and she opened her eyes.

Soleil sighed. "You aren't feeling it. Magic is emotion, even elemental magic."

"What kind of emotion am I supposed to feel about fire?"

"It's whatever you want to feel about fire. You're angry?

You get a raging fire that destroys. You're content? You get a comforting fire to warm the fae-lings who grow cold at night. Feel it!" Soleil hit her again, and Clover resisted the urge to jump up and take that silly little switch from her.

Clover gritted her teeth. Her eyes remained open and she felt the cold swelling inside her. This time, it turned to heat. The sparking came back right before her eyes, and she focused on it. In her heart, she wanted a single, candle-like flame, the kind she had struck with a match the night Grant asked her to marry him. Love flooded her heart and warmed her insides like the cold had chilled her, but it was stronger now. She urged the emotion to grow, holding onto how she felt that night.

It flitted to life in front of her, a flickering flame, and Clover concentrated on it, the world seeming to fade away. The flame grew until it lit the clearing before it faded and went out, leaving no trace behind.

"There you go, a fire. Nicely done," said Soleil.

Clover let the heat in her chest fade, and she felt tired, a good, accomplished kind of tired. But as the heat faded, so did the memory she'd brought to the surface. Most days, Clover could keep herself busy, and that would be enough to keep the sorrow away. But now it came back, and tears welled in her eyes. She needed to focus now. This was the kind of magic she could use—maybe even the kind that could somehow help her find Grant.

"Thank you for your help." Clover got to her feet.

Soleil grinned. "You're welcome." She gave Clover another thwack before Clover lunged at her. Soleil screamed and ran off into the woods, grinning. Clover followed for a bit before giving up. She needed sleep, so she made her way back to the manor.

KNOX WAS NODDING OFF. CLOVER KEPT WATCHING HIS EYES trying to close while Dr. Van Doren gave him a lesson in anatomy. Knox's head nodded forward, and he pretended to have a coughing fit. Clover gritted her teeth trying not to laugh as she held the tray with all their instruments on it.

The dead body on the table had been a young boy who experienced a mishap in Hirane. Donating bodies to doctors paid exceedingly well, apparently. Grant once explained to her that the doctor had tasked him with writing polite rejection notes to the morgue in Hirane for fresh bodies. The one they had now was starting to smell and Clover's stomach churned.

"Are you paying attention?" asked Dr. Van Doren, reaching in and holding up the boy's heart. Knox stared at it in horror before leaning over and throwing up, which effectively froze the bile in Clover's own throat.

Dr. Van Doran grimaced, turning his eyes to her. "Clean it up." He looked back at Knox, who was coughing. "We'll pick this up in an hour."

Knox looked at Clover pleadingly and Clover searched through her brain for an excuse to get Knox out of doctor duties.

"Master Van Doren, it's going to rain, would you like to have dinner early?" she asked before closing her eyes, expecting a slap of some kind.

Dr. Van Doren was silent, and when she opened her eyes, he nodded. "Fine, but have this cleaned and have dinner ready in an hour."

Clover bowed. "Yes sir."

Once the doctor had left, Knox stood upright and took

one look at the body before grimacing and gagging. "I owe you one."

"One what?" asked Clover.

"A favor. Can I help?" Knox gestured to his own sick.

Clover shook her head. "No, it's all right. I don't want you sticking around and getting sick again—uh, that's more for my benefit instead of yours. I'm the one who'll have to clean it up."

"Thanks, Grim," he said before leaving. He staggered a bit, but he got out of the room all the same. Once he was gone, Clover got to work cleaning up the mess.

CLOVER TRIED TO HOLD HER BREATH AS THE ACRID SMELL OF Knox's vomit filled her nostrils. She had cleaned up plenty of sick in her life and much more, but she never got used to it, though it no longer made her equally nauseous as it had when she was a child.

"He was never known for his iron constitution when it came to blood," said Grant, and Clover let out a whimper. His visage kneeled beside her and tried to reach forward and help, but as before, his hands went right through hers and anything he tried to touch. He smiled sheepishly. "Worth a try."

Clover let go of the rag and wiped her hands on her apron, not that it mattered, as she couldn't touch him, but she still reached out.

"Why is this happening?" She hovered her hand across his face. He closed his eyes as though actually feeling her touch.

He sighed. "I wish I knew. I feel weaker all the time. I dream of a great fall."

"You know nothing else?" she asked and he shook his

head. "Grant, your father faked your death. There was a funeral and everything. I know you're alive—somewhere. But I can't find you."

He took a shallow breath. "Are you certain?"

"Yes," she said. "Can't you tell me anything?"

He shook his head. "I know nothing else."

"I'm going to find you. Knox is helping me; I promise I'm not going to stop until you're back," she said.

"Be careful," said Grant. "If my father did what you believe, then he is more dangerous than either of us have imagined."

Clover nodded, eyes welling. "I'll be careful..."

"Please don't cry. It kills me that I can't be there truly to comfort you."

"It's getting harder to tell what's real. I don't want you to go away again," she said, trying to smile.

He began to flicker. "I'm real. I know I'm real and I'll come back. I..." He reached for her before his image faded completely.

Clover's lips trembled, so she pressed them together hard along with her teeth. She blinked the tears out as she reached back for the rag. Vomit was her job for the moment. Then she would focus on Grant. She had to find him—now she'd promised.

WHEN SHE FINISHED, THE SMELL OF SICK WAS GONE, BUT IT WAS replaced by another aroma altogether. The smell of freshly baked bread and spices was coming from the kitchen. Clover's heart leapt. Her mother hadn't been able to clean, but maybe she had found it in her to cook—maybe she was finally starting to heal.

Clover rushed into the kitchen. Knox stood in front of a large pot and a beautifully braided loaf of bread was on the wooden table.

He turned and smiled. "I am in your kitchen."

"Yes, I see. What are you doing?" She went to the bread. It was perfect but she didn't want to say that. She thought of telling Knox about her conversations with Grant, but she couldn't risk him thinking she was crazy now. He could have thought that before, of course, but this was different. Or maybe she just wasn't convinced that her visions were real yet.

"I asked you if I could help, you said no—but I wasn't going to let you clean up my vomit and sit in my room waiting for dinner. I'm not a child, and I can do my part and help you."

Clover picked at a splinter on the table, thinking about what Grant said in the autopsy room. "You really do get sick when it comes to blood and organs and—"

"Please! Not while I'm cooking," he said and she smiled, letting it turn into a laugh. "So until dinner is done, this kitchen is mine."

"What am I supposed to do?" she asked.

He shrugged, turning to the table to carve up some meat. "Why don't you do some of that nothing we were talking about the other day...and by the way, your mother is resting in her room, so don't worry."

Clover sat in one of the chairs and put her hands on the table before moving them to her lap. It didn't feel right, so she moved them back up.

"You are pathetic," he said, and she put her hands back in her lap.

Clover's face heated with embarrassment and frustration. She had never done *nothing* in her life. What was the point when there was work to be done? What did other people do when there was no work? Sit around and stare out their windows? Clover reminded herself that other people could read and write.

"Well, you seem to be the expert." She held her arms out, waiting for instruction.

He raised an eyebrow, frowning before coming over. "Maybe you could start by relaxing." He lowered her shoulders, which she hadn't realized were raised. She kept them down and he went back to the meat.

"Do you sleep with your hair like that?"

"No," she said. "But it keeps it out of the way when I clean. It's practical."

"It looks painful, are you sure it's not a torture device?"

Clover gave him a look.

He laughed before turning and pointing the wooden spoon at her. "Shoulders."

Clover huffed before lowering her shoulders. Again. Clover just wasn't like other people. This exercise was pointless and a waste of time. She stood, slamming her hands on the table, making Knox jump out of his skin.

"I can't just do nothing."

Knox frowned. "Sit down," he demanded.

Clover did and crossed her arms, which seemed a little more natural than having them on the table or in her lap.

"You may busy yourself by judging my cooking."

"It's actually good."

"Ah! She can give compliments," he said, focused on his cooking, and Clover shook her head with a grin.

KNOX FINISHED DINNER AND HELPED CLOVER SET THE TABLE.
Dr. Van Doren was still up in his study, but he would be down
in a few minutes. That gave them some time to talk, and she
wanted to know how the investigation was going.

"What news?" she asked.

Knox raised an eyebrow, looking between two similar forks.
"What do you mean?"

"You said you'd called in favors from friends in Hirane to
check the other towns," said Clover. She flexed her hands and
the joints strained and her bones cracked, relieving some of
the anxiety they held. "Have you heard anything?"

"Grim, I told you that a day ago—if that. These things
take time."

"How much time?" she asked.

Knox scoffed. "Well, the Fae Road has made travel easier,
but not everyone wants to travel it, and it's still quite a
journey."

"That answer would be helpful if I had asked if people
preferred traveling the Fae Road or not." Clover frowned. He
was purposefully dodging the question, like he was trying not
to lie. "Knox, how long is it going to take?"

"Until midwinter." He shrugged. "Maybe if they conduct
thorough searches, which is what I explicitly asked them
to do."

Clover set down the plate she was holding a little too hard
and it nearly shattered. Midwinter? It was late fall now, but it
would still be weeks, nearly two whole months until midwinter.
What could possibly take that long?

"They are small towns—"

"They're also searching Hirane—"

"How hard could it possibly be to find one—"

"My uncle has many connections. Don't suppose you have any of those—"

Clover coughed out a sob before turning away. She didn't know if she was more sad or angry. She wasn't angry at Knox, there wasn't really anything he could do about this problem. She was angry at Dr. Van Doren. This was all his fault. His pride had been wounded by Grant's love for her. His only son, his heir, his successor in love with a half-fae. Now Grant was gone, and she wanted Van Doren to suffer.

Clover felt out of breath, and she tried to banish the thoughts even as the whispering of Cypress's dagger called to her. Knox came over and put a hand on her shoulder. Clover saw a deep sadness in his eyes. She wasn't the only one who had loved Grant. They hadn't seen much of each other but they communicated often, to the point where Grant had relied on their connection to pick up his whole life, including her, and move closer to Knox in Hirane. That had been the plan, anyway.

"I'm doing my best," he said.

"I'm grateful." She wiped her eyes. "I am, I'm sorry. I'm just...I'm just so tired of this. I want him back and I'm impatient—I know it's not your fault."

"You're right, you are impatient," he said. She frowned at him, and he smiled. "Hey, Grim's back and ready to fight. We've still got one place we haven't eliminated yet."

"The church," said Clover.

Knox nodded. "Exactly. We'll need a plan, but for now, just focus on staying strong, keeping your mother healthy, while I focus on keeping the doctor happy. He needs to be convinced that nothing is going on."

Clover sighed. "I can do that."

"Good, because I'm probably going to struggle. I fear you may have to clean up much more of my vomit before we get Grant back."

A door opened upstairs, and Clover pulled Knox by the shoulder of his shirt back into the kitchen.

"Go out through the servants' entrance and come back in through the garden doors. He'll be none the wiser, his office doesn't have any windows."

"I noticed. Does he have an affinity for coffins or something?"

Clover smiled. "Just go."

Knox took off down the corridor and out the servants' entrance. For all of Knox's strange mixture of personality traits, he was a help to her and a hope. She was glad he was here.

❧

VERITAS WAS GETTING READY, HOLDING ITS BREATH AND waiting for the Blood Solstice, the one day a year when Death would wander freely during the day. With his whip in one hand and his shackles in the other, he would be searching for souls who escaped during Eve of the Grey. He would take them back to the Grey where they belonged.

Clover's teeth chattered. She hated everything about their holidays. They were always so cold, so...grim. She hated using that word now that Knox had chosen it for her nickname. If anyone was Grim, it was the humans and their lifeless religious practices. But she would wear the red just like the rest of them. Though they wore it to show death that they were alive so it wouldn't mistake them for lost souls, she would be wearing it simply so they would not decide that her scorn of their beliefs would be the last straw.

Clover kept her back pressed hard against the general store. Her eyes scanned Veritas for signs that its inhabitants were waiting to pounce. For a moment she thought she felt hands grabbing at her skirt, but it was just the icy wind and she shuddered. She clutched the edges of her gray coat hard, making it stretch around her. Her breaths came out in a mist, and she tried to keep them even as she scanned the streets for Benjamin and the Vale twins. They hadn't been waiting at the gate this time. She supposed they couldn't wait around forever for her to show up.

Mr. Mulligan came out with boxes for her as well as a bag of flour. She quickly pulled the cord of the bag around one shoulder and took the boxes.

"Where's the fire?" he asked.

Clover was looking around. She thought she saw a Vale twin peeking out from behind a building.

"No fire here. Thank you." She put the money in his hand and walked away before he could say anything else.

Outside, Clover crept around the edges of buildings and looked down every street. She still had to check for mail from Knox's mother. As she approached the post office, she could see Mr. Winetrout rushing around his counter. Not a moment too soon, Clover stopped, and the door slammed an inch away from her nose.

"Go away, you horrid creature!" he shouted.

Clover frowned. "Mr. Winetrout, Dr. Van Doren and his nephew need their mail."

A few slips of paper shot out from under the door and into the dirt. Clover picked them up and stared at the door. This was definitely new.

Clover turned and shouted when she came chest to chest with the person who'd been standing behind her. For a moment, she cowered before she saw who it was.

"Angela."

"You remember me." Angela's smile was like a ray of sunshine, but it faltered, and she looked around. "Did you hear?"

Clover shook her head, her mind fogged by fear. Benjamin and his gang were waiting to kill her, and she couldn't comprehend why this girl kept stopping to speak with her. Angela was nice, so maybe their conversation would protect Clover.

Angela took a deep breath to steady herself. "Poor little Stephen Whitmore's gone missing. His father said he went in and saw his bedroom window open. He claims the fae took him. You need to leave, it isn't safe." Angela began leading her back to the gates of Veritas.

Clover frowned, thinking about Cypress. "But how did Stephen get past the gate? He couldn't have gone through by himself."

"You know very well logic and reason have no place in this town," said Angela, nearly laughing.

"So why do you have it, then?"

"Because I was educated in Hirane with my grandparents. I only came back to Veritas recently to..." She hesitated, and the damp smell of wet cloth and mold filled the air. Sorrow. Angela went on. "...Well, it doesn't matter now. My grandparents are old-fashioned at the best of times and even they think Veritas' ideas about the fae are ridiculous."

"What about your brother?"

Angela paused. "I don't know what happened to Marvin... but I know it wasn't your fault. It just wouldn't make any sense."

They got to the gate and Angela opened it for her.

Clover was about to walk through but she hesitated. "Why are you helping me?"

"I haven't been around long, but I saw the way you looked at Grant," said Angela. Clover expected to see a smirk but instead she saw glistening tears. "I know what it's like, not being with the one you want. The Book of the Veil says that 'People who help people are people who get helped.' I figure that applies to humans and fae alike."

"You...want to be with Knox, right?" Clover asked before she could stop herself. She didn't even know why she asked it. Maybe she felt she and Angela were more similar than Clover originally thought. Maybe she just felt sorry for Angela.

Angela smiled and sniffed. "We met in Hirane. I thought he was going to ask me to..." She shook her head. "Nothing to be done about it now."

Clover wanted to ask about Benjamin, but she didn't want to stay any longer for fear of townsfolk or the Justice Riders seeing them. She stepped through the gate and Angela closed it.

"Clover, wait," said Angela. "You know, I can see that tower from my bedroom window. If you ever need help, maybe coming through town...just give me a sign."

Clover stared at Angela for a moment. She had just shared a strange connection with Angela, and she found herself warming to the girl. "Thank you."

Angela gave her a beaming smile and Clover returned a polite one back before turning toward home. More people were going missing? Was this Cypress's doing? She would have to ask if Soleil could look for Fanny Logan's body or see if the forest or the other fae knew anything about her disappearance. No light fae ever took humans. This could only be

Cypress. Clover would have words with him if she saw him again.

❧

STREAKS OF GRAY WENT THROUGH HER MOTHER'S DARK HAIR. Clover ran a wood comb through it, gently getting the tangles out before putting it back in a long braid. She rolled it into a bun and stuck a pin through it.

"Does that feel all right?" She moved her mother off the pillow on the floor and up to her own bed. Clover leaned around to make eye contact with her mother, but it was like looking through a window into the foggy marshlands. "Mother, can you hear me?"

No response.

"Can you just give me a sign?" Clover moved around to kneel in front of her and took Torryn's hands. Clover pulled a little harder than necessary, but she felt desperate, a longing ache to have her mother back. "Please. It's me, Clover. Can't you just...can you just say my name, or nod, or *something!*"

Clover's voice cracked and she began to cry before putting her head on her mother's knee. Her crying grew more out of the sudden pain in her head and less about the loss of her mother. Clover looked up when she heard her mother's voice —only it wasn't coming from her mother, it was coming from a memory of her.

Torryn sat in the rocking chair near the window, both Clover and Grant on her lap. They were small, no older than three or four at the most, and they held very still. Grant could be a devil at the best of times, but he valued Torryn's affection as much as Clover had. Neither of them wanted her to slip away because she was telling them a story.

"It was a window very much like this one. Only it looked out on the sea—so closely that when I laid in bed, I would watch the sails billow through the window panes like clouds. The ships would come and go, and the crew would sing songs about the sea with their voices deep and booming like thunder." Torryn's voice began to fade away into memory, but it was all right then, because young Clover and Grant had fallen asleep. The memory faded and Clover lifted her head from her mother's shoulder. The pain was fading back into the tolerable throbbing.

Clover could be strong. Strong until winter. Grant would come back, and they would leave Dr. Van Doren to live in this big old house all on his own. Her mother would heal eventually. Knox could go back to Hirane.

She just had to make it to winter.

Chapter Twelve

THE RED DID NOT SUIT her. In the dingy mirror of her room, Clover smoothed the long sleeves of her red Blood Solstice dress, the only color she was ever allowed to wear. She had never liked the red, the reason it was worn, the fact that she was forced to wear it, or the way it made her look. Sallow.

Clover closed her eyes, and when she opened them her room was filled with memory.

The bedroom door in her memory opened and Grant stuck his head in to look at her. The memory of herself, rather. A smile spread across his face. "Ah, a winter rose."

"Stop it," said Clover. "I'm no rose. More like a weed."

Grant looked behind him to make sure his father wasn't about before stepping into the room. He took her hands and moved them out so he could see her entirely.

"Yes, you're right, that impervious weed. I see it now, though I forget the name of it. Only comes out in the summer and fall—green leaves, thick stems with the thorns—red blossoms. What's that one called?"

Clover smothered a smile. "You're not funny."

"No?" He gave her a false pout, sticking out his lower lip. Clover stood her ground on the subject and shook her head. Grant finally smiled. "Don't I at least get charming?"

"You always get charming. You would even if you didn't try."

Grant tilted his head. "So upset you don't even know what I've gotten you yet."

"If it's not a kiss, I don't want it." She tried to walk past him. He grabbed her from behind and spun her around. Clover tried not to laugh aloud. He set her down and she leaned back so he could kiss her cheek. He let her go.

"It's not a kiss, though I'm flattered by the request."

She sighed. "You shouldn't—"

He pressed a hand over her mouth. "I preemptively refuse your refusal."

She pinched his arm and he winced, removing his hand.

"Be grateful I didn't bite you."

"Well, that would have been my Blood Solstice gift." He chuckled. "Meet me in the tower?"

"Not if you're bringing a gift," she said.

He shrugged. "Fine. No gift."

"You're such a liar." Clover laughed.

"Clover, please meet me in the tower. I swear I won't displease you in any way," he said.

She raised an eyebrow.

"In any way that can't possibly be mended through time and effusive apologies," he said.

Clover couldn't smother her smile as she leaned forward and kissed him...

The door in reality opened behind Clover and Knox stuck

his head in. The memory faded. Clover had been sitting on the ground while she was lost in memory.

"What are you doing on the ground? Did you fall?" he asked.

Clover shook her head. Her eyes welled with tears, and they spilled over. Knox checked behind him to make sure Van Doren wasn't around before coming in and gently helping her to her feet.

"Hey, it's going to be all right. Remember what we're doing," he said before frowning. "You do remember what we're doing, right?"

"I remember. I wish I didn't," she said, referring to the memory he wasn't privy to.

Knox squinted at her, clearly confused.

Clover shook her head, clearing away the lingering sorrow from the memory. "I remember. I'm ready."

"I hate the Blood Solstice," said Knox, nervously straightening his bow tie only to turn it askew. Clover reached up and straightened it.

"So do I," she said. This one posed a new threat. If she was caught sneaking around where she shouldn't be, no one could save her from whatever punishments the Tavertys would give her. Even a minor punishment from them would be brutal, especially now that the Justice Riders swarmed their small village. No violence could be committed on the Blood Solstice, but they could lock her up overnight and deliver her punishment tomorrow.

Clover steadied her breath and her voice. "Let's get through this as quickly as possible and hope that it all ends here."

"Agreed." Knox held out his hand and she shook it.

೭ಿ

CLOVER MADE SURE ALL THE FOOD HER MOTHER COULD EAT
was laid out on the chair next to her mother's bed for her to
see. Torryn Grimaldi could not be brought to Veritas. If she
interrupted the Grey Service...Clover shuddered. The punishments were severe, and as much as she didn't want to leave her
mother home alone with the ill and the doctor, she also didn't
want her to be abused for some silly mistake.

That was Clover's role these days.

"Come along!" snapped Dr. Van Doren from the main
hall. No coat for Clover—only red may be worn and since she
didn't have a red coat...

She rushed out into the main hall where Knox and the
doctor waited for her to open the door.

"You represent this family—and therefore me. Do not
embarrass me." He gripped her arm. The whispering began
gathering at the edges of her hearing, but she ignored it.

"Yes, Master Van Doren," she said. He would not be going
to the Grey Services. Not only did he secretly believe the religion to be for the dull of mind, but he had patients to attend
to. She had to prepare all *his* meals beforehand as well.

He let her go so she could open the door. The handle
clicked and the heavy door swung open. She let Knox pass
before locking the door behind them and walking in Knox's
footprints. They were bigger and farther apart than hers, but
at least she didn't have to carve a path through the snow for
herself.

"The Blood Solstice," Knox muttered under his breath. "I
thought I was finished with these things when I was a child—
here I am, trekking through the cold to be lectured at for four
hours."

"Don't you believe at all in your people's religion?" asked Clover.

Knox scoffed. "There has to be something better when we die than an endless gray void to wander through. You're half human, do you believe in it?"

"Of course not. The fae have a religion. It seems better but I never asked about it—I've been meaning to but...I guess other things seem more urgent." She stumbled when her foot fell through the snow a little too quickly but she righted herself.

"A fae religion...I don't know anything about it. It doesn't come up much in the city. Do they have holidays?"

Clover shrugged, though he wasn't looking at her. "Probably, but Soleil sought to teach me about the forest, not all fae customs. She's not the talkative sort."

"Am I ever going to meet this mysterious figure?"

"No. She never leaves the forest and she hates humans."

Knox drove his foot through the snow. "Can't say I'm overly fond of them myself. I've seen just how bad they can be."

"Grant believes in the goodness of people," said Clover. She smiled at the thought of his eyes. They could shine like the sun at midday while he laid their future out before them, all of it optimistically perfect.

Clover held onto the thought with white knuckles. "I guess both perspectives are right in a way. I used to believe there weren't any good people other than him."

"What changed your mind?" he asked and she rolled her eyes, staying silent. He laughed. "Oh Grim, you flatter me."

"It's not just you...it's others. People like Angela. But I have a question."

"Do tell."

Clover stopped to catch her breath and use some of the

courage she was building to be so bold. "Why didn't you ask Angela Hallows to marry you?"

Knox stopped walking too and he let out a sigh. "I was going to."

"So why didn't you?" Clover caught up to him.

"I..." He sighed. "...waited too long. I wasted time worrying that she wouldn't want to spend the rest of her days with a poor journalist."

"When I spoke with her, she seemed very sorry that you didn't ask her," said Clover.

Knox frowned. "I know you're trying to help, but that doesn't make me feel better. You know—knowing I disappointed her."

"I thought you'd like confirmation that she did in fact want to spend the rest of her life with a poor journalist, as you put it."

"You know, you're not supposed to say stuff like that." He smiled. "I'm supposed to be the optimist and you're Grim." He began walking again.

Clover followed in his footsteps. "She's not married to Benjamin, they're only courting. You can still get her back."

"One thing at a time, Grim. First, I've got to find my kidnapped cousin to reunite him with his true love, then I can worry about mine."

"If you say so, but I'm not letting this go."

Knox turned with a grin. "Yeah, I'm sensing a pattern."

Clover smiled to herself. Meeting Knox and Angela and having them defy all expectations of what humans were supposed to be like had changed her mind. Not entirely, since she still believed the majority of humans were terrible, but she was more confident that there were some out there who were different.

ONCE INSIDE VERITAS' GATES, CLOVER AND KNOX NO LONGER
had to forge a path through the snow and they easily made
their way to the church. On the way, they passed Benjamin
and his family. He snarled at her but no violence could be
committed on the Blood Solstice. For once, she wasn't worried
about being attacked by Benjamin and his gang.

Everyone stood stark and red against the dismal dark gray
of their buildings and the pure white of the snow. It was
almost beautiful—but a different kind. A hauntingly beautiful
spectacle, less of a miraculous beauty than nature provided.

The church loomed ahead of them across the town square.
It was the tallest building in Veritas, square in shape with
tower-shaped points on each of the four corners and another
over the door where people were going in and out. It reminded
Clover of the way Grant explained how blood flows in and out
of the heart. Even the Justice Riders sported red versions of
their usual crisp uniforms.

Something caught underfoot and Clover stumbled,
sprawling hands first into the hard-packed snow. Her teeth
were already chattering, and the tips of her fingers and toes
stung, along with her nose and cheeks. Red-clothed children
laughed as they ran past her and she pushed herself up and
brushed snow from her dress.

Stick to the plan, she told herself in her head. Stick to the
plan and resist the urge to burn down the church.

Reverend Taverty, similar and birdlike to his wife who was
beside him were greeting people at the door. They beamed
when they saw Knox, who gave them a formal introduction as
Warner. Their smiles fell into scowls when they saw Clover.

Someone grabbed her roughly by the arm and yanked her

backward. She slipped on the ice-slick snow, so the only thing holding her up was whoever grabbed her.

"What is the meaning of this halfbreed entering a holy place?" said Captain Dawson.

Clover didn't dare struggle, but the more off balance she became, the harder he gripped her arm, and her mouth opened in a silent shout.

"As a favor to the Van Doren family, we allow her into this holy place once a year in the off chance that her soul might be saved," said Reverend Taverty.

Knox looked between Reverend Taverty and the captain, probably weighing his odds. Clover caught his eye and shook her head. She had to get into that basement. The plan was still on.

Captain Dawson seemed to consider this before slowly lifting Clover and setting her on her feet. "Very well. Make sure to keep a close eye on her."

"We will. Pay attention, creature," said Reverend Taverty.

Clover gritted her teeth and nodded once before passing them. The inside of the church was nothing extraordinary. Six windows covered every wall, and all the decorations were red, black, or white. It was...something. Definitely not beautiful. Catching, perhaps? Whatever it was, the effect fascinated her.

Clover went to the back of the church near the door—the only place she was permitted to be. Knox was shown to his seat at the front of the church. On his way there, he waved subtly to Angela, who smiled back at him.

Clover's heart was mildly warmed at the sight, but another wave of worry overwhelmed her when she saw a Justice Rider watching her nearby. While people were still coming in, Angela turned to her and Clover gave a subtle bow of her head. Angela did the same back with a smile. Clover didn't want to smile. For her, this was not a day of smiling. But it was Angela, and if there was anyone good in this town, then it was she. So, Clover gave her a smile back. Angela's smile only grew brighter before she turned around in her seat. Once everyone was in the church, the Grey Services began.

FOUR HOURS OF SERVICES. CLOVER FELL ASLEEP TWICE AND SHE was forced to stand the whole time. Sleeping was only punishable if you were caught and over the years, she had seen many adapt to the length of the services. The Vale twins, for example. One of them would bow their head to pray or fall asleep, rather. Then the other would wake his brother so he could get a turn. Clover had seen outright hiding under the benches, pretending to lean down and tie shoes. Children fell asleep into each other only to be pulled up and woken by their parents—it was disastrous if someone began to snore.

During these services, she couldn't help but feel a moment of pity for them. She only had to attend service during the Blood Solstice. They had to attend a service every fourteenth day. Those services weren't as long, but were just as boring with Reverend Taverty droning on.

Clover snapped herself awake for the third time as Reverend Taverty was conducting his final prayer. A little boy sitting in the pew in front of her had thrown a small pebble at her that hit her in the forehead. Both his parents were dozing on either side of him. At first, she was a little annoyed by the act, but then she realized he probably saved her some grief. She did what she thought she might never do.

Clover smiled at the little boy. She didn't know what she was thinking. This boy, this human would probably grow to hate her and her kind. He would grow to be like Benjamin—want to cut her open and experiment on her or simply cast her out or kill her altogether. But she couldn't deny that right now, he was just a little boy.

And he smiled back at her.

A collective sigh of relief came from the town of Veritas as the final prayer was finished. They stood from their pews, stretched, shook hands, or embraced each other, and now the real celebration would begin. More candles were lit, the pews were cleared away by the men and the tables were brought in by the women.

"You! You there! Get to work!" said Mrs. Taverty.

Ah, yes, the great honor, Clover thought before picking up a broom by the door and sweeping around the church like she did every year. Her penance for being born, she supposed. But this year was going to be different. Her task was a benefit, as she needed to be able to move about the room to get to the door at the back of the church. It was the only way to get into the basement.

THIS WAS IMPOSSIBLE. IT SEEMED LIKE EVERYWHERE SHE WENT, all eyes were on her. Whispering or simply speaking out loud how they suspected her of stealing their children out of their beds and killing them in the forest. Apparently, Fanny Logan's body was found in the woods the day before. Clover sighed—between the townsfolk, the Justice Riders, and the Tavertys, she was never going to get behind that door. She needed a bigger distraction than the one they had planned.

"Servant!" Knox called with a fake smile.

Clover resisted the urge to roll her eyes, but she made her way over with the broom.

"Master Van Doren?" she asked, and he pulled her away from people trying to overhear their conversation.

"What's the holdup?"

"Everyone is looking at me," she whispered with her eyes cast to the ground. "We're going to need more help."

Knox huffed before looking around. "Angela would help us."

"We don't have time for you to tell her everything."

"Have a little faith, Grim. Angela is my best accomplice," he said. "Just get yourself in position by that door and we'll take care of the rest."

Clover bowed before taking up her broom and continuing to sweep around people. She swept up their garbage and cleaned their spills all the way over to the door. She flicked her eyes up to Knox, who took a sip of his drink. A signal asking if she was ready.

Clover tucked her hair behind both her ears. Knox grimaced and she knew what he had to do. Knox made his way over to Mrs. Taverty and began flirting with her. She could hear them from where she was sweeping, and she tried not to laugh.

"Good Solstice, Mrs. Taverty. I've been meaning to ask if you arranged these decorations?"

Mrs. Taverty raised her nose. "I did."

"They're just lovely, not even the churches of Hirane compare. There's no heart in them there, you can tell they're just thrown about. These! These were done with great care."

"Oh...well, that's kind of you, young man. It's good that you've come to the country—it's the city itself that has no heart. Out here, the church is what keeps the faith alive."

"I definitely see that. I can tell you dedicate much of your life to the church," said Knox. "You would have made an excellent Grey Priestess."

Mrs. Taverty smiled and placed a hand on her chest. "My mother was a Grey Priestess…"

Just then the high windows opened with a bang and all the candles in the church blew out at once. Clover saw Knox before all the light was gone and she smiled to herself. Angela. The girl must have cut the ropes for the counterweights that kept the large windows either opened or closed. In the sudden darkness, people began to panic, and Clover dove through the door and closed it quietly behind her. Her minutes began now. Time to find Grant.

※

THE TAVERTYS WOULD WANT TO KEEP HIM HIDDEN, BUT HE wasn't a prisoner. He was the good doctor's son. They would want him to be comfortable, so as much as Clover hated it, she had to check their room first. It was sparse with few places to hide a boy like Grant, and she passed over it quickly. Then it was onward to the basement.

In the middle of the hallway, her feet stopped working. Her entire body froze as a jarring pain crept through the top of her head. Clover doubled over, pressing her palms to the crown of her head. Her eyes watered with pain, but she bit her lip to keep from crying out in case someone heard her.

"Not now," she whispered to herself, but it didn't matter. The pain began to dull and thankfully, no memories appeared.

"So…what are we doing down here?" asked Grant, standing beside her.

Clover let out a sharp breath of shock. "Grant? You can't be here."

"But I'm not here." He tried to take the broom that was still in her hand. She propped it against the wall and began walking.

"I guess you're right. We need to hurry. I'm looking for you."

"And you think I'm in the Tavertys basement?" he asked before taking a moment to think about it as they got to the end of the hall. "It would make sense, they're sick enough to do something like that."

Clover opened the door that was capable of being locked from the outside, which was both horrifying and curious. "I don't have a lot of time." She pushed the door open into utter darkness. A lantern hung outside the door, so she took it to light the narrow steps that led downward.

An old, dank smell came from the darkness. A chill ran up her spine but she forced her feet to move forward against the will of her body, which wanted to run away. There wasn't much to see until the staircase ended and the basement opened before her.

It reminded her of Dr. Van Doren's office with lots of desks covered in beakers and books and ink and notes. In the middle of the room was a metal table but nothing was on it. This wasn't sort of the place she imagined they could keep Grant, but she also didn't understand why the Tavertys had a laboratory in their basement.

"No," said Grant. "I don't feel close. I also don't like this place." He began coughing loudly and she was going to shush him before remembering she was the only one who could hear him.

"What's the matter with you?"

He cleared his throat. "I feel ill and tired."

He definitely looked it. His eyes were sunken, and his cheeks seemed more hollow. Was he…no. No, he couldn't be. Van Doren wouldn't take his son and hide him away just to kill him. Grant wasn't dying.

"What's that?" asked Grant, pointing.

Clover went to one of the tables with raised shelves over it and found a book full of notes.

"Fae Exper…experiment—" Clover frowned before lifting the lantern higher. She clamped a hand over her mouth as she came face to face with a severed head. She stumbled back and her lower back painfully hit the edge of the metal table. Was that the head of a fae? There were more jars holding other body parts: hands, eyes, in one case, a heart. Clover was going to be sick.

"All right. Stay calm. Breathe, breathe." Grant stepped in front of her but she could still see through him. "You have to focus. If they find you down here, you'll end up in one of those jars."

Clover nodded. In through the nose, out through the mouth. She strode forward and grabbed the book of fae experiment records. As she rushed for the exit, she shoved the book down the front of her dress—it had room to spare. Knox would know what to do with what she found.

SHE TOOK THE STAIRS TWO AT A TIME, BREATHING HARD OUT of fear—a newfound fear of the Tavertys and a fear of being caught. She closed and locked the door behind her, and Grant stepped through it with raised eyebrows of shock. Clover hung up the lantern before rushing to the end of the hall.

She grabbed her broom and opened the door an inch. Some of the candles were re-lit by now. People were rushing about, trying to get the hundreds of candles re-lit. She stepped through the door and closed it behind her with Grant still by her side. As she suspected, no one else seemed to see him.

"You, girl! Get to work on lighting these candles or I'll light you up myself!" snapped Reverend Taverty.

Grant grinned. "Better do as he says, now that we know what he's really up to."

"I failed you," she said quietly, her throat growing tight. "I'm running out of places to look—you're getting weaker. I can feel it."

He shook his head. "I have the utmost faith in you. I always have." He leaned forward as though to kiss her cheek and she closed her eyes. "Merry Solstice, love."

When she opened her eyes, he was gone. She let out a strained sob before holding her breath, attempting to contain herself.

"Girl!" shouted Reverend Taverty. "Don't make me tell you again!"

Clover clenched her fists hard and closed her eyes. Her anger burned like a flame unyielding. Could he not give her a moment? Was there nothing in him that sensed her pain? Of course not! He was evil! A vile murderer!

People began shouting and gasping and Clover opened her eyes to see the whole church lit up. The candles had all come to life and burned fiercely. Her fists unclenched as she realized what she'd just done. Knox stared at her from nearby. He quickly came over and grabbed her by the arm.

"It's been a lovely Blood Solstice! Best I've had in ages! Reverend, Mrs. Taverty—I do hope you'll have us back next year. Everyone, please enjoy the rest of the festivities!" he said jovially, all the while dragging Clover toward the door, which he opened and closed behind them quickly. The doors opened again behind them. Clover turned to look, thinking it might be Angela, but Knox stopped her.

"It's Justice Riders, don't look," he said.

"You there! Stop!" shouted Captain Dawson but they didn't stop and he didn't give chase.

They didn't talk until they were outside the gate.

"Are you out of your mind?" Knox nearly shouted. "You're lucky they were too shocked or else they would have put you in chains right then and there."

Clover's eyes burned. "I didn't mean to." She forced her tone to be even.

"You didn't mean to? Clover, somehow that makes it worse!"

"I just wanted a moment!" she shouted back at him before pressing her hands over her face to cry. "Couldn't I just have a moment?"

Knox groaned before gently putting a hand on her shoulder. "All right, all right. I'm sorry, Grim. I don't want you to end up on the wrong side of a Justice Rider." He took his hand away.

Clover wiped her eyes and caught her breath. She reached down the front of her dress and held the book out to Knox.

"Uh…" He flicked his eyes between it and her a few times. "Aren't you full of surprises? What's this?"

"I found it in the Tavertys basement, along with their fae laboratory."

Knox's mouth fell open. "What?"

"Well, the fae body parts in jars gave it away mostly. I couldn't read what was in the book. I thought you might want it." She began walking and he followed behind. She could hear him flipping through the pages.

"I'm sorry you didn't find Grant, but Grim…this is the find of a lifetime. If I can find a link between this lab and the one in Hirane, I could unlock a whole chain of laboratories. People like the Tavertys would go to prison for the rest of their lives," he said as he caught up to her trekking through the snow.

Clover raised an eyebrow.

Knox cleared his throat. "After we find Grant, of course." He put the book in his pocket.

"I'm glad I could help you back in some way," she said.

He grinned. "Are you trying to thank me?"

Annoyed, Clover waved him off, going back to focusing on pushing through the snow on the road back to Van Doren Manor. She hadn't failed—Grant was still out there, he just wasn't in the church. That still left many other places for him to be. Hope wasn't lost, just a little dimmed by her disappointment. This was far from over.

Her mother was still in her room where Clover left her but had eaten none of the food Clover set out for her.

Clover wanted to stay and take care of Torryn, but she knew Van Doren would want her to see to whatever he needed first. So she left her mother and made her way to the hospital wing, where Dr. Van Doren was looking through his notes. The whispers emanating from her pocket grew stronger.

"Is there anything I can do for you, Master Van Doren?"

He glowered. "I require the assistance of your mother."

The whispers grew louder and for a moment, she thought

she heard the whispers become more pronounced. Like they were saying something.

Clover closed her eyes, trying to clear her mind. "Couldn't I help you instead? My mother is resting and she's very—"

He dropped his notes and surged toward Clover before she could finish. This would be the point where she held her ground. Closed her eyes. Waited to be struck to the floor.

Instead, she stepped back and the hand he'd sent out to strike her missed completely. She kept backing up and Dr. Van Doren's expression grew even darker and viler as he advanced toward her. The whispers grew louder like a torrent of rain against the roof of the manor. But she also began to hear words. A jumble of words that filled her head so she couldn't hear anything else.

Knox stepped out of a hospital room directly between the two of them. Clover's hand slipped into her pocket and the whispers solidified into coherent words, three phrases overlapping each other:

THEM THAT KILLS A KILLER IS A HERO.
Kill the doctor and bring me his heart
I'll be waiting for you

THE WORDS CONTINUED TO OVERLAP BUT SHE COULD HEAR them all and make them out perfectly.

"Bring me the woman. Now," Van Doren demanded, but his voice sounded funny and far away.

Knox stood firm. "No. Clover can help you with whatever you need. Torryn is sick—she'll die if you disturb her."

"It would be wise for you to stop defying me—don't think I

can't take away everything that you are," said Van Doren. "Into the room with me, girl. I still have patients to treat."

Van Doren turned his back and Clover gripped the dagger harder in her hand. It would be all too easy. Drive the dagger into his back or hook her arm around his throat and drag the blade across his skin, pushing down hard. She took the iveen dagger far enough out of her pocket to allow it to flash in the lamplight.

Knox grabbed her arm. "Please tell me that's a spoon."

Clover tried to pull away, but he was stronger than she was. He quickly pushed her arm aside and took the dagger for himself.

"You need to get that temper of yours under control. Killing him won't solve anything." He walked away with the dagger. He pointed upward, gesturing to the tower. Clover nodded and stepped after him to retrieve her dagger.

"Girl!" Van Doren's voice halted her steps. "Don't make me ask you again."

"Yes, Master Van Doren," she said before stepping into the room. She helped him assist patients into the night.

WHEN SHE WAS FINISHED WITH VAN DOREN AND HE HAD GONE to bed, Clover leaned against the wooden kitchen table, resting her hands on it and sighing. This truly was the longest night of the year. She left the kitchen and went to her mother's room, wrapping her in another blanket. She tried to get her mother to eat, but it was no use.

"This is no holiday." Torryn stared at the ceiling. "This was never good."

Clover nodded. "I know..." Even though she didn't know.

She hardly ever knew what her mother was talking about. So much about her was so hard to decipher. "Go to sleep, mother. You're all right now." She kissed her mother's forehead before making sure the blanket was secure and the fire was warm.

She took a few moments for herself—warming by the fire while she made sure her mother went to sleep. Once Torryn's breathing became even and her features relaxed, Clover made her way up to the tower. Knox was inside when she pushed the door open. He had a blanket around his shoulders and was beginning to nod off.

"Ah, Grim, always ready with a cheerful expression. I can tell from your smile you had fun tonight," he said.

Clover's frown deepened. "Did you thank Angela for helping us?"

"I would say so," he said, nodding, but he just kept nodding. "Yes."

"What did you do?" She narrowed her eyes.

He shrugged. "I have no idea what you're talking about. Back to the problem at hand. Anywhere else in Veritas Grant could be kept?"

"No." Clover shook her head. "No one else would be loyal enough to hold him without gossiping and Angela would have heard something and told me by now."

"All right. We've still got letters to receive from my contacts," said Knox. "This is what investigation is all about. Ruling out suspicions until you're left with the facts. It was good work."

She rarely got compliments on her work, and it gave her a little pleasure to know that she was decent at something other than housework. She could be an investigator, couldn't she? If she were free, she'd have the option to consider it. As it was…

"Thanks," said Clover before remembering all the fae body parts. "It didn't feel like good work."

"It's one more place to cross off the list, with our prime suspect being, of course, the good doctor himself," said Knox.

She crossed her arms. "So now we wait for the letters?"

"We wait for the letters, preferably with patience, but considering patience is a good grace you lack, I won't set my expectations too high," he said.

Clover rolled her eyes. "Ever the charming."

"If I wasn't, you wouldn't have had time to find an entire fae laboratory," he said.

"Then I guess we'll be expecting a letter from Mrs. Taverty as well, won't we?" asked Clover with a smirk. Knox grimaced.

So maybe she wasn't the most patient, but she'd have to wait for these letters whether she liked it or not. At least the Blood Solstice was over for another year.

Chapter Thirteen

THERE WERE NO STARS. The mist blocked out the sky, but through it snow gently fell. It touched the ground around Clover in an arc, none of it reached her as she manipulated the air around her body. That was as far as she had gotten with her training with Soleil. She ran her fingers through the snow beneath her, feeling the cold.

Clover felt the closest to Grant here in the forest, and she didn't know why. It was as though the tether between them was so short, she could reach out and touch him. The sky seemed closer here, though she in no way thought Grant was up in the sky. She just missed him. He loved everything to do with winter, except the mist. He always complained about how he wanted to go into the forest, but it wouldn't let him see.

Her eyes drifted shut as she tried to remember him as he was. Running around the yard as a child playing in the snow. Him climbing up the back wall to try peering through the forest mist. He would always be that way in her memory, but she wanted him that way now. Even if he felt close here, he was still beyond her reach.

Clover turned on her side in the snow and curled in on herself. The morning would wake her. She closed her eyes and forced herself to drift to sleep even though her waking mind clawed at her to remain conscious. Darkness overwhelmed her and she clung to it. Grant was somewhere in that darkness; she would get him back. No matter what it took. The iveen blade in the pocket of her Blood Solstice dress whispered for her, trying to get her attention. She closed her eyes hard, willing it to go away, but it refused. She had to get back to the manor now, but she didn't want to go back. She never wanted to…but she always did.

Frost danced upward across the windows. Laundry was now done inside and hung in front of the large fire in the kitchen. Snow laced every surface and the cases of Grey Fever increased every day. Most were treated at home with information given to the town by Dr. Van Doren, but serious cases came to the manor.

All five of their patient rooms were filled and Clover stood in one of the rooms Mrs. Taverty had recently filled. The woman was wailing and carrying on even though most of the worst symptoms had passed quickly in the three days she'd been there. Clover had no doubt the only thing remaining was a cough and a stuffy nose. As she stood holding a tray of instruments for Dr. Van Doren, she resisted the urge to roll her eyes.

Mrs. Taverty rolled her head back and forth. "Oh, good

doctor, will I make it? I promised my grandchildren in North-burry I would come visit them in the spring."

"I believe you'll be just fine, Mrs. Taverty," said Dr. Van Doren.

Unfortunately for your grandchildren, Clover thought to herself.

If Dr. Van Doren was irritated with Taverty's moaning and groaning, he didn't show it, and Clover hoped she didn't, either. Mrs. Taverty looked fine. Her birdlike self was a little thinner perhaps, causing her to look more skeletal, but she'd barely been sick in the first place.

"Don't you sneer at me, creature," said Mrs. Taverty and Clover frowned before turning away. She was reminded of the laboratory in the Taverty basement and she clamped her teeth together to keep from shivering.

Mrs. Taverty went on, "Grey forbid you ever have a chance to procreate. I doubt your tainted womb is even capable."

Clover took an even breath. She had never considered having children before. She wasn't sure she wanted to but maybe she would just to spite Mrs. Taverty. This scenario meant that they had finally found Grant and they were married. Clover buried her anger in a hope for the future.

Grant had once asked her if she had ever wanted more out of life. He wanted to help people, but she never really thought about what *she* wanted. Clover didn't know what she was good at. Knox was good at solving problems, and it was what he liked to do, as well as write his discoveries down and turn them into a story for the people of Hirane. But Clover Grimaldi? What could she do? She could clean and do laundry and get back up when someone knocked her down.

Not exactly skills you could use to strike out into the world.

Clover shook her head, and she was brought back to the

patient room where Dr. Van Doren was finishing Mrs. Taverty's patient assessment.

"Mrs. Taverty, you are right as rain, another day should do it. Take your time gathering your things and I'll have Miss Bell send a carriage to pick you up from town the morning after tomorrow," said Dr. Van Doren.

Clover put down the tray and followed him out of the room. Mrs. Taverty sniffed, lifting her nose into the air and scowling, offended by the result of her diagnoses, as though she wanted to suffer. And Clover was supposedly the strange creature.

❦

THE DOCTOR TURNED TO HER. "GO CHECK ON THE OTHER patients, see if they need anything—but don't be so foolish as to give them anything cold."

"Yes, Master Van Doren." Clover walked past him.

Mrs. Taverty had been in the very last room. In the room next to hers was a young boy who looked deathly pale. He was asleep and Clover frowned at the wet, ragged sounds of his breathing. He had knocked his stuffed bear off his too-large bed, so Clover picked it up and put it next to him. The young ones usually died, but he was still hanging on. She gently reached up and brushed the hair on his burning forehead to one side. He was human, bound to grow up and revile her just like his parents probably did and his grandparents would have as well. She should have the same feeling toward him, but she couldn't. He was innocent. Even Benjamin Freeman had been innocent once. This one would grow up and maybe he would be different.

She left the room. In the next room was another young

one, a girl this time. The girl was a bit older and in the throes of it, coughing and hacking while reading a book. Clover placed another clean linen on the girl's lap before gently taking the bloody one and putting it in a lidded bucket by the door.

"Do you know this word?" asked the girl.

Clover looked back at her. The girl was holding up the book and pointing. She didn't seem all too worried about her condition, but Dr. Van Doren was revered. Her parents had probably convinced her she would be fine. Clover hoped she would be fine, too. The very inner edge of the girl's lips was red with blood and Clover held back a look of pity and fear.

Clover shook her head. "I don't. I'm sorry, I can't read."

"Oh, sorry. Could I have some water, please?"

"I'll bring you some."

"Thank you."

Clover left her room and her eyebrows flicked up. *Thank you?* What sort of heathens were these new children? Thanking the half-breed? They must be the disappointments of their race.

In the last two rooms were older people. In one was a man who was asleep, in the last was a woman. She screamed when she saw Clover and Clover was so startled her knees nearly gave way.

"Get away from me!" she howled. "You evil, evil being! You're making me sick! Get away! May the Grey protect me!"

Clover slipped out of the room and closed the door quickly, eyes wide. From within she could still hear the woman shouting. Well, the doctor had told her to give the patients what they needed. Clover went back and got a warm glass of water for the young girl before letting out a sigh and smoothing the front of her apron.

ASSISTING THE DOCTOR DURING THE DAY, REOCCURRING SPELLS of darkness that stabbed through her like a blade, her usual duties, and magic lessons at night were wearing on Clover. It was winter and every day, Knox begged her to be patient. He told her that the information would come in at any moment, but Clover was beginning not to care, or maybe she just didn't have the energy to worry about it until it arrived. She had other more present matters to worry about, like her mother.

Torryn was sitting on the stairs dusting the spindles and Clover watched her carefully as she passed by on the way to the parlor. Torryn's teeth were chattering slightly, and Clover made a note to get her mother's shawl.

Her mother seemed blank but she moved with purpose and Clover supposed that was something. Torryn still wasn't speaking but more than once Clover had seen the barest spark behind her mother's eyes. It would get even better once they had left this place. If or when Clover had children, Torryn would be there to know them. Torryn had been mostly catatonic since Clover was ten. That was an awfully long time to be missing from one's own life. But Clover had to hope there was still part of her mother inside the shell. If not...well, she didn't want to think "if not."

As for her current duties, Clover figured she'd better step into the parlor to make sure there wasn't anything the visitors needed, the fire to be stoked or something to eat. In the parlor were several people, including Knox, who was speaking to them quietly. Maybe reassuring them? That *was* part of a doctor's duty and Grant had been proficient at it. The visitors in the room were two pairs of young adults, probably the parents of the younger patients. There was an old woman and an old man who were talking to one another—probably the spouses of the older patients. The older people looked at her and frowned before turning back to each other, and the younger parents did the same. The only difference was that the younger parents reeked of fear. The whole room reeked of the corrosive smell and it made her nose tingle.

Knox seemed to sense the tension and rushed over. "How is everyone?"

Part of her was annoyed. She was doing his job, after all. But she also didn't want to be the one dealing with these parents who were more scared of her effect on their children than the deathly sickness their children were infected with.

"I saw all the patients. Matthew is sleeping peacefully. Evangeline is still getting through the harder part. The older gentleman is asleep, and the woman is well enough to shriek at the sight of me."

Knox nodded. "Yes, well, you are frightening. I'll alert the parents."

"You could at least pretend to be a doctor. I can't watch the patients. I have to cook lunch soon," she said.

"Right. I'll wrap it up. Thank you for your help," he said.

Clover bowed and he rolled his eyes before putting on a smile and turning back to the parents. Clover checked on the patients one last time before Knox showed up to make the rounds himself. Dr. Van Doren didn't make rounds as often as Grant did, and maybe Clover was being paranoid but the last thing she wanted to see was a small coffin. Small enough for a child like Matthew or Evangeline.

‹❧›

CLOVER CAME BACK TO THE STAIRCASE WHERE HER MOTHER was still dusting spindles, though not the same ones as before. Torryn was making steady progress up the steps and her teeth were still chattering. Clover stopped her mother's hands and put Torryn's arms through the slits in the shawl before closing it with the buttons on the front. Clover was about to leave when she saw the cloth that her mother had been using on the spindles.

It was tinted with red. She forced Torryn to face her and parted her lips slightly to see blood on her mother's gums.

"Oh no," she said.

Torryn leaned forward and put her head on Clover's shoulder. She began to cough, and Clover held the rag up to her mother's mouth. Only a little blood was coming, but it would get worse. It would get much worse.

"You're going to be all right. Let's get you to bed."

Clover pulled her mother off the stairs, and slowly led her toward the dining room. She didn't want the patients' families to see that her mother was sick, too. There was tromping as Dr. Van Doren came down from his office.

"Servant! I need you."

"My mother is ill, Master Van Doren. She needs rest," said Clover. *That* was bold. She kept walking. She was about to be punished; her mother didn't need to be part of that. Clover pulled Torryn quickly through the dining room, the kitchen, and the servants' quarters before laying her down.

"Stay here, try to sleep," said Clover. She rushed out and only made it as far as the dining room before Dr. Van Doren was there. Clover took a step back, but he grabbed her by the shoulders and swung her to the side. Clover connected painfully with one of the wood walls. She hit her head so hard that at first, she didn't hear what the doctor was saying.

"…and you will come when you are called! You are nothing! How many times must I explain it?" He pulled her off the wall and threw her toward the door. Clover went stumbling and her shoulder hit the partially open door painfully. She fell to the floor, gasping in pain.

Dr. Van Doren walked past her. "Get up."

She tried, she definitely tried but it wasn't fast enough, because Dr. Van Doren came back and pulled her up by the hair and dragged her along.

⁊⃘

DR. VAN DOREN HAD HER CLEANING UP BLOOD, CLEANING out bedpans, and washing the patients, all with her shoulder, which ached and burned every time she moved it. Finally, it was closing in on lunchtime and she was sweating from the strain in her shoulder. He dismissed her. Clover went toward the kitchen, stopping first by the parlor. Many visitors had left—the spouses of the older patients and the fathers of the two children, leaving Matthew and Evangeline's mothers behind.

They stood when she entered, and though Clover could still smell their fear, she sensed something else. It was hard to tell if it was compassion or pity but either was welcome compared to Dr. Van Doren's cruelty.

Clover clasped her hands together before speaking. "Your children are both fine. I came to ask if you were interested in lunch. I'll be serving a mild broth for the doctor and patients alike."

Neither woman said anything, so Clover bowed before leaving the room.

"Do you…" Evangeline's mother started, and Clover

turned back to her. The woman finished after a little more hesitation, "...need any help?"

Clover shook her head. "No thank you. I'll be ready in a while." She left the women, holding her arm to her body as it began to throb again, and went into the kitchen where Knox was waiting for her.

"Infiltrating the kitchen again, I know." He held up a hand at her frown. "I came to help with something else. Sit."

"Knox, I don't have time for games."

Knox frowned. "What a shame, I really wanted to play Kill the King with you. Sit." He sat on one of the stools and patted the other.

Clover sighed before sitting. "Hurry up, I have to make lunch."

"Ease up," he said. Clover relaxed her shoulders, and he reached forward and took the arm of her bad hand. "The whole house heard the scuffle in the dining room."

Clover's eyebrows went up. Maybe that's why the women had offered to help her.

"Back in Hirane, I see this particular injury every other week, it seems. Something I actually know how to treat, doctor or not." He did some slow and gentle arm movements, and with a small pop, Clover flinched, but the pain diminished significantly. It no longer felt like a blade was trapped between her arm and her body.

She narrowed her eyes. "How did you do that?"

"Street smarts. Dislocated shoulders are a Vincent Syndicate favorite for nosy reporters," said Knox before standing. "Go easy on it and good luck with lunch." He stopped at the door and turned back. "Can I help?"

"Rounds!" she warned, pointing her finger at him, and he nodded.

❦

"MASTER VAN DOREN, MY MOTHER HAS COME DOWN WITH Grey Fever." Clover stood in the doctor's office. It seemed darker than ever, as he was no longer lighting the candelabras on the far walls. It only made the room seem smaller.

Dr. Van Doren didn't look up and he didn't respond. Clover didn't know what to do now. Her mother needed help.

Finally, he sighed. "I'll look into it if I have time. Dismissed."

Clover frowned but left the room without a word. She had no confidence that he was going to take care of her mother but what else could she do? She followed her feet out into the main hall and saw Knox sitting on the staircase. He was holding something in his hand and when he saw her, he brandished the off-white square of paper in the air.

A letter.

She rushed over and he stood. They went through the kitchen and into her room, closing the door. Dr. Van Doren couldn't possibly hear them from in here.

Knox ripped open the letter before reading it aloud. " 'Dear Knox…' blah, blah, blah, he's talking about how things are in Hirane. Here! 'I sent Dougherty and Wain out to Northburry and Laewaes looking for your cousin, and I personally searched the city. I am sorry to report that…' " Knox's reading slowed. " 'There was no trace of him found anywhere. If he's missing, then he's close. Deepest regrets…etcetera.' "

Knox let the letter fall to his side. He looked at her warily, like she would break down crying, but she didn't see how this was bad news. He was acting like it was over.

Clover shrugged. "So he wasn't anywhere else? So what? That only means what your friend said—he's close by."

"Maybe…" Knox looked down at his shoes. "Logically, there's only two options left. He's either in the forest…or he's in the grave."

"He's not in his grave," said Clover. "That would mean he's dead."

"Are you sure?"

"How would I not be sure? He's not there."

"Did you see that it was empty? Did you see it?" Knox demanded.

Clover said nothing. Her mouth and throat dried as her eyes burned and welled with tears. She didn't have to see the grave, she just knew. But how was she supposed to convince Knox of that? The visions? He would only think she was insane, especially now that he was doubting her.

"He's not in the grave. I will prove it to you." She took a shuddering breath before opening her door.

His jaw set, its muscles flexing before he nodded and folded up the letter. "I hope you can prove it. I don't want you to be wrong."

Clover wasn't able to read Knox's face before he left and she worried that she might have estranged him. She didn't just need him as an ally, he was also a friend.

Why was he so willing to give up? Why couldn't he feel that Grant was alive like she could? She knew Knox wasn't fae, there was no tangible tether he could look at or feel—but he and Grant had loved each other. Couldn't he feel Grant in his own human way? Or was he clouded by his doubt?

Clover sighed and laid down on her bed. Her forehead was burning but only because her head was hammering along to the beat of her heart from the fight. Grant wasn't an idea; he was a person with a heart that was still beating somewhere. She could feel it, as though he were right under her hands.

Clover could feel the steady rise and fall of his chest like he was sleeping. She wasn't giving up, so she reviewed all the facts in her head. Grant's death had been faked, and now that she knew he hadn't been anywhere else, it narrowed down the places for her to search. Her mind went back to the day when Soleil told her to see the truth—the truth being Grant's body. But Clover hadn't gotten the chance before the funeral was over and—

Clover sat up. "The funeral," she said aloud. Grant's coffin was empty, Clover knew it, so it was never in the cards for Knox. She could tell him about the visions, but that could possibly add to him thinking she was crazy. But if she could prove to Knox that Grant's coffin was empty, maybe she could get him back on her side and they could continue making progress. This convincing meant that she and Knox had to dig up Grant's coffin. Knox. Who could barely stand the sight of blood.

It was going to take some convincing, but she knew she was right. She wasn't going to give up on Grant. She loved him and if it were the other way around, he would be doing the exact same thing she was.

Chapter Fourteen

THE COLD WAS BITING, and Clover's feet were numb before she made it across the yard and into the forest. The wind howled, snowflakes whipped at her face, and she swore she could feel them through her coat. The snow ended where the forest began but the cold did not. The trees and plants were stripped bare of their foliage, but to keep outsiders away, a thick fog shrouded the forest like a coat.

Clover walked through it without a second thought. Soleil was waiting for her in the clearing she had created before winter. She was still wearing that lighter-than-air outfit, using an internal fire to keep herself warm. Clover hadn't quite mastered that yet. Since that first flame, Clover had grown more familiar with both fire and water. Soleil said the darkness that caused Clover's head to pound and her mind to fade into memories was the same thing keeping the elements from responding to her. Clover suspected Soleil was trying to soften the blow. It was becoming more apparent that Clover just wasn't as powerful as full fae.

"You must be prepared to use magic in harsh environments. When you are in pain or uncomfortable," said Soleil. "Your magic must be powerful at all times."

Clover took her hands out of her pockets. "Agreed, but first, there's something I need to ask of you." Soleil waited, so Clover went on. "My mother is ill with the Grey Fever. Is there anything you can do for her? I don't know how much experience the fae have with human sicknesses."

"You'd be surprised," said Soleil quietly, her face a grave mask. "The Grey Fever has been a plague of the northern forests since before the treaty. Fae don't catch it, of course, but the humans are easily taken by it. Sympathetic fae near the border of Hirane are adept in treating it."

"So you can help?" asked Clover.

Soleil sighed. "I would have to send for their knowledge. It's different in the south, we hardly ever come into contact with humans. It wouldn't take long to get the medicine, maybe a day or so."

The tension in Clover's shoulders relaxed and she let out a breath of relief. Clover had gone to Dr. Van Doren again, asking about her mother, and his reply had haunted her.

"Your mother's health is of little concern to me. She's no longer my assistant and she's barely a servant. She is simply another chore for you to take care of. Better that she dies."

Clover gritted her teeth. After everything Torryn had given to the doctor: time away from raising Clover, years of hard work, years of blood and torture, years of abuse while her mind wore away, and he wouldn't help her just this once? As though helping Torryn birth Clover absolved him of every debt he was bound to pay. Clover knew her mother was still in there, deep inside somewhere, and if the *great* Dr. Van Doren wasn't going to help, then Clover would take things into her own hands.

Grant would have helped.

Clover's breath came out and added to the mist. "Thank you. The illness is still in its beginning stages. She has a little time."

Soleil put her hands on Clover's shoulders. "Worry no more. Now we train."

How to dig up a body when the ground was frozen solid? Clover wondered as she washed the windows in the spare room which now belonged to Knox. The frost outside blocked the view of the town. She could use her magic, but she would have to get through the snow first. Dig through the snow and force the earth to push the coffin to the surface. Then there was the problem of Knox. There was no polite or vague way of asking someone to help dig up a grave to prove a point.

She would just have to come right out and say it. She was going to prove to Knox that Grant was alive. Knox only went by hard evidence and what was more fact than an empty grave? There was no use deceiving him. Knox doubted her love for Grant? Well, she would show him. She would give him evidence he couldn't ignore.

"Ha!" she cried aloud, tossing her rag into the bucket at her feet.

"Victorious window washing?" Knox stood behind her, nearly scaring her to death. Her body curved inward as she jolted, and she hit her forehead against one of the panes of glass.

Clover rubbed it. "No. Can I help you with something?"

"The doc wants you," he said.

Clover walked toward him, still rubbing her forehead. "I'll be cooking after I'm finished, any requests?"

He stopped her at the door with a hand in the crook of her elbow. "How long are you going to be upset with me? Just so I know how long our conversations are going to be terse and hollow."

"Oh, I wouldn't get too worried about it." She leaned toward him. "We need to talk. Meet me in the tower tonight."

He nodded, eyes turned toward the ground as he rocked on his heels like a child caught in a lie, but Clover would put his worries at ease soon enough. She wouldn't be in such good spirits if she didn't know how to prove to Knox once and for all that she was right.

Clover hurried down the stairs and to the hospital rooms. Dr. Van Doren was in the room closest to his office, tending to the old man.

"Mrs. Taverty is leaving us. Please help her and then clean up her room once she's gone," Van Doren said without looking away from his patient.

Clover grimaced behind his back before going over to Mrs. Taverty's room. The woman was trying to put on her coat and Clover stepped in with her hands out.

"Back, you filth!" Taverty snapped.

Clover's hands fell to her sides. Mrs. Taverty still had a cough, but the doctor was letting her go. He would let the old man leave as well; they were still sick but could recover on their own. Beds needed to be holding patients who were in serious sickness, not ones who were past the worst of it.

Mrs. Taverty put on her coat with a bit of a struggle before picking up a small sack of her things and leaving the room. Clover shook her head as she watched the old woman go. Mrs. Taverty would sooner throw herself off a cliff than be helped off a ledge by a fae or even a half fae. But that old woman was the least of Clover's worries.

She opened a window, letting in cold but clean air before she got to cleaning—scrubbing the floors, changing the linens on the bed, cleaning tools and straightening medicine bottles. As she cleaned, her mind turned to memories.

Grant had been sick with Grey Fever once, in his sixteenth year...or had he only been fifteen? Clover couldn't remember. She did remember that he was strong, and he made it through without Clover having to worry too much.

Grant was an intolerable flirt, and not even the Grey Fever could stop him. Her mind was overcome with the sound of knocking. Clover was knocking on Grant's door...and she was pulled into another vision, watching it walk and move around her as though it was real.

꧁

"DON'T COME IN. I'M WRETCHED," GRANT SAID, AND CLOVER smiled before going into his room. He was lying on his bed—which he was beginning to outgrow—with his arms crossed over his face.

She set down the tray she'd been piling dirty dishes and tissues on. "Any requests for lunch?"

"Licorice sweets and blackberry milk." His voice was muffled.

Clover laughed. "Broth and bread it is."

"I'm in a prison! You are my pitiless warden!" he shouted.

Clover sat on the edge of his bed and tapped his arm. "Let's see."

Grant shook his head—or rather his whole upper body rolled back and forth with his head.

"Grant, you're acting like a baby. Come on, look at me," she said.

He put down his arms, crossing them over his chest and turning his face into his pillow. He was grinning though—he liked the attention.

Clover felt his forehead. "You're barely warm."

"Then stay close to me." He reached up and wrapped his arms around her waist before turning so she was lying next to him.

"Grant!" she hissed, but she was also trying not to laugh. "Let go."

"No. I want you to stay here. Consider it an order," he said.

Clover let a laugh slip, trying to push him off. "I don't take orders from you."

"Just this once?" He held her tightly. "Please? The final wishes of a dying man."

Clover couldn't make him let her go, not that she was trying very hard, and so she let him keep her there. "You get a minute."

"A whole minute," he said with reverence before pulling her closer. Clover sighed before turning toward him and kissing his forehead.

"I'm glad you're all right," she said, letting her hands run up into his dark brown curls. They were messy for his lack of neat attendance.

He smiled. "I'm glad too. While I was coughing up blood,

I had time to ponder the nature of sickness, but I could only manage a single thought."

"What thought?"

"Gratitude to whatever magical or scientific pattern in you that spares you from such an illness." He shuddered.

Clover held him close. "Happy to be of some comfort to you, dying man that you are."

He began to fake a rasp and clutched at her. "Oh, bring me something sweet. The last thing I want is well…" He raised an eyebrow at her.

"Grant! You know what? Your minute is up," she said as he began laughing. Smiling, she pushed him off, got off the bed and smoothed her dress. She picked up her tray and stepped toward the door.

"Clover," he said seriously, and she turned back to him. He had such a sincere smile and mischievous glint in his eye.

She smiled. "I'll be back with lunch. I'm sure you'll survive until then."

He dramatically flung himself back onto his mattress as she left the room, swinging the door shut with her foot…

THE SLAMMING OF A DOOR BROUGHT HER OUT OF MEMORY. Her heart was pounding, worrying that she was in trouble, but when she heard the doctor's feet heading up to his office, she realized he had slammed the door to the stairs. She stood and looked around the room. While she had been lost in memory, she had continued to clean the entire room. Fear clutched her spine. Is this how her mother lived, then? Trapped in memories while she did tasks her body had memorized for her?

Clover backed up and hit the edge of the counter holding

medical tools. She slid down, breathing hard, and clutched her knees. She didn't know why this was happening to her now. Maybe it was Cypress, maybe it was something her mother had passed down to her, maybe something else entirely. Her teeth clenched hard as she focused on driving away the cold of fear.

"Find Grant. Escape. Find Grant. Escape..."

Clover repeated it over and over in her mind before pulling herself together. She needed to get to that coffin, but she needed Knox's help to do so.

CLOVER WAS WAITING IN THE TOWER BEFORE KNOX FINALLY joined her. It was freezing, so she'd worn her coat and an extra blanket, and she was warming herself with a small fire she held in her hands. Knox scooted into her former spot and looked at the fire, giving it an impressed nod before warming his own hands.

"What did you want to talk about?" he asked.

"I have a way to give you evidence that Grant is alive."

Knox sighed, pulling his hands away.

"Just listen," she demanded, so he looked into her eyes. "When Grant was buried, no one saw his body before his coffin was put into the ground. So that's the most logical place to look."

He was silent for a long time before he took a deep breath.

"You want to dig up Grant's grave?"

Clover shrugged. "He's not in there."

"All right, but what if—and just hear me out—he *is*!" he snapped. "What then?"

"Then we re-bury him. You were right. I was wrong. You

finish up your time with Van Doren and we part with mutual uncomfortable feelings and a secret we'll take to *our* graves," she said. "I swear, Knox, if he's in there, then this is over. I'll never ask you another favor. But if he's not there, then I don't believe you can give up the search for him with good conscience."

Knox rubbed his hands over his face. "Do you know how difficult it's going to be to dig up his grave? Not only is Veritas small, but the graveyard is out in the open and the ground is frozen solid."

"I already have a plan," she said. "Do you want to hear it, or do you want to keep complaining?" He scowled, so she continued. "Tomorrow night, a…friend is going to push the forest mist into the town of Veritas. It happens sometimes and when it does, it scares everyone inside—probably even the constable, who makes a single round per night anyway. Even if he is brave enough to be out, he won't even see us."

"What about the Justice Riders?"

"They'll only see us if they've made a deal with a fae to be able to see through the mist. It can be granted…" Clover thought back to their treatment of the fae criminal in the woods. "…I doubt they have it."

Knox frowned. "You're not sure? Even if I'm with you, do you know what they'll do to you if they catch us?"

"I'm aware, I'm just undaunted. It won't just be the mist, it'll also be dark—can they see in the dark?"

"How will we see?" he asked after rolling his eyes.

Clover pointed at herself. "Once we get through the gate and to Grant's grave, all you have to do is help me dig through the snow. I'll do the rest. You'll have to pull the nails off the coffin because they're iron."

"I'll leave that first peek up to you."

"Of course. Wouldn't want my plan uncovered by your sensitive bowels," she said.

Knox stared at her; eyes narrowed. Clover could practically see the cogs going around in his head, looking for flaws in her plan. But he wasn't coming up with any.

"Fine," he said. "If he's in there, we're done."

"And if he's not, the search continues," she said.

His brow furrowed. "I can't believe I'm going to dig up my cousin's grave."

Clover sighed, exasperated. "He's not—"

"Yes, yes, he's not in there. I'll believe it when I see it."

"You mean take my word for it," she said, raising an eyebrow.

He scowled. "I'll look in there if I have to," he said, but even as he did, his face became pale and a little green around his mouth.

"Tomorrow night," she said. "Be ready."

ON HER WAY OUT OF THE TOWER, CLOVER FOCUSED ON THE wick of the candle standing in its window. She let the cold of the magic turn to warmth before the candle came alight on its own. It was still fairly early, and Clover waited nearly an hour before blowing the candle out and leaving the tower. She just had to hope that Angela saw it. Tomorrow she had to go into town to pick up medicine refills for Van Doren.

None of which would be given to her mother.

She pulled Torryn into a sitting position so she could cough up the blood and phlegm easier. Knox often checked on her when doing all his patient rounds, but Clover had to take care of her through the night. She was getting worse. If Soleil didn't get back with the remedy soon, Torryn would die.

But Clover was optimistic. Soleil had failed her in the past, letting her fear get in the way of helping Clover with Clover's admittedly foolish plans. But Soleil would help Clover save her mother. She couldn't see a reason why her fae friend wouldn't or couldn't. She had to be patient...*that* again.

Her night was restless, mixed with fear for her mother and fear of what she might see in her dreams. By the time the sun rose, Clover had been awake for an hour at least. After breakfast and a few small chores, Clover left for Veritas. Knox was in the middle of a lesson and the only worry he could express was a glance, but Clover just had to have faith that Angela saw the candle—and if not, maybe if she screamed loud enough, Angela could somehow...what? Come to her rescue? Her footsteps through the snow stopped. It was too late to go back, and Van Doren would punish her if she didn't get these supplies. When she reached the gate and saw the Justice Riders standing on either side of it, she considered turning around and going back once more, but who should come walking to meet her but Angela. The girl sported a royal blue dress, abnormal against the common black, but there was nothing common about Angela.

The two met in the middle on either side of the gate. Angela shooed the Justice Riders away. They moved but watched the two intently.

Clover let out a breath. "I was worried you hadn't seen the candle."

"Oh, I saw it. No worries. But you must stay out there." Angela turned and looked behind her at the Justice Riders.

"What's happened?"

"Someone else went missing," said Angela. "Evette Appleton. It's not safe. Tell me what you need, and I'll get it for you."

Clover reached into her pocket and passed Angela the key through the bars. "A delivery of medicines for Dr. Van Doren. That's all."

"All right, wait here and I'll bring them back," said Angela. "It'll be all right." She sounded like she was trying to reassure herself as much as she was trying to reassure Clover.

Angela rushed off and Clover waited just on the other side of the gate. Now she couldn't even go into Veritas? Not that she enjoyed doing so, but this was getting out of hand. Cypress was behind this—he had to be. He was the only dark fae in the area. Was Soleil trying to find him? Perhaps dark fae were especially hard to find? She would have to ask.

Angela came back and handed Clover the packages and the key through the bars of the gate.

"I'll still be watching for the light." Angela put her hand through the bars.

Clover took it and grasped it hard. "Thank you." She let go.

Angela looked behind her once more. "All right. You better hurry home—don't want anyone to catch you on the road, either."

"Stay safe, Angela. Dark fae about. No light fae will call you into the woods, remember that," said Clover. She couldn't have Angela falling to harm—not after the risks Angela had taken to help her find Grant. And if Cypress hurt her, Clover would give his blade right back to him, though perhaps he would have preferred it in his hand rather than his heart.

"I will. Hurry," said Angela. Her eyes flitted around, and her hands shook as she raised them to grasp the bars.

Clover turned and hurried home. Every finger in Veritas was pointed toward her and Van Doren Manor. Who was going to protect her then? Knox? He was a formidable fighter, but she doubted he could take on all the Justice Riders. Tonight, she needed to prove to Knox that Grant was somewhere out there, alive. Somehow, someway, this nightmare would end. Whether or not it would end well was still unclear.

THE NIGHT AIR STUNG HER CHEEKS AS SOON AS HER BOOT FELL through the soft snow gathering on the ground. Clover stuck her head out through the servants' entrance door and looked up and down the side of the house. This was it—Clover and Knox were to dig up Grant's grave. The thought made the hairs on her arms rise. She blamed it on the cold. She wasn't about to relinquish her determination to fear.

"Who do you think is going to see you?" asked Knox behind her, nearly making her jump out of her skin. "Or are you having second thoughts?"

"Of course not. Let's go." She continued her outward journey through the snow. Before they left the manor grounds, they both grabbed shovels from the tool shed. On the other side of the wall that surrounded the manor, moonlight illuminated the road like a silver thread. Beyond that lay an endless darkness. It was a stretching, death-like darkness that chilled her deeper than any snowfall.

"It's eerie, isn't it? Almost like the spirit of the forest is still there. Like it's waiting for something. Watching," said Knox.

Clover frowned. "I know. Now that we're both properly terrified, we should continue on to Veritas."

"Onward, fearless leader," he said, and she scoffed.

They continued their walk in silence. Clover felt her heart pounding two and a half times for every step, she felt her breaths shuddering in and out, but the fear was entangled so deeply with the cold that she couldn't truly tell one from the other. No one came along the road while they were there. No one really traveled at night around these parts.

When they got close to Veritas, Clover steered them closer to the edge of the forest, walking just barely within the mist. On the other side of the gate were two Justice Riders. Behind them, all the homes were darkened, and all the streetlights were dimmed.

"I thought you said there would be mist," said Knox.

Clover leaned her shovel against a nearby tree before she rubbed her hands together. "Keep your voice down."

She held her still freezing hands out and watched the space between them closely. She could see her fire, a warm hearth, Grant's laughter. There was a spark and finally she had a fire. Clover held it in her hand and took a firm stance in the snow before reeling back and throwing her fire into the thick wall of mist that was the forest. The light it made was as dim as the lamps in the town. They looked back toward the Riders but neither of the Riders made a move.

The wind whispered sharply. Individual snowflakes hit the ground as Clover's heart pounded and her breathing stuttered with cold. Just when Clover wasn't sure Soleil had received the signal, the fog began to move. It swept in their direction like a blanket was being pulled over them. Knox flinched a little when it hit them, only it felt like nothing. Clover watched it envelop building after building and douse streetlamps. The Justice Riders looked around, taking their crossbows out, but they made no move away from the gate.

"I can't see a thing," said Knox. "Give me the mist sight."

"I can't. I don't know how."

Knox huffed. "Well, that would have been nice to know beforehand."

They both picked up their shovels.

Clover grabbed his wrist and began leading him to the gate. "Can you climb over?"

"Yeah, I think so. How are you going to get over?"

Clover turned and looked at the trees—why not? "I have my ways. Just hurry."

Knox grabbed the bars and began climbing while Clover stepped a little closer to the trees and closed her eyes. She let the cold magic swell inside her chest. "I need your help," she whispered. "Please."

There was a creaking and a fluttering and Clover opened her eyes when she felt something touch her back. She was enveloped in the branches of a tree, and she let it lift her over the gate. It went no further, so she dropped down and watched the tree retract its branches into the forest.

"Thank you," she whispered before she reached back through the gate and grabbed their shovels. She handed Knox his.

"Where to now?"

She peered into the darkness. Even she was having trouble seeing, but her eyes would adjust.

"Just follow my lead." Clover took Knox's sleeve and pulled him along. She skirted buildings and made sure to check around corners for Justice Riders. They only seemed to be posted around the fence and main streets. Clover made her way past them easily, and after squeezing between houses and climbing through yards, they came face to face with the graveyard.

KNOX FOLLOWED HER STEP BY STEP AS SHE WANDERED ALONG the stones for a moment. It was much too dark to see the names printed on them unless she traced them with a finger.

"This is taking too long," she said. She created another fire in her free hand and held it up to the graves, one after another after another, until she finally found Grant's.

GRANT AILLARD VAN DOREN

"FIND HIM?" KNOX ASKED, FEELING AROUND.

Clover put out the small fire she made before she guided his hands to the headstone. In Knox's other hand, he gripped the shovel tightly.

"Where do we dig?" he asked.

Clover led him around until he was facing Grant's headstone. "We dig until we can't anymore."

She was first to dig her shovel into the snow. It was noisier work than she hoped and the two of them stopped every now and then to make sure no Justice Riders were sneaking up on them. Finally, after what seemed like hours, there was no more snow to dig through. The frozen earth threatened to chip away the metal of their shovels.

"All right," he said, breathless. "Now what?"

She stood at the foot of the dug-up snow. "Now I do the rest." She kneeled in the snow and let out a few breaths.

The earth was stubborn and even harder to coax than fire. She had to dig in with her soul, command it as firmly as the stones were lodged far below her. Clover gritted her teeth and clenched her fists—even clenched her frozen toes in her boots.

"Open up," she commanded. Her skin hardened as though she were freezing, her blood slowed like a muddy river. She closed her eyes. "Open up."

The ground began to rumble. The dirt before her began to rise and fall to either side of a large wooden mass. The ground slowly stopped shuddering and settled.

Knox swore quietly. Then he swore again. And once more.

"Do you mind?" she asked. "Come over here and help me get the rest of the dirt off it so we can open it up."

Knox stepped forward and kneeled before reaching out blindly. His hands hit the dirt and he began pushing it off before touching the wood of the coffin. "You did it. I mean, I can't believe it actually worked."

"I told you I was going to do it. What did you think was going to happen?"

"Little Grim, always so glib." Knox reached behind him for the shovel, which was out of reach. Clover stood and handed it to him. He shivered, using the blade of the shovel to take the lid off the coffin.

Knox cringed after every iron nail pulled out to the point where Clover wanted to push him aside and do it herself, even if it caused her pain.

"I swear to the Grey, if my cousin is inside this coffin, I'll never forgive you, Grim," he said in a wobbly whisper.

Clover huffed. "Would you just hurry up? I'd rather not be caught."

"All right, all right, last nail." Knox yanked it out and quickly stepped back. "I'll um...I'll stand back here and let you do the honors."

"Just make sure no one's heard us," she said.

Knox stepped away to listen for approaching footsteps, hugging himself and letting his teeth chatter freely. Clover reached for the coffin lid. She pushed it off with a heave and gently set it in the snow. Knox flinched away and Clover rolled her eyes.

She couldn't see what was inside the coffin, so she focused on making a fire. The warmth swirled within her, but fear clouded her magic. Was there anything in the coffin? Grant? Part of her didn't want to see, and it was stopping her. She sparked a few times before dropping her hands and letting out an angry sigh. She *had* to see. She had to convince Knox that Grant was alive and that this coffin was empty.

Clover raised her hands again and the spark caught fire right away into a thin, subtle flame. She looked past it to the inside of the coffin.

There he was.

"Grim?" asked Knox. "Just waiting blindly over here."

She stood and continued to stare at the body. This couldn't be possible. He shouldn't be here. He *couldn't* be here. It didn't make any sense. Somewhere along the way, something had been twisted, and now she was more lost than ever.

"Clover," said Knox, his tone serious. "What is it? Tell me!"

She gritted her teeth and swallowed, forcing her voice to remain steady. "Well, the bad news is that he's here."

"You say that like there's good news!" said Knox, nearly shrill. "I knew it! We shouldn't have done this. Oh, Grey, I should have listened to my mother, and *you* should have listened to me. She always said leave the dead out of it and—"

"Would you shut up!" Clover snapped. "There *is* good news."

"Oh, well, by all means, tell me. I can't wait to hear what it could possibly be."

"The good news is that it's not Grant."

Knox was silent for a long time. His eyes narrowed in confusion as he tried to fit this new information into his puzzle. "It's not? Well then, who is it?"

"It's Marvin Hallows."

Chapter Fifteen

KNOX HAD WANDERED a bit away to vomit while Clover continued to look at the placid face of Marvin Hallows. Something was off about him, and she finally put her finger on it.

"He doesn't *look* dead," she whispered.

Knox made a heaving noise. "Grim, please, I don't need you to describe Angela's dead brother to me."

"I mean, he's been missing for months. If he'd been dead all this time, then there would be some kind of decay. He just looks like he's sleeping...but he's not breathing." Clover reached out with the hand that wasn't holding the flame and touched his cheek. It was warm. She jerked her hand back and shivers ran down her spine. "He's definitely alive."

But there was something else. When she touched his skin, it was as though there was a shroud or covering over him, dark, as though a shroud of death, and yet he was alive. She put out the fire.

"Something's wrong with him. It might be magical—we

need to take him to the forest," said Clover. "I suppose it's time for you to meet Soleil, though she will not want to meet you. We need her help."

Knox came over, wiping his mouth. "Okay, now you're really and truly out of your mind. First this young man goes missing, supposedly stolen by the fae. Now he turns up— apparently alive—and now you want to take him to the forest and give him to the fae? How are we going to get him over the gate?"

"I don't know. You get his shoulders; I'll get his legs."

Knox gritted his teeth before feeling around. He touched Marvin Hallows' chest before flinching and turning away to put his hands on his knees. "I can't do this."

"Knox, for the love of all that is good, stop whining like a child and pick him up. He's not even dead," she said. She had expected Knox to be a baby, but she had also expected the coffin to be empty. Her irritation with his squeamishness was rising, but the faster they got this done, the faster they could figure out what exactly was going on.

Knox rolled his head on his shoulders before letting out a sharp breath. He came back over and, sightless, he knocked his knees against the edge of the coffin before closing his eyes and reaching inside. It took nearly five minutes for Knox to lift Marvin Hallows out of the coffin.

"What about the shovel?" asked Clover.

"Shovel? What about the entire unearthed coffin?!"

Clover sighed. "Forget it. Who's going to trace a shovel back to us?"

🍃

THEY CONTINUED TO CARRY MARVIN HALLOWS BACK THROUGH
Veritas. He wasn't a small boy, and even though Clover was
carrying the lesser half of his weight, she still struggled at
times. The snow and cold weren't helping. Yanking her boots
out of the snow while not really being able to feel her feet
proved difficult as she moved as quickly as possible toward the
exit.

"I think I'm starting to be able to see again," said Knox.

Clover huffed. "That's terrible news."

By the time they got to the fence where they'd climbed
over, Knox claimed he could see the streetlamps in the
distance. Clover was breathing hard and so was Knox. She
didn't know if it was from fear or exertion for either of them.

"Right. Now, to get him over," said Knox as they set him
down.

Clover huffed out a sharp breath. "Right."

"Who's there?" called a loud voice and both of them froze.

Clover's heart was skipping beats, she was sure of it. If
they caught her, there would be no explaining, there would be
no listening, there would only be death. She didn't know what
to do.

"I heard you out there. Show yourself!" It was Constable
Gennady.

What was at hand? The spellbound body of a missing boy,
Knox's fighting skills, Clover's mediocre control over fire and
earth and a little water, and the weather, a long shot at best.
She was running out of time.

Clover stood, turned, and held out her hands, palms facing
Veritas as she focused on every flame in the city. Now that the
mist was slowly fading, they had all blinked back to life. They
were flames of security, flames of need—to drive away the
cold, to drive away the darkness. She felt all of them as though

she were gathering them in the palms of her hands. All she would need to snuff them out was to clench her fists around them. So that's exactly what she did.

All the flames went out: flames in street lamps, flames in windows, flames in fireplaces, all of them gone. The town of Veritas plunged into darkness. There was a whimper and a pounding of feet not far from her, probably Constable Gennady. Clover held her ground and her breath as Constable Gennady ran right past her, trailing a small stream of air that tugged at her coat and stray hairs as he passed.

"Captain Dawson! Something is happening!"

When he had passed, she let herself breathe. When she turned, she could barely see Knox by the light of the moon.

"We need to move, now!" he said.

Clover turned toward the forest and let the cold churn in her chest. She let it flow down into her stomach and through her arms and legs before it reached her mind.

"We're trapped," she whispered. "Help us!"

She closed her eyes and clenched her hands hard. She could feel the forest pulling and she pulled back, crouching as she kept her whole body tense, unwavering. Eventually, she heard the creaking and groaning of the trees.

"Whoa!" Knox said.

Clover opened her eyes and saw him reeling away from the reaching branches as the trees leaned over the fence to grab them.

"Don't fight it." Clover went forward and grabbed on. "They're trying to help."

The branches picked up Marvin on their own and curled him tightly in their twigs, like fingers. Knox stepped forward and grabbed on as well. The tree then bent the other way, into the mist of the forest, and set them down in the snow. Clover let the cold flow out of her body as the forest pulled back.

Knox stared breathlessly up at the tree that had helped them. "Thanks."

Clover slumped fully in the snow, thoroughly tired from using all that magic, but she sat up again when she heard the shouting of the Justice Riders in Veritas.

"Time to go," said Knox, grabbing Marvin under the arms while Clover grabbed his legs. They both moved as quickly as they could deeper into the forest.

❧

"SOLEIL!" CLOVER WHISPERED INTO THE MIST SURROUNDING them. It had been nearly ten minutes since they left Veritas and dragged Marvin into the woods. "I know you're there. He's human, but he isn't going to hurt you—he's completely blind! He's not even going to speak. He's my friend, too, and we need your help!"

There was movement not far from her. Clover moved to step toward Soleil only to find the stiff branches of a sleeping bush wrapped around her ankles.

"Soleil!" she snapped.

Soleil ran forward with a knife and tackled Knox to the ground.

"Soleil! For night's sake!" Clover hissed. She urged the sleeping forest to release its hold.

"Blind as I am, I can see that you're quite capable with a blade," said Knox. His hands were raised in surrender to his unseen foe. "Please don't hurt me. I just want to find my cousin."

Soleil took her knee off Knox's chest but kept her little iveen blade to his throat. "So this is Knox?"

"Yes," said Clover. "So please let him go."

Soleil gritted her teeth and Clover wondered if she was debating whether it was worth it to turn dark just to take the life of this human who had come into her forest. Finally, the light won in her—as it usually did. Soleil slowly removed the blade.

"Lovely meeting you." Knox slowly sat up. He sat there with his hands where Soleil could see them. Clover silently applauded his tact.

"We have a problem," said Clover.

"You always have a problem," said Soleil, still scowling at Knox, her knife held up and pointed at him. "I'm assuming it has something to do with this thing." Soleil nudged Marvin's leg with her bare foot.

"You assume correctly," Clover said. "There's a spell over him. What is it? And can you take it off?"

Soleil gave Knox another look to make sure he wasn't going to move before she went around to kneel over Marvin's head. Clover watched as Soleil took both sides of it in her hands, closed her eyes, and pressed hard. A translucent black blanket like a death-shroud began to lift off Marvin Hallows' body before it sank back down.

Soleil let out a breath. "A preservation spell. This is strong magic. I've never seen a dark spell like this."

"Why? What's different about it?"

"Whoever cast it is skilled. When fae turn dark, they choose the light eventually. But the more hatred festers, the stronger the magic, and this magic is very strong." Soleil rolled her head on her shoulders. "I'll need your help."

"I've never done anything like this." Clover shook her head. "I don't even know if I'm capable of doing this."

"Perhaps you should actually try first," said Soleil.

Knox shrugged. "She's got a point."

Clover and Soleil shushed him at once.

"My hands are starting to freeze," he complained.

They shushed him again.

"All right, tell me what to do," said Clover.

Soleil moved to Marvin's side and Clover moved to the other.

"One hand on his forehead, the other on his chest," said Soleil and Clover did. "Do you feel that...the covering, the protection?"

Clover nodded. She saw the shroud once more but it was heavy, like it was made of iron. Marvin wasn't breathing and he had no heartbeat, but he was alive underneath the iron blanket.

"We have to lift it," said Clover.

"It's going to hurt, are you sure you want to do this? Wouldn't it be better to just leave him like this? He's human."

"I need to know who did this to him," said Clover. "It could be the same person who did this to Grant. He might even know where Grant is. Even if he knows nothing, he's Angela's brother...and she's my friend, she deserves her family back."

"Uh, Clover—"

"Silence!" Soleil snapped before turning to Clover. "Fine. Then close your eyes, feel the shroud, and start peeling it back from the feet upward."

Clover closed her eyes and felt the heaviness of the shroud. She saw it covering Marvin Hallows' body, and she hooked one hand under it and began to peel it back. She kept pace with Soleil and when they got to the chest, Clover felt Marvin Hallows' heart begin to beat. When they pulled the shroud off his head he gasped, and his eyes flew open. He looked around and saw Clover before scrambling back.

"Fae?" he said quietly. Then his voice rose. "Fae! Get away from me!"

Knox shot forward and grabbed Marvin by the front of his coat and knocked him out with one punch.

"So much for your questions." Soleil stood and brushed snow off her knees. She seemed pleased with herself, which annoyed Clover.

Clover turned to Knox, glowering. "Why did you do that?"

"Well, before I was summarily silenced, I was going to warn you that something like this might happen. Now he's seen all three of us," said Knox.

"Do you have any sort of memory tampering magics?" Clover asked Soleil.

Soleil crossed her arms. "I could give him an illusion-like dream, but I can't tamper with people's memories."

Knox stood and held a hand out for Clover. "Better hurry, it's getting late, and we need to get back to the manor before sunup."

Soleil kneeled and pressed her hands to Marvin's forehead. When she pulled away, she put her hands on her hips. "A confusing dream. That's the best I can do."

"I'm sure it'll be fine," said Clover, but she was not sure. Even dreams could be powerful. They'd swayed people more than once and for both good and bad.

"So what do we do with him now?" asked Knox.

"Now we take him back to Veritas—uh, inside the gates, and hope that his own people don't turn against him," said Clover.

Knox sighed. "Back to Veritas, then. Miss." He held his hand out to Soleil, who looked disgusted and bashed it away from her.

"Come into my forest again and I will kill you."

"Pleasure's all mine," said Knox with a grin before bending down and picking up Marvin under the arms. The young man was bleeding heavily from the nose.

Clover turned to Soleil. "Thank you for your help."

"You're welcome—and here, a treatment for your mother." Soleil reached into the pouch at her side and took out a bottle of what appeared to be mashed-up green leaves. Clover took the bottle and tilted it this way and that.

"What does it do exactly?" she asked.

Soleil shrugged. "I don't know. All I know is that this has been known to speed up healing and even cure the sickness entirely."

Clover shook her head at the little bottle. The Grey Fever was as powerful as any plague to the humans. How many lives could have been spared if both sides would stop fearing and hating each other?

Clover wrapped her arms around Soleil, who held her back.

"Be careful of the company you keep." Soleil narrowed her eyes at Knox, who made a face back at her.

Clover nodded, mocking seriousness. "I will." She picked up Marvin Hallows by the ankles and they began carrying him out of the forest.

AT THE EDGE OF THE FOREST, THEY MADE SURE THE COAST WAS clear before they went farther. The Justice Riders, who were supposed to be at the gate, were missing, so Knox opened it and they slid Marvin through. The Justice Riders would be back, they would find him.

Teeth chattering, feet numb, bones aching, Clover and Knox took off running back down the road toward Van Doren Manor while the sky lightened. When they neared the manor, they slowed to a walk and caught their breath. Some of the feeling had come back in Clover's feet, but she would need to spend some time by the fire.

"Well, you certainly made your point," said Knox. "Grant is alive somewhere but there's nowhere left for him to be."

Clover took her hair out of its bun and ran her hands through it. "I know. I know I said before that Dr. Van Doren would never go into the forest—but if he were desperate enough to seek out a fae, put a spell of preservation over both Marvin and Grant, and bury Marvin's body in his son's coffin, then I'm thinking it wouldn't be all that improbable that he would hide Grant in the forest."

"You'd think Soleil would have stumbled across him though if he were somewhere out there."

"I know it's strange but it's all we have left," said Clover.

They got back to the manor and went in through the servants' entrance before sneaking through the kitchen. Knox grabbed some food out of a cupboard while Clover sat on one of the stools. She was too tired to stop him or kick him out.

"All right, starting tomorrow, we look for Grant's body out in the woods," said Knox with a mouthful of bread.

Clover waved a hand around the lightening kitchen. "It *is* tomorrow."

"Well then, you're going to need to get some rest," he said.

She sighed, putting her head down on her arms.

Knox stopped at the door. "Thank you for proving me

wrong. I'm sorry for what I said...even a blind person could see you love Grant."

"It's okay. See you in a few hours," she said. She was a mixture of exhaustion and excitement. They were close, so close, but she didn't want to miss a single clue, and for that, she had to get *some* sleep.

He laughed. "In a few hours, then."

BEFORE SHE WENT TO HER OWN ROOM, CLOVER WENT TO HER mother's room. Torryn was asleep and Clover gently shook her awake. She was burning with fever.

"Mother, I need you to take some medicine," said Clover.

Torryn's eyes opened but she didn't seem to register anything Clover was saying. So, Clover had her sit up. She scooped out some of the slick green leaves and the oil it was in onto a spoon. It smelled fruity and like spring flowers. She pushed it into her mother's mouth, making sure she actually swallowed it. Clover gently opened her mother's mouth and checked under her tongue and behind her teeth to make sure she didn't miss any before laying Torryn back down. Clover surrendered her blanket to her mother and decided to sleep by the fireplace in the kitchen.

The end was in sight. Clover was starting to see the light at the end of this horrible nightmare. Yes, the forest was vast, but Dr. Van Doren couldn't hide Grant very far into it, not without someone noticing that he was going in and out of the forest. She would find Grant and they would take her mother and leave this all behind. Knox would go back to Hirane, live his dreams as a journalist, and marry his beautiful true-love Angela. And Soleil? She didn't know. Maybe Soleil would stay.

Maybe she would go somewhere else—the entire forest was her home, and Clover would always know where to find her, even if they left.

Things would be good, and wholly good—no partialities left. She could hardly wait for that moment.

Chapter Sixteen

CLOVER'S DREAMS were brief but terrible. She was running through the mist-filled forest and she was injured, a deep pain in her leg as she ran. There were footsteps behind her, gaining with every moment. Her heart was pounding so hard it hurt and there was no escape. Where was she to hide? How far would they follow her into the forest?

Clover felt a hand on her arm, and she woke with a scream.

Knox jumped back in shock and landed on his rear before putting a hand over his heart, clutching it as though it was trying to escape.

"What is wrong with you?" he demanded.

"Bad dream." Clover rubbed her eyes. "What are you doing? I thought I told you to get some rest."

"I did, and so did you. Clover, do you know what time it is?"

Clover looked around. There was a small window in her room that didn't open but she could clearly see that the day was early—but too bright. She should have been up hours ago. She kicked off the covers and Knox turned away.

Clover quickly pulled on one of her gray dresses and began pulling tight the laces from behind as she rushed into the kitchen.

"Whoa, wait." Knox followed.

Clover did not wait. "Where's my mother? Have you seen her?"

"No, she's not here," said Knox.

"What's that supposed to mean?" she asked, trying to get things ready as she still held the laces. Knox pushed her hands off and grabbed the laces himself, which stopped her from moving around. "Hey!"

"Just listen!" he snapped. "Your mother is gone, and so is Dr. Van Doren. I checked the whole house. They're not here. The patients are still here, and their families are going to start arriving soon. What do I do?"

Clover stared at Knox, not fully comprehending what he was saying. It wasn't possible for either of them to simply be gone. The fear in the dream that had begun to wear off in her waking had returned. If Van Doren and her mother were gone, they could be together—which meant that he had taken her somewhere. It didn't make any sense, where could they possibly go?

"I don't—I don't know." She was still trying to clear her head from sleep and the dream she'd had. Had she been herself in the dream, or someone else?

"Clover!" snapped Knox, turning her around. "Snap out of it. What do we do?"

Clover closed her eyes tight. "All right, go tend to Dr. Van Doren's patients as best you can. Come get me if there's something urgent. I'm going to make them something to eat, and when their families come, we reassure them—tell them the doctor is very busy. I'm going to check the backyard. If my mother wandered into the forest, she couldn't have gotten far."

She remembered the images from her dream and shuddered.

"Okay. Okay, I can do that." Knox quickly left.

Clover made a quick breakfast of oatmeal while she thought about what was going on. Had Dr. Van Doren taken her mother? Clover and Knox had planned to search the forest for Grant. Could the doctor have taken her mother in there, or was it a coincidence that they were both missing at the same time? A sense of urgency plagued her, but she couldn't put her finger on why.

Clover spilled hot oats on her hand and shouted. She wrapped her hand in her apron and quickly began dishing out servings of breakfast onto a large tray. If the doctor wasn't around, what would happen if one of his patients began to die?

Clover rushed back into her room, grabbed the bottle of Soleil's Grey Fever treatment, and put that on the tray, too. She assumed that it worked for her mother. Why not the rest of them? If Dr. Van Doren found out what she did, he would beat her within an inch of her life, but she wasn't about to let those children die in there.

THERE WAS DEFINITELY A TRAIL OF FOOTPRINTS THAT LED INTO the forest through the snow. Clover followed them for a time. There were two sets of prints, and they were going deeper into the forest than she had time for right now. It was still snowing—soon, the tracks would be gone. She had to hurry.

Go back and get Knox, get a coat, and they could look for her together.

Clover ran back to the manor. When she stepped into the entrance hall, two people were coming in through the front doors.

"Hello?" asked Clover.

Angela turned and with her, none other than her brother, Marvin Hallows.

"Oh, Clover, thank goodness you're all right. You have to leave; they're coming for you," said Angela, rushing to her.

"Who?" asked Clover. She couldn't tear her eyes away from Marvin Hallows.

He stepped forward. Clover could smell his guilt—like a room that hadn't been aired out in years. "The whole town. I-I was confused and scared. I'm sorry!"

"You're not making any sense," Angela scolded him before addressing Clover. "He didn't understand you were the one who saved him—not the one who took him. You and the other fae out in the forest."

Clover gritted her teeth. There wasn't time for this.

Angela turned and looked at Marvin. "I don't know exactly what happened either but the whole town is coming— they're coming for you!"

Clover began to walk to the hospital rooms to get Knox.

"What are you doing?" Angela grabbed Clover by the sleeve, stopping her. "You need to leave right now. Clover, they're bringing a cage. An iron cage."

Marvin shook his head. "Angela's right—Benjamin and his friends were made honorary Justice Riders and he's gone mad."

"Aren't you one of his friends?" asked Clover.

"No, not this Benjamin. I don't know what's happened to him."

Someone pounded at the door. Angela and Clover looked at each other. There was too much to think about. Too much to do. Clover felt frantic but she couldn't force herself to move.

Finally, the tension was broken.

"What was that?" Knox came out of the hospital rooms. "Angela?"

No one answered.

"Someone tell me what's going on!"

Angela whipped around to the front door. "They'll have surrounded this place by now. You need to go somewhere and hide. This is a big house; I'll try to stall them."

"Open up!" shouted Benjamin from the other side of the door. "We don't want any trouble, Van Doren! Just give us the fae girl and we'll give you no grief!"

"Go," said Angela.

Clover ran up the stairs, breathless from fear and trying not to be afraid, which only made it worse. When she got to the top, she looked out the window to see that Angela was right. The towns-folk circled around the back of the manor. Clover continued—she pushed open the door to Grant's room. This wasn't her intended hiding place, but if she was going to end up running for her life like she had in her dream, then she wasn't going without a coat.

Even the smallest of Grant's coats were a bit too large on her, but it didn't matter. After leaving Grant's room, she made her way back out to the hallway and ran across to the door leading to the attic as the door to the manor broke open. Clover made it through the door and the last thing she saw was a flood of black-clothed people coming through the doors only to be met by Angela.

Clover rushed up to the attic, up the small ladder hidden carefully on one side of the room. She was halfway up the ladder when her name was called.

"Clover Grimaldi!"

It was Benjamin.

"I know you can hear me...oh, you're here. I can practically smell your filthy blood. You're going to come down here, because if you don't, I'll kill your friend."

Angela? He wouldn't, Knox and Marvin would never let him, not to mention the Justice Riders...it couldn't be anyone human. Soleil? No. There was no way. He would have had to go into the forest to catch her and he never would have even seen her.

"It was no easy task, but I had some help. Amazing what you can get a dark fae to do for you when you give them what they want," said Benjamin.

The Justice Riders shifted uncomfortably, but they made no move of disapproval toward Benjamin. Guess it didn't matter what was being done as long as they were killing fae.

Clover frowned. A hollow pit of disappointment grew in her chest. Cypress? Would he help a human? What would he even ask for? The same thing he had asked for from her? All those missing people. Had that all been Benjamin? If he had help from a dark fae, then Benjamin's capture of Soleil didn't seem that improbable at all.

She came down the ladder and went back to the attic door. Clover was not about to abandon her best friend. Bartering with Soleil's life was the last thing she wanted to do, but if she didn't do this right, Benjamin might hurt Soleil either way. This needed to be handled carefully.

"Be clever, Clover. Be clever," she said to herself.

"I'm not a patient man, creature. I'll give you another

fifteen seconds before I slit your friend's throat and come searching for you myself!" shouted Benjamin.

The stairwell hall was clear, so Clover got on the ground and crept to the edge of the second floor and looked over into the main hall.

Benjamin stood at the foot of the stairs. In his arms was a bloody and battered Soleil. Her clothes were torn, and iron shackles around her wrists and ankles burned her. Benjamin held a knife to her throat. Soleil's eyes met hers and Clover knew Soleil was thinking about her parents.

A lump grew in Clover's throat. This was her fault; she had taken too many risks, pulled Soleil into a problem that should have remained her own. Clover held her breath along with a sob. This wasn't the time for self-pity, she needed to save Soleil.

Now.

There was no guarantee that if Clover gave herself up that Benjamin would let Soleil live. He wanted Clover alive, so the only thing she had to barter with was her life. If Benjamin took her, she would never find Grant—but Knox would. Her heart sank at the thought of never seeing Grant again, but she had gotten herself in this mess. Clover's life was not worth that of her friends, not after everything Soleil had done for her.

She couldn't wait any longer.

"Here!" she called, standing and producing a flame in her hand. All eyes turned to her. Some gasped and shrank away.

Benjamin grinned.

"I'm right here." Clover's voice shook. Her heart was galloping, and it took all her strength to keep her knees from failing her. She walked around to the top of the stairs, still holding the flame. "But if you want me, you have to let my friend go."

"I will," said Benjamin. He had not gotten his prize

without injury. There was a jagged cut from hairline to chin on the right side of his face. It was barely cleaned up, damp from the snow, and his eyes were sunken but wide and wild. Any semblance of a clever man holding all the cards was abandoned.

"Either you let her go now, or the only thing you'll get from me are the charred remains of my bones." Clover's nostrils flared. She forced herself not to cry, clenching her jaw as she pulled the flame closer to her chest.

"Clever beast." Benjamin grinned.

"Unchain her and let her go. Once she's far enough into the forest, I'll go with you. No fight. No hassle." Clover's eyes landed on Knox. He had the fight beaten out of him by the Vale twins and a few other men. He was a mess, but his head was still raised, eyes still shining with defiance. He was being held at knifepoint by Walter, but Knox relinquished no hint that he wasn't still the one with the upper hand here—and his attitude bolstered her own. Clover felt stronger, more confident. She couldn't see Angela or Marvin—she hoped they were hiding.

"Swear it," said Benjamin. "Fae deals are binding. Swear on your life."

Benjamin was capable, but he wasn't as smart as he thought. Dark fae were bound by deals, not light fae. Even if she lost her life by what she was about to do, it would be better than going with him and being tortured to death.

Clover crossed her heart. He took the knife away from Soleil's throat and produced a key from his pocket to unlock her. Once the shackles were off, Soleil slumped against one of the bannisters at the end of the stairs.

"Go on!" Gerard kicked her.

"Enough!" Clover screamed.

Walter was distracted by Soleil's release, so Knox made his move—a single move, to be specific. He disarmed Walter and began swiping his knife around. Everyone backed off in an arc as he made his way to Soleil. Knox picked her up, and still holding the knife, made his way out of the house.

Clover rushed to the window that looked out over the land leading to the forest behind the manor. Knox ran across the yard and into the forest. She let out a breath of relief. Now, it was time to double cross Benjamin and get out of here. Only she hadn't gotten this far with her planning.

There was no way out down the stairs. On her right, the second floor led to Van Doren's windowless office and bedroom. But to her left were the library, Knox's room, and Grant's room. There was no more time to decide. Benjamin stepped toward her with the shackles.

Clover took a deep breath and with the swirling cold forming, she managed to produce a small blast of air that knocked Benjamin backward down the stairs. She turned to the left and leapt up the stairs to the library. On the last step, she stumbled, and when her hand hit the ground, the runner carpet in the hallway caught on fire. No time for that.

"Get her! Get that filthy double-crossing half-breed!" shrieked Benjamin.

Clover pushed herself up and stumbled into the library, slamming the door behind her. Now she needed a way to get out of here, the most obvious being the windows facing Veritas. Panicked, she turned and ran waist-first into a table, nearly knocking the wind out of her.

The door to the library was open, so Clover reached out

and grabbed the first thing her hand landed on. She turned and bashed Gerard Vale right across the face with a statue of some long-gone Van Doren. He fell to the ground and Clover kept running.

People flooded into the room, trying to grab her, the Vale twins giving the most effort. They tried to trap her between them on one side of a long table. Clover pushed herself up onto the table and ran down its length. Walter Vale grabbed the edge of her skirt. It ripped away slightly from the bodice and the jerk tripped her. She fell onto her back.

She kicked Walter hard in the face and he let go but his brother, Gerard, had already grabbed her around the shoulders. His hands slipped up to her neck and she clawed at him as he cut off her air.

"Don't kill her, you idiot!" shouted Benjamin from the doorway.

More shouting came from the main hall. Clover reached around and her hand landed on a small but thick book. She picked it up and whacked Gerard with all her might once again. He let her go, shouting.

She picked herself up and began running. At the end of the table was the long window. If she threw herself at it hard enough, would she break it? Would she simply knock against it like a witless bird?

Clover would never find out. From one side of the table, Benjamin and Walter, having recovered from her vicious kick, tilted a bookshelf right at the place where she was running. She was going too fast to stop so suddenly and the first thick volume struck the side of the head. Time slowed and darkness framed her vision. Clover fell off the table and hit the ground hard—but not as hard as the dozens of books still cascading over her body.

HER THOUGHTS SCATTERED, BOUNCING AROUND HER HEAD SO
loud and fast that she could barely comprehend them before
they were gone. Grant's death, and her mother's illness. Had
Soleil gotten to safety? Was Knox going home to Hirane soon?
Where had the doctor run off to?

The sharp burning of iron shackles on her wrists and
ankles focused her mind to the present. The books were gone,
but she was still in pain. Clover screamed as she was hauled to
her feet. The world was a blur, and she smelled smoke. Her
feet and knees bounced along the ground as her sight and
hearing finally sharpened. The Vale twins were dragging her
out of the library. Clover got her feet underneath her but
screamed as the iron pressed against her bare skin.

The entire main hall of the manor was a furnace. Had she
started this fire? One little flick of her hand and everything up
in flames? If she even wanted to, could she stop it? Clover
wasn't sure. She coughed, hacking on the acrid smoke burning
up everything she'd ever known. Half of her home had been
one of torture, pain, and misery—but the other half had been
a wonderful love, friendship, and family. And her heart ached
at the thought that they would both be burned up together.

When they pulled her out of the front doors, the rest of
the town was out on the lawn. The Justice Riders were with
them. Clover suspected they were waiting to see if the newly
initiated boys of Veritas could complete their task alone. The
patients had been moved to the back of a cart and were
preparing to go back to Veritas. There was another cart
waiting for Clover. It was an iron cage supported by the strong
wood of a carriage, pulled by two horses.

Clover gritted her teeth and struggled against the twins.

She yelped as the iron seared her skin. Her heart pounded faster than she ever thought possible. The twins kept pulling her.

"No!" she screamed.

Someone shoved her from behind.

"Get in that cage, you beast!"

"Filthy creature!"

"Go on, half-breed!"

"Abomination!"

Clover felt the cold swirling in her chest. She didn't care that she was drawing her power from the forest. She would not beg for her life. The grass began to grow up out of the ground and lash at the people standing on the lawn.

"She's using her dark magic against us!"

"Burn her!"

The vines wrapping around the outer walls grew around the gate, closing it and grabbing at the townspeople on the lawn. Clover was shoved into the cage, and she landed hard on her hands and knees, both of which were burned by the iron. She sobbed. Benjamin locked her in the cage and put the key in the pocket of his coat with a wild grin.

"Make her stop!" shouted Captain Dawson.

Batons of iron were stuck through the bars of the cage, and they pressed painfully against her face, her back, and her exposed legs until she could barely breathe. The magic stopped. Clover was spent. Despair, fatigue, and regret took over. Consciousness remained, though she wished it wouldn't. Her prison began its journey forward, undoubtedly toward her demise.

While her past, good and bad, burned away behind her.

Chapter Seventeen

CLOVER LAID ON HER SIDE, curled against the pain. Grant's coat and her dress subdued some of the stinging pain the iron caused, but only for so long. She would have to move or turn, and when she did, the shackles around her wrists and ankles would sear her and make her cry out. This would anger Benjamin, or the accompanying Justice Riders, and they would shove their iron batons through the bars, which would only make her cry out more. Benjamin was wasting no time in getting her to Hirane, risking the Fae Road through the forest. The Riders clutched their crossbows tightly, eyes darting to the wall of mist on either side of the road. Even they were not immune to fear.

"Not so hard to catch, were you? I lost the other one but all I needed was you." Benjamin had been keeping up a steady stream of talking to himself. The others either didn't mind or enjoyed his crazy chatter.

"Oh yes, yes, yes, my name will be in the Hirane papers now. Maybe they'll write stories—no, books about me. Oh, yes. Benjamin Freeman. Everywhere. In the papers. The scientific papers."

Perhaps in his deal with Cypress, Benjamin had unknowingly paid the dark fae with some of his sanity as well. While he kept talking, Clover watched the mist-covered forest pass. The snow had surely erased all footprints left by Dr. Van Doren and her mother by now. She hoped Knox and Soleil were all right, not back at the manor—but somewhere safe. One thing after the other kept getting in the way of her finding Grant. Maybe something beyond any of them was trying to keep them apart. That thought hurt worse than any iron.

All around her, the winter world shone bright white. The cold drove her to want to sleep, but the heat of the iron kept her awake. In her half-sleep, her mind wandered to the scientists of Hirane. Did fae have rights there? Did they apply to Clover, or did she fall into some sort of gray area? Lawfully or not, they were going to cut her open and study her insides as though she was some kind of plant. Would they do her the courtesy of killing her first? Or did they want a live subject? A different kind of burning came—tears down her cheeks. She didn't want to die. Who would take care of her mother? Where *was* her mother? Question after question filled her mind as the road to Hirane seemed to last forever.

"Stop!" shouted one of the Vale twins. Clover didn't know or care which one he was, but it might have been Walter. "Benjamin, stop!"

Benjamin did, pulling the horses to a stop. "What is it?"

"Where's my brother?" he asked.

Clover tensed as she lifted her head and looked around. She hadn't noticed before, but the longer they traveled the road, the more the mist encroached on the passage.

"He was just there and now he's gone!"

"Well, call out to the idiot. He can't have gotten far," snapped Captain Dawson. The other Justice Riders readied their crossbows. There were about eight of them in all, four on either side of the cart.

Walter turned back the way they came and cupped his hands to his mouth. "Gerard!" he shouted. "Where are you?"

There came no reply, but neither Walter nor Benjamin seemed keen on wandering away from the cage. Clover looked up when she thought she saw something dart through the mist. She wasn't sure if it had been real or if she was so tired that she was beginning to see things.

But then she saw it again. Something moved in the mist—the mist that was growing ever closer. It now drifted around the feet of the two boys.

"Forget him," said Benjamin. "We press on."

Walter scowled. "He could freeze to death."

"It's his own fault for wandering off!" Captain Dawson snapped. "And if you're going to snivel and cry and prance about, then do so. We have a delivery to make." He waved his hand and Benjamin whipped the horses into moving forward once more.

From beyond the mist, there was a groan. It was loud enough for all of them to hear and Benjamin jerked the horses to a halt once more. This was no human sound.

"Gerard!" Walter rushed for his brother. He rushed straight through the mist without hesitation, but as soon as he was out of sight, even his footfalls could not be heard. Nothing could be heard but the breathing of the men, the impatient stamping of the horses.

"Ready your arrows," said Captain Dawson. There was a long, slow silence that followed until a shriek, loud and terrified, came from the mist. Clover's heart seemed to stopped beating and it left her breathless. The mist built all around them, surrounding them, so both directions of the road were cut off.

"Steady," said Captain Dawson.

Immediately after the word left his mouth, roots sprang out of the ground and grabbed him by the wrists and ankles. Clover sat up and gasped as he screamed. The roots knocked him off his feet before dragging him into the mist.

"Captain!" one of the men shouted, trying to grab him, but Dawson was gone before the man could get to him. He stumbled back from the mist.

A Rider turned his crossbow on her. "She's doing it! Kill her now!"

"Don't!" shouted Benjamin.

Clover curled in on herself. As the Rider fired the arrow aimed at her heart, a massive snow-white owl grabbed him by the shoulders and jerked him backward. Clover shrieked as the arrow entered her shoulder. With a single beat of its wings, the owl pulled the Rider into the mist. Clover grasped the arrow tightly before yanking it out with another shriek of pain—the iron tip was thankfully no longer in her skin.

The horses, afraid for their lives, began running. Benjamin, it seemed, had no control over the horses, who ran this way and that, throwing Clover around in her cage. Not only did the bars burn her, but now they struck her as well. In the distance, she could hear the other Justice Riders screaming.

Finally, something jostled loose and the horses broke free of the cart. The ride for Benjamin and Clover was not over, since the cart went reeling off the road and down an embankment.

Clover cried out as she landed hard on her side. The bars

burned her face, but she was also quickly enveloped by a thick, freezing sludge. It was slowly rising, with some of the cage already submerged beneath it.

"Clover?" Knox called through the mist.

Hope and fear were a toxic mixture inside her. She didn't know whether to laugh and clap or be sick. She rushed to the edge of the cage. "Here! Knox, I'm here!"

He and Soleil ran into view. Knox was in no state of celebration, since there was still a cage between them. He frowned in concentration before he grabbed the cage and dug his feet into the snow on the bank of the muddy, icy bog. It stopped sliding. Soleil came forward and grabbed the lock, only to jerk her hands away, hissing.

"Key," Knox grunted. He was using all his strength to keep the cart still.

Clover shook her head. "Benjamin. I saw him put it in his pocket."

Soleil looked past the cart at the bog, and she rushed into it without a word. Knox let out a few quick breaths before pulling the cart back.

"Not the day you imagined?" he asked.

Clover shook her head. Her tears flowed but no sobs tried to burst from her. "I'm sorry."

"Ah, what are friends for?" he grunted, changing his grip. The cart slid a little but he steadied it.

Soleil surfaced from the bog, dragging an unconscious Benjamin behind her. Dripping thick mud, she dug through his pockets and pulled out the key. She tossed it into the snow like a hot coal.

"What do I do?" she demanded.

Knox sighed heavily. "Be creative."

Soleil reached for the key again, but Benjamin suddenly

roared to life and grabbed her. Soleil shouted, reeling back, but he already had her. He rolled her beneath him and wrapped his hands around her throat.

"Knox, do something!" Clover shouted.

He looked painfully between Clover and Soleil before gritting his teeth. He let the cage go and tackled Benjamin off Soleil, who gasped for air. She rolled to her hands and knees and scrambled around for the dropped key.

Clover pressed herself to the edge of the cage as the frozen mud in the cage reached her lower back. Some of her hope was beginning to fade but she grasped at it like the bars of her cage. This was far from over and she needed things to be moving faster. Clover sniffed and cleared her throat.

"Soleil...I don't mean to rush you—"

"I'm trying!" Soleil shot back.

Knox and Benjamin rolled around in the snow, throwing punches. Knox was experienced, but Benjamin was wild and desperate—both were dangerous. The mud came up to Clover's armpits now and the cage sank faster.

Soleil shouted at the sky in frustration. "I can't find it!" She ran off and came back with a rock. She bashed at the lock over and over, screaming like a furious animal until the lock broke. Soleil pulled the door open as the mud and still water of the bog swallowed up Clover's neck. Clover reached out for her friend, who grabbed her.

"I've got you," Soleil said through her teeth as she pulled Clover out of the mud. When they got to the bank of the bog —where hard-pack snow meant they were safe— they both fell to the ground, breathing hard.

Clover looked over where Knox and Benjamin were on their feet and trying to push each other into the bog. The ice was uneven where they fought—it could break under them at any moment. Knox brought his knee up and caught Benjamin in the stomach, but Benjamin reached up and clawed at Knox's face, pushing him deeper into the bog. Clover rushed forward.

Benjamin stood upright and tried to throw a punch at Knox's face. Instead, Knox grabbed his arm and spun Benjamin around toward the bog, so Knox's back was to them. There was a deep, echoing crack, and faster than Clover could blink, Benjamin was gone, sucked down into the bog.

Knox toppled forward at the sudden disappearance of Benjamin before Clover grabbed the back of his jacket. He was heavy and she nearly slipped but Soleil grabbed the back of her dress and the three of them stumbled into the snowy bank behind them.

All of them were breathless.

"Where did he go? One moment he was there, then..." Knox gestured with his hand to the bog, where Benjamin was clearly no longer.

"Lightning mud," said Soleil. "Nearly invisible to the untrained eye. Wander onto it and you're a hundred leagues down before you can scream."

The three of them sat up and looked at the place where Benjamin had been pulled into an unintentional death. There was an ever so faint trace of bubbles around the area where the lightning mud was located.

Knox nodded—he looked like he was in shock. "Thanks."

"I guess that's what friends are for," said Clover.

Soleil and Knox nodded. Knox grimaced and dug around beneath him before pulling out the key.

Soleil scowled before she flopped back down in the snow while Clover held up her shackled limbs. Knox unlocked her and tossed the shackles into the bog.

The three of them stood, still staring at the hole Benjamin had been pulled into. Clover knew Benjamin wasn't sane, and he had tried to hunt her down for dissection on multiple occasions—but she realized she never hated Benjamin. She certainly hadn't wanted him dead. He had been a child once, hadn't he? He was still somebody's son. Maybe in their own twisted way, they had loved him.

"I feel like we should say something," said Knox. His face was stuck in a concerned pinch, like he was in pain. "I mean— no one is pure evil. Well, except maybe my uncle."

Soleil held her hands out, palms up toward the sky. "Great Spirit who watches over this forest, who gives everything life and gathers all peoples like the mother bird under her wing— we ask that you take this soul into your great place and give comfort to those who watched his untimely end."

Soleil brought her hands together toward the earth and clasped them. With that, she opened her eyes. Knox and Clover gave each other a look—that sounded far better than the Grey nonsense, and though she still felt sorry for Benjamin, the thought that his soul was in some "great place" gave her comfort. She hoped Knox had some too.

"We should go back to the manor," said Knox. "Recoup a little."

Clover nodded, shivering. "Agreed."

The three of them left the bog and made their way through the misty forest back to Van Doren Manor, or whatever was left of it.

§

VAN DOREN MANOR HAD BEEN CLEAVED IN TWO BY THE FIRE. The middle was black and charred, leaving a skeleton of posts and beams. On either side, the manor had been licked black by the flames, but remained intact. They entered the manor through the servants' entrance. A little coaxing was needed for Soleil, but Clover was fairly certain the doctor hadn't returned from wherever he'd run off to. On their way back to the manor, Soleil had used a quick remedy to heal iron burns for fae, and even though the scars would remain, the pain from the burns was gone. The same magic couldn't be used to heal the burns on Van Doren Manor. Clover didn't know how Grant felt about the house, but she certainly didn't mind seeing the old prison go—even if there *were* a few good memories to be found within.

Clover's nose wrinkled at the smell of cloth and wood eaten up by fire. Luckily, her clothes had been spared. Knox and Soleil ate whatever they could scrounge while she changed her clothes. She kept Grant's coat, however, simply beating the mud off it with a towel. When she came out, Soleil was munching on an apple and Knox was biting into an entire loaf of bread, uncut, and shoving slices of meat into his mouth along with it, like some sort of heathen. Given the circumstances, she let it slide. He offered some to Clover and she accepted some of the meat but left out the bread.

"Now what?" Soleil grabbed another apple and shoveled dry oatmeal into her mouth. Clover's lips raised in disgust at the action.

Clover focused on answering Soleil's question. "We figure Grant is out in the woods somewhere. That's where we intend to look for him, and my mother."

"What about Dr. Van Doren?" asked Knox.

"Let him rot," said Clover angrily. "He lied to us about Grant's death. He probably made a deal with Cypress to put a preservation spell on him. Business has been good for that dark fae around here. Who knows what he gave Cypress in return?"

Knox nodded thoughtfully, biting into his loaf. "We should check his office."

"Why?" asked Clover, eating more of the meat.

"Because there could be something in there that would narrow down our search. He wouldn't hide Grant in the woods—or even let someone else hide him without knowing where Grant was," said Knox. "There could be some useful information in there."

"I agree," said Soleil. "Everyone leaves traces...if there's something your pitiful human senses don't catch, I will find them."

"Thanks, I guess," said Knox, grimacing. Soleil nodded her welcome, not catching onto the complete lack of thanks in Knox's statement.

&

WHEN THEY'D ALL HAD ENOUGH TO EAT, THEY LEFT THE kitchen. Knox and Clover had to slam into the door leading from the kitchen into the dining room in order for it to open. A beam from the roof had fallen across the doorway on the other side. They pushed it away and it fell, scattering ash and making them all cough.

The center of the dining room table had crumbled away, and most of the chairs were piles of sticks on the ground. In the main hall, the wood floors had given way to the stone beneath, but the hospital ward was entirely untouched.

"Did all of the patients make it out all right?" asked Clover.

Knox nodded. "I think so. Thankfully, after we put out the fire, there were no bodies."

The wall separating the stairway up to the doctor's office and the main hall had burned and crumbled away but the stairs were still intact. Knox and Clover passed over the threshold to Dr. Van Doren's office easily, but Soleil hesitated.

"I am not entering this sick room," said Soleil. "Whoever called this place one of constant habitation was not well in mind, body, or spirit."

Clover couldn't have put it better herself. It was good to know other people felt the same way she did about Van Doren's office. "You're right, but we need you in here. It'll only take a moment, then you never have to come in here again. I promise."

Soleil grimaced, still looking around at the windowless room and its complete separation from all things light and natural before she finally stepped into the room. Knox was already looking around.

"Dr. Van Doren seems to have had some strange fascination with the fae," said Knox. "Almost all his books are about them in some way or another."

Clover began going through the drawers of his desk. "Maybe he needed information on how to locate a dark one."

Knox held up a book as though that proved her point but then he seemed to remember that Clover couldn't read.

"*The Commoner's Guide to Surviving an Encounter with dark fae,*" he read aloud.

Soleil shook her head, sniffing around. "No human survives an encounter with dark fae. The human we struggled with was a perfect example." Soleil lifted the stopper off a bottle of alcohol, tasting the rim before spitting and hissing, revealing sharp teeth.

Clover tried opening one drawer only to find it locked. "Knox, come here."

He did, kneeling next to her. Knox himself tried to jerk it open before he frowned.

"I'll go get my lock picking kit," he said. "Keep looking around."

⁊⋒

HE LEFT AND CLOVER KEPT LOOKING BUT ALMOST EVERYTHING else was a book or writings that she couldn't read. She found herself wishing she had taken Knox's offer to continue her lessons in Grant's absence. Too late for that. She felt useless without the skill. Her frustration drover her fingernails into the palms of her hands.

"Strange markings." Soleil looked over something on a counter nearby. Clover went over and saw a map. She couldn't read any of the names on the map but according to positioning, she knew they were looking at Van Doren Manor.

"It's a map of this land, Soleil," said Clover. "Apparently, the Van Doren estate used to be much, much larger."

"Yes," said Soleil, as if she already knew.

Clover frowned. "What do you mean?"

"Many things has the forest grown over. Statues, graves, fountains...the forest reclaims all. Even this evil town...many houses did it reclaim before the iron bars."

Knox came back into the room with his lock picking kit, but Clover was still thinking about what Soleil had said. If the forest had overgrown parts of the Van Doren estate and the doctor knew that, then maybe Dr. Van Doren hadn't gone very far at all.

"Knox, come here. I need you to read something," said Clover.

Knox sighed. "Knox, open this drawer, Knox, read this. I'm only one man, you know."

"One man who complains a lot. Hurry up," said Clover. Normally, she would have been annoyed by Knox's whining, but she was too interested in what might lay hidden inside this box that Van Doren seemed to care an awful lot about to hide this way.

Knox focused on his lock picking. There was a click and he smiled and pulled open the drawer. His smile turned into a frown as he lifted whatever was in the drawer out and put it on the desk. It was a large metal box.

"What is that?"

"I don't know...and I'm no scientist, but I'm fairly certain this is blood," he said, looking at the top of the box.

Both Clover and Soleil went over. There were three finger-prints of blood on the top of the metal box. One large, one medium, and one so very tiny. Clover touched the box—it wasn't iron, but it was sealed shut with what looked like wax or some other hard substance.

"I sense great darkness within this box." Soleil ghosted her own hand over the top of it. "Something very evil was contained in here long ago."

"Open it," said Clover. Maybe it was something they could use against Van Doren. She wasn't optimistic, but *something* had to be in their favor.

Knox turned to her. "Look, I'm just as curious as you. But did the words *great darkness* and *very evil* not put you off? Not even a little?"

Clover raised an eyebrow at him, and he sighed before reaching into his pocket and taking out a knife, not the dagger

he'd taken from Clover on the Blood Solstice. Soleil growled
and tried to knock it out of his hand.

"Hey! Quit it! It's made of iveen—that means even you
can kill me with it," he said.

Soleil grabbed his wrist and pulled it to her, examining the
knife.

Knox pulled his hand back. "Stop it! I'm trying to open
the box of many bad things." He began chipping away at the
seal around the edges of the box while Clover was fixated by
the fingerprints at the top of the box. With a gentle brush of
her fingertips, she could feel the old blood tied to the energy of
her and her mother. Those were *their* fingerprints. Whatever
was inside this box was going to make things clear. Questions
she didn't even know she had were about to be answered.

When the last of the seal was chipped away, Knox opened
the box. Inside, resting on a velvet covering, was a knife made
of the most curious substance. It was pitch black, as though a
knife-shaped hole had been carved out of the universe and
there was nothing left but darkness. Two other indents
suggested the presence of other knives, but they were missing.

"What is it?" asked Knox.

Soleil stared at it, hypnotized. "A spirit blade made of soul
flint."

"What's a spirit blade?" said Clover. She wanted to ask if
they could use it against Van Doren somehow, but one question at a time. She needed to know all the details. The appearance of the knife had chilled her.

"No." Soleil shook her head, frowning. "That doesn't make
any sense."

"Soleil." Clover went to her friend and jerked her, pulling
Soleil's sight away from the spirit blade. "What is it?"

"A spirit blade, when bound, can allow the wielder to drain

another being's spirit. To increase their own power, sometimes even to increase their own life span..."

"So what doesn't make sense?" Knox's eyes were attached to the spirit blade, transfixed and horrified by it at the same time.

"Spirit blades can only be wielded by dark fae," said Soleil.

Knox's face went slack with sudden understanding. "Would this draining cause mental degradation?"

"Degra..." Soleil squinted.

"A sort of fracturing of a person's mind. So they wouldn't be entirely themselves."

Soleil nodded. And then, with the strike of a match, Clover understood what Knox was really asking. Everything in Clover's mind was illuminated. The two missing knives, her mother's insanity, her own increased mindlessness, Dr. Van Doren's ability to treat even the most impossible of patients, his lack of aging, his strength, the fact that nothing in Van Doren Manor was made of iron...he was fae. Dark fae.

"Stop it," said Clover. Her shock had caused her breathing to pick up. Her heart raced, but this could be stopped, couldn't it? Couldn't it? "How do we stop it?"

Soleil sighed. "It's nearly impossible. The effects can be dampened by the bound breaking their own blades...but that would only return a fraction of their life force. Much of their life would still rest within the binder's spirit blade. In order for the bonds to be completely broken, the binder, Van Doren, must break his own blade. Even if the other blades weren't broken, the breaking of Van Doren's spirit blade would release the bound."

Clover took a moment to decipher that. "So if I break this blade, Van Doren's spirit blade, my mother and I would be free. We don't even need our own blades?"

"No," said Soleil. "He must break it...and it must be of his own free will."

Clover sighed. Wherever Van Doren had gone, he'd taken the blades with him and the only one left was the most useless to them. In order to be released, she would have to find him—and even if she did, she wasn't sure she could fight him if he was draining her life from her.

"I hope you see the very big problem with that statement," said Knox. "Van Doren's been draining them for years. If there's anything I know about people with power, it's that they'd rather die than give it up. How are we going to get him to break his blade?"

The three of them were silent with thought for a long while—but time was wasting. Torryn and Grant were still out there, waiting to be found.

Clover looked at all the books on Van Doren's tables. "Are all his books about fae?"

"They appear to be," said Knox. "Fae artifacts, fae abilities, fae biology. Why?"

"I think I have an idea—but first, we're going to need a fae artifact."

Soleil crossed her arms. "I might know where one is. But it's not going to be easy to get. What did you have in mind?"

"I'm going to do what humans believe fae do best," said Clover with growing determination. "I'm going to trick him."

Chapter Eighteen

Knox picked up the map and spread it out after closing the box and shoving everything else off the desk. They all gathered around the map.

"Well, look at this." Knox pointed to one square plot with a word beneath it. "It must be out in the forest. It's the most obvious place for Grant to be, so perhaps we should start there."

Clover squinted. "M—maw—maws—" She huffed. "I don't know that word."

"It says mausoleum," said Knox. "It's the Van Doren Mausoleum."

"What is a mausoleum?" Soleil squinted at the word. At least Clover knew the letters. To Soleil, it must seem like random marks on the paper.

"Some human families liked to be buried together, so they put them in these stone buildings for generations," said Knox. "We know Grant is most likely out in the forest, and what better place to keep his preserved body than in the family mausoleum?"

Clover took a deep breath. They had somewhere to start, and even if they were wrong, it felt good to have a real place and a good possibility. "All right, we'll start there. How far away is it? Soleil, have you seen it?"

Soleil shook her head. "No. The forest claims things in many ways, holds them, swallows them, lifts them up. I have never seen this place."

"I'm not exactly a cartographer," Knox said. "We'll just sort of aim for it and hope we get remotely close."

Clover ran a hand through her hair. "Then we need to get the fae artifact now. It's going to get dark soon, I don't want my mother out in the cold after dark."

Soleil stood. "I'll talk to the forest—it will bring me the artifact."

"It will?" asked Knox.

"My intentions are pure," said Soleil.

"Right. I'll bring the blade," said Knox. "Clover, you should get a blanket and another one of Grant's coats. When we find him and your mother, they'll probably be cold."

"Good thinking," said Clover before leaving Van Doren's office. She entered his bedroom, which was untouched. The thick woolen blanket in the cupboard by his bed would do much better for her mother than the patchy quilt Torryn usually used.

Leaving Van Doren's room, the smell of burnt wood hit her like a slap but she continued on. The fire had carved even the grand staircase in half, leaving a cleft into burned darkness. Clover leapt over it to the other side, where her foot broke through a charred step. She yanked her foot out and went on to Grant's room.

Earlier, she had rushed through it. She didn't have much time now, but she selected his favorite coat with care, sniffing around for a lingering scent. She couldn't detect his scent, and why should she? Grant had been gone for two seasons. But now it wouldn't matter. She was going to get him back and her longing would be over.

&.

CLOVER SHOVED THE BLANKET AND THE COAT INTO ONE OF Grant's traveling medical bags after emptying out the contents. As she left his room, the whispering that had plagued her since meeting Cypress grew loud, and though it echoed like it was all around her, it was definitely pulling her in a single direction.

Clover ignored the twisting of fear in her stomach as she pushed open the door to Knox's room. The hinges creaked but the whispering was deafening, and it drowned out all other noise, including her rapidly beating heart. She knew what was calling her now, and if she wanted it to stop, then she had no choice but to answer.

Inside the drawer of Knox's desk, she pulled out the iveen dagger Cypress had given her. As soon as it was in her hand, the whispering stopped, leaving a ringing sound behind. The dagger looked just as sharp and evil as when she first received it. What was she going to do about Dr. Van Doren once he broke his spirit blade? He couldn't be allowed to do any more damage, but how was she supposed to stop him? Benjamin's demise had been the only thing that stopped him. How could Dr. Van Doren be any different?

But if she killed, killed with intention and hatred, then she would turn dark, just like Cypress. Soleil said turning other fae dark was the aim of all dark fae—but Clover wouldn't let Dr. Van Doren hurt anyone else, even if it cost her own light. Soleil said that even dark fae could be led back to the light.

Clover would only use the dagger as long as it was her last option, and then she would trust the faith of the people around her to help her back to the light. It would be painful… but worth it to protect her friends, her family. Clover slid the dagger into the inner pocket of her coat.

❦

THERE WAS NO MORE TIME TO WASTE. SHE LEAPT ACROSS THE divide, intending to go back up to Van Doren's office, but was jolted off her feet when someone called out.

"Clover! You're alive!"

Clover put a hand over her heart and recovered, looking down the main hall at Angela. Marvin trailed behind her. Clover broke through the spindles of the stair rails and dropped into the main hall.

"I'm all right. Angela, what are you doing here?" she asked.

Angela's eyes were puffy. "I came to apologize. I thought if we hurried, we could get you out in time—I didn't know about your friend!"

"Is Benjamin…" Marvin looked pained, like he didn't really want to know but was forcing himself to ask.

"Yes. It was an accident," said Clover.

Marvin relaxed noticeably.

"It's just as well, really." Angela took Marvin's hand. "I don't think he was himself anymore—I don't think he ever would be again."

Marvin's smile was soft and sad. "I know, you're right—it's

still such a shock to see the sudden change. He was my friend once."

"I'm sorry," said Clover. As the siblings stood side by side, she saw their similarities in the shape of their faces and the straight lines of their noses.

"Angela." Knox stepped into the room. Clover stepped aside and she and Marvin looked away as Knox and Angela kissed.

"Shame about the old house," said Marvin.

Clover looked around. "I know. It could always be rebuilt…transitioned into a true hospital."

"No doctor to fill it, though. Angela explained that Grant might be alive. Don't suppose you and Grant would want to be staying after…everything that's happened."

"We'll put in the good word in Hirane." Clover smiled as she turned back to him, but her smile fell as she looked closer at his hairline. "Is that gray hair?"

Marvin's brows pulled together in confusion before his face relaxed. "Oh, yes. It seems to have happened while I was gone." He frowned. "I believe I may have been…dying or drained somehow. It was cast by dark fae, wasn't it? I can't imagine anything benevolent happened to me."

Clover took him by both shoulders and stared into his eyes. No other part of him had aged, but she sensed a shortness about it. His life. Could it be that he had some of his years on this earth stolen away by the spell?

"You're going to be all right," she said, relaxing her face so as not to scare him.

He nodded, seeming relieved. "You think so?"

"Yes." Clover held out her hand as she'd seen others do and he shook it. She turned. "Knox, we have to go."

He and Angela let go of each other. Angela turned back to

her. Never in Clover's wildest dreams had she thought she would have a friend who'd been born and raised in the town of Veritas—she never thought she'd have a human friend at all. But now she had Knox and Angela in addition to Soleil and Grant and she felt…grateful.

"We are in your debt," said Angela, stepping back toward Marvin.

"No," said Clover. "No debts between friends, and you have been a very good friend indeed. I'm afraid this next part is up to the three of us alone."

"If you ever need me…"

Clover smiled. "I'll light a candle." She pulled Angela into a hug. If it hadn't been for Angela's protection, Clover would have been on the road to Hirane long before this point, with a much different ending. She never would have gotten this far without Angela. If only Grant could see her now, trusting other humans, even calling them friend. Clover could just see the smug smile spreading across his face and couldn't stop her own smile at the thought.

"And Knox...please bring him back to me," Angela whispered.

Clover nodded. "I will."

"Clover," said Knox.

The girls separated. Knox and Soleil stood on the other side of the divide, ready to go.

"We only have a few hours until dark," Knox said.

"Keep each other safe," said Angela. Marvin put an arm around her shoulders, and she leaned against him for support.

Clover adjusted the strap of her bag. "You two do the same."

THE THREE OF THEM STRUCK OUT FROM THE BACK OF VAN Doren Manor, the snow crunching loudly beneath their boots. Grant's coat provided much more warmth than Clover's own threadbare one, but the cold still stung her cheeks and her legs. Soleil was in the lead, stepping through the snow barefoot.

"Where exactly are we going?" asked Clover.

Soleil looked around. "The forest will lead us. It's not far."

"Why do you have light fae artifacts lying about in the forest?" asked Knox.

"When an object becomes important to our history, it is given to the forest to hide away. Many believe if you look hard enough, you may find it yourself—this is not true. You must make a plea, ask for the forest to reveal it to you. If your intentions are pure, the forest will do just that." Soleil gave Knox a scowl. "Otherwise, you could look for a hundred years and never find it."

Clover found that to be a relief, even though she knew there was part of her that was contemplating murder. Soleil took a twisting, turning path through the forest, and even though it didn't seem to lead anywhere, Clover could sense it too. That the forest was leading them to something.

"This is getting a little long—"

Soleil shushed Knox before stopping in front of a small pool in the roots of a tree. Clover leaned over and saw herself in a perfect, glassy reflection. There was no way to tell how deep it was or what lurked beneath the water. Still, there was no time to waste. Clover steeled herself before plunging her hand into the water. She thought it would be ice cold, but it was actually hot and it seared her skin. She shouted as she kneeled, sinking her arm into the water up to her shoulder. Finally, her fingers brushed the bottom and her hand tangled in something. She grabbed whatever it was and pulled. Her arm came out completely dry and tangled in her fingers was a leather strap with an iveen charm on the end.

"It's a necklace?" asked Knox.

Soleil gave him a frown. "It was worn by one of our best warriors. Aviana was wearing that necklace when a human marksman fired upon her. The arrow was blocked by the necklace and the necklace protected her from many such attacks."

"It'll do." Clover put it around her neck and took a deep breath. "Now we have to find the mausoleum."

Knox looked at the map before sighing. "We're lost."

"Soleil, don't suppose you know where we are?" Clover asked.

Soleil looked at the map with a frown before looking around. "Manor is that way." Soleil pointed. "So the mausoleum would be that way."

Clover began walking. "No time to lose."

CLOVER WALKED AHEAD OF SOLEIL AND KNOX WITH THE MAP. She couldn't read words, but this map was more pictographic than literary. Perhaps she could be a carto-whatever-Knox-had-said. Cartographer! Knox had said investigator before. It was a strange feeling, believing she could be something other than a slave. Clover smiled to herself, but it fell. First things first: find Grant and free her mother. Then she could just be the simplest of things—free.

Clover stopped and held up the map, marking their approximate progress with her eyes. They were getting closer. They had passed the ruins of a fountain, which was mostly enveloped into the side of a growing tree.

"We should be coming up on it quite quickly now." Clover

lowered the map but trying to see into the forest was a useless task.

"I hope so, this thing just seems to keep getting heavier," said Knox. He put the box down, but when it began to sink through the snow, he quickly picked it back up.

Soleil walked past him, leaving no footprints behind. "Your larger stature has a singular use. This is it. Cease your complaining."

"You're rough around the edges, you know that?" Knox grumbled. "And I thought Grim was grim."

Clover shook her head and kept walking, looking down at the map every now and then until they passed beyond the tree-line into one of the most special places from Clover's memories.

The hill in the center of the pond was white with untouched snow, and the water around it had been frozen but was broken now. The single stepping stone to the hill was covered in snow and ice as well.

"This must be it," said Soleil. "I sense something hollow beneath us."

Clover turned to her. "What? No. This can't be the place."

"Why not?"

The map fell from Clover's hands and landed in the snow. Her heart picked up speed and a chill went down her spine. Grant had been here the whole time? Clover had never felt so foolish in all her life. This place she had come back to time and time again, each time feeling so close to Grant, like she could reach out and touch him. Only to find out she really could have.

"Grant and I had our first kiss here...right on that hill," said Clover before she could stop herself. She hadn't meant to say it aloud and she looked at Soleil and Knox for reaction. Soleil's face pinched with disgust.

Knox took a deep breath. "Well, I'm sure it was much more charming when it happened. If it's below us, then how exactly do we get inside?"

"I don't think that hill is actually a hill," said Soleil before stepping into the water. She didn't even flinch.

"How does she do that?" Knox shuddered.

Clover stepped after Soleil. Pins and needles went down to her bone, and she pulled her lips into her mouth and bit them to keep from crying out. But whimpers still fought their way out of her throat anyway.

"Here," said Soleil on the far side of the hill. She was in the water up to her shoulders. Clover was barely in up to her waist and she felt faint.

"Soleil," she wheezed.

Soleil turned and frowned. "Hurry up, the faster you get through it, the faster the pain ends."

"I'm in no mood for logic," said Knox through his teeth. He was holding the box over his head.

Clover closed her eyes and forced her feet forward. By the time she got to Soleil, who stood at a stone doorway, she was breathing as though she'd run a great distance. Soleil pushed her way inside and Clover followed, huffing and puffing. Soon, she heard Knox behind her. Soleil began to rise out of the water and Clover's feet struck stone steps.

Soleil and Clover stood side by side in a room that was rather small. All around them were squares with names on them. Beside each of the squares was a small plate of oil that was already lit. The doctor must have come down here. All the names on the squares were Van Dorens, though she didn't know what their first names were or what the numbers meant.

Knox fell to his knees beside them. "Where are they?" he asked, looking around. Clover did too, remembering the mission. She didn't see the doctor, or Grant, or her mother—who she hoped was with the doctor—anywhere.

"I don't know." Clover shuddered. It wasn't much warmer in here, but it was a sun-baked rock compared to the water. "We should look around."

Knox got to his feet, and they began looking around at all the names. The room was about as large as Dr. Van Doren's office, longer than it was wide, with names from floor to ceiling. The room sloped downward from the doorway, and they descended carefully. Clover saw no sign of anyone having been there, other than the lit oil plates, and she began to worry. Where could Dr. Van Doren and her mother have gone?

"Clover," said Knox. "What was Grant's mother's name?"

She turned to him. "Ailara, why?"

"She's here." Knox stood in front of a square.

"That's impossible. When Ailara died, she was sent to her family to be buried with them. That's what Dr. Van Doren said."

Soleil came over. "The same man who has probably never told the truth in his life?"

"Yes," said Clover. It disgusted her to think that Ailara's coffin was empty, and she was actually here in this horrible place—just like her son.

"I know she only died when Grant was young—still a child. Which either means this place was only recently submerged, which is probably not the case, or Dr. Van Doren took her down here to be buried—which solves nothing. It's just horrifying."

The whole room shuddered, and Knox shouted as he stumbled back. A darkness opened beneath his feet, pulling him down. Clover rushed forward and grabbed him by the elbow as he suddenly sank. But instead of helping him, he just dragged her with him.

"Clover!" shouted Soleil, grabbing her by the back of her coat, but to no effect. The three of them tumbled into a world of darkness.

Chapter Nineteen

CLOVER'S MIND swam with memories. Washing Grant's blood off her hands, then instead of blood, Knox's hands were holding hers. He smiled but his face changed into Soleil's and the girl hugged her. When they separated, she was hugging Angela, who turned into her mother. Clover was a child again, and her mother was having a good moment. Her gaze was clear of the distant fog, where her eyes would wander, and Clover couldn't find her.

Torryn smiled. "Did you know that your father could close his eyes, reach out and pluck four-leafed clovers from the ground like he was picking blades of grass? He would pick bushels of them, weave them into crowns and place them on my head. He would have loved everything about you."

The memory faded, replaced by the cold of the smooth stone pressed to her throbbing cheek. Clover's body ached as she remembered where she was, having just fallen through the floor of the Van Doren family mausoleum. Her teeth chattered and her dress was heavy with water that was rapidly turning into ice. It felt like her heart was skipping every other beat. Her hands shook as she felt around. At least she wasn't dead. Her friends could be, though, so she brought one hand up, palm open. A spark lit and she held a small candle flame. It shook as badly as her hand was shaking but light was light.

When she looked up, the hollow eyes of a skull glared back at her, and Clover sucked in a hard breath. She sat up and scrambled away, causing the light to go out. She was swallowed by darkness which was worse than having a light—even if what she saw was terrible.

The flame came back. From the looks of things, they had fallen into an underground stairwell and were on a landing which was partially a room filled with junk. All of it was iron, twisting metal, hooks, beams, what looked like part of a fence. More steps led down to yet more darkness. Then there was, of course, the skeleton.

Knox was lying nearby, along with Soleil. Both were breathing but something was wrong with Knox's leg. On closer inspection, Clover saw an iron bar going through his right calf.

"Knox." Clover reached up and gave his cheek a little slap. He groaned and rolled his head away from her hand. "Knox, wake up!"

Knox gasped awake and as soon as he tried to move his leg, he sucked in a sharp breath. Clover pressed a hand over his mouth to muffle his scream. At the sound, Soleil roused and she coughed.

"Easy," said Clover to Knox, who was still struggling. "Stop moving, you're just making it worse."

He was breathing hard, but he stopped moving. Tears streamed out of his eyes, and Clover noticed how young he looked now, like a scared little boy.

Soleil frowned at the body. "Who is this?"

"I don't know." Clover winced. "I hope it's not Grant's mother."

"It smells fae," said Soleil. "But the forest did not take her? Dark fae, perhaps?"

Clover was curious but Knox's whimpering drew her attention. Soleil came over and inspected the injury. She gently touched the bar before pulling her hand away, flinching.

"Iron," she said.

Clover took a deep breath. "All right, here's how we're going to do this. Soleil, you're going to brace yourself on that statue and you're going to hold Knox's leg. I'm going to pull the bar out."

She pulled her hand away from Knox's mouth now that he seemed a little calmer and he sucked up his tears.

"Do we have to take the bar out?" he asked. "I mean, can't we just leave it in there for the time being?"

"It's going to come out sooner or later," said Clover. "Better that it happens now."

"I do not consent," said Knox.

Clover's teeth chattered. "You've been overruled. Soleil, ready?"

Soleil grabbed Knox's leg and braced herself so she wouldn't move around. Clover pulled the sleeves of Grant's coat over her hands and grabbed the bar.

THE IRON BAR MIGHT HAVE GONE THROUGH BONE. FOR whatever reason, it fought Clover and it took her several minutes to finally pull it free. Somewhere along the way Knox had passed out, which was probably for the best. If Van Doren was here, he surely knew they were too by now, but he wasn't coming to stop them and she didn't know why.

Clover set down the bloody bar and cooled her hands on the stone beneath her while Soleil ripped off the lower part of Knox's trousers and bound his wound with the cloth.

"What do we do with him now?" Soleil's eyes were wide with fear and the braids in her dark hair were quivering. "Wait for him to wake up?"

Clover shook her head. "We're running out of time; we'll have to leave him here."

"In the dark? What if he wakes up?" asked Soleil.

Everything around them was metal or stone. Nothing would burn...but then Clover remembered the little plates of oil next to the graves above them. Clover hurried up the stairs and passed through a little hidden door made of two of the nameless squares. She grabbed one of the plates off its holder and carried it down to Knox, where she placed it in the hand of a nearby angel statue.

"There," said Clover. "We'll get him when we leave."

Clover found the box Knox had been carrying and she took out Dr. Van Doren's spirit blade, putting it in the bag still at her side.

Soleil looked past Clover, who followed her friend's worried eyes into the darkness of the stairwell.

"We can do this," said Clover. "Are you with me?"

When Clover held out her hand, Soleil took it.

"I'm with you."

Clover made sure Cypress's dagger was still in the inner pocket of Grant's coat before creating a fire that lit their way as they went ever downward.

"What is this place?" Soleil whispered.

"I don't know," said Clover, out of breath. She couldn't

shake the tight feeling in her chest. "I feel the darkness pressing in."

"Look at the walls," said Soleil.

Clover raised her hand with the flame and saw the skulls, both animal and human, embedded in the stone walls. Clover backed away only to hit her shoulder on another skull-covered wall. Her bones were stiff with fear and her skin—what wasn't numb from cold—tingled with raised hairs. She wanted to turn back, to leave this place, to come back when she was braver. But she would never be braver. Clover knew she was growing closer to her mother and Grant and the darkness of Dr. Van Doren.

She forced her numb feet to descend, and Soleil followed closely behind, clearly just as afraid but not showing any signs of wanting to retreat, which bolstered Clover's confidence. The air grew more chilled and damp. Clover wasn't sure if she was smelling true rust or her own fear.

They both stopped when they heard the sound of a voice ahead. Clover closed her hand and put out her flame before slowly feeling her way forward. The closer they got, the clearer the voice became.

"Mother loves her tricks. That's why she built this room. I was born right here on these stones..." It was Dr. Van Doren.

The staircase opened into a chamber lit by flames. Candles were spread out in circular patterns across the floor, grouped together in wall notches or decaying candelabras. The stone tables that went in a circle around the room were covered in them as well. The light they gave was unnatural—a cold green light that made Clover's skin crawl. Soleil leaned over and tried to blow one out, but the flame continued to flicker.

Dr. Van Doren's back was to them as he stood between two stone tables. On one was Grant Van Doren, and on the other was Clover's mother. They were both on their backs, hands folded over their stomachs like corpses.

"Do you know what happens when a fae has a child with a human, Clover Grimaldi?" asked Dr. Van Doren.

Clover and Soleil shared a look before stepping into the chamber. He was waiting for her to answer, so she did.

"The child is half-fae," she said.

Dr. Van Doren turned toward them. "The true trick of the half-fae is that they can look just like everyone else…if they're lucky." He looked her up and down and she scowled at him. His skin rippled from its normal pale tone to a darker shade similar to Clover's. Dark fae and their illusions.

The doctor continued, "Even Grant has some fae in him, you know…eventually he'll succumb to the darkness, like his father and my mother before me."

"You're wrong," said Clover. News that Grant had a little fae in him wasn't as much of a shock as she thought it would be. It made sense—how the forest simply welcomed him, the reason he wasn't afraid of it, or nearly anything to do with fae.

"I will not be manipulated by you," said Clover. Dr. Van Doren was a liar, and he always would be. This wasn't why she was here. "Just give me Grant and my mother. We'll leave. You never have to—"

"Leave!?" he interrupted so loudly her heart skipped a beat as his voice echoed all around the chamber. "Why would I let you leave?"

Clover didn't have an answer.

"So it seems you did not think this through. How common of you." He turned around. "You think this is just about your little infatuation with my son? This is bigger than all of us! Humans were never meant to rule—they are so easily manipulated. Kill a few of their children and all they can do is quiver behind their gates."

"You?" Clover grimaced.

Van Doren smiled. "Names are a powerful thing, you know. Own the names—own the people."

Clover thought back to his endless list of names.

"Have they sent a few more glares your way recently? Could you smell their fear grow into hatred? All I need is their birth names and I can twist their minds in any which way I desire...but I only desire one way to twist them. I will kill you and them and burn down the forest if I have to. After the new war, we'll make this world our own. We lost once—we won't lose again."

"The war is over!" Clover shouted. "Both sides lost."

"And yet we are the ones they hunt, we are the ones restricted to the forest, to every day look upon the desolation they wrought."

Clover shook her head. "You hypocrite! I'm not going to let you start a war and I'm not leaving here without Grant and my mother. The spell you have him under is killing him!"

The doctor's confidence wavered slightly. "If you want them—then you'll just have to kill me."

Soleil turned to her. "Don't do it—that's what he wants."

Dr. Van Doren pulled out a dagger, turned, and sliced through a rope. Clover was barely aware of what was coming down on their heads before it was there. Soleil pushed Clover to the ground as a metallic slam crashed against the stone behind Clover. After pushing herself up, Clover could see that what had come down on them was a cage, a small iron cage that Soleil was now hunkered down in.

When Van Doren came close, Soleil reached through the bars and scratched at him, baring her sharp teeth. Van Doren stayed just out of her reach and smirked at her before moving on to Clover, who shot to her feet and moved away from him.

"You have been a thorn in my side since the day you were born," said Van Doren, still holding his dagger. "If it wasn't for your power, I would have killed you then."

"And now? Now you'll just drain my power through this?" Clover reached into her pocket and pulled out the spirit blade.

Dr. Van Doren stopped moving.

Clover looked between him and the knife. "Are you afraid of this knife?"

"I fear nothing. Especially not some witless halfling like you." Van Doren took out a spirit blade of his own. His was thin, like glass, and though it was the same substance, it was weaker, liable to shatter at the tiniest bit of pressure. The frailty of it could only mean it belonged to one person.

It was her mother's.

Dr. Van Doren grinned. "So we're at an impasse. I hold your mother's life in my hand, you hold mine...let's trade."

"I might not be as smart as you are, but I'm not stupid," said Clover. "And unfortunately for you, you're the one lacking information, not me."

"Don't be coy," Dr. Van Doren growled. "You're not strong enough to kill me. I'm done talking." He surged forward with the dagger and with nowhere to run, Clover's only option was to fight. So she did.

LIQUID COLD FOUND ITS WAY INTO HER CHEST. THE CEILING above them broke open, showering them with cold earth. Through the break rushed roots, sturdy tree roots that grabbed at Van Doren as Clover skittered away from him, hiding behind the stone table her mother was on. He slashed at them with his knives. The air grew colder and the darkness in the cavern shifted—along with it came a surge of ringing pain. Clover cried out from it and the roots withered and died.

He laughed. "There can't be light without darkness. Life wouldn't be life without death!"

Clover jumped to her feet with a flame in her hand and with a powerful breath she blew a jet of flames at Dr. Van Doren. He shouted and staggered back, most of his clothes on fire. As he fell to the ground trying to pat himself out, she heard skittering. She rushed forward, searching for the spirit blades.

She had barely reached for a blade when her other hand pressed against a stone with a hole in the center. The stone sank into the ground and an iron spike came through and skewered her hand. Clover screamed, feeling Knox's pain and the burning ache of the iron in her skin.

Van Doren finished putting himself out and he stood and kicked her in the stomach, knocking the breath out of her. When she sank to the ground, gasping, he pressed a foot into her back.

"Here we are again." The doctor reached down and picked up the blade she'd been trying to grab before she was speared through the hand. "You see, you were raised to be weak, to serve, to stay down when you've been beaten. It's not your fault that you always end up here. It's just in your blood. You'll never be powerful enough to beat me, not because your magic isn't strong—but because your mind isn't. And it never will be."

Maybe he was right, Clover thought to herself. All her life she had ended up here, on the ground with Van Doren standing over her. She wanted freedom, but it wasn't enough

—there was still something inside her that would always try to keep her head down, to bow before something more powerful.

And she'd found Grant, hadn't she? She'd known he was alive. She proved to Knox that he was. She knew that he'd been hidden out in the forest. And she'd been right. And Torryn? Clover's mother had once loved her, held her, been her safeguard—but somewhere along the way, they'd switched roles and Clover was tired. Tired of seeing her mother slip further and further out of reach. Maybe it was better this way.

But if it was better, then why was she still so angry?

"Grim!"

She picked her head up off the stones as a pale, limping Knox threw himself onto Van Doren. They fell to the ground and the pressure was taken off Clover's back. She pushed herself up and ripped her hand off the spike with a cry of pain.

Soleil pressed against the side of her cage, skin sizzling under the burning of the iron as she reached for a spirit blade. Her fingers brushed it before she held it in her hand. Once she got it, she threw it to Clover, who caught it in her good hand.

In the blade itself, she could feel its pull toward her, she could hear her own voice speaking within it, overlapping sentences, laughter, crying. This blade was hers. If she broke it, the bond wouldn't be completely severed, but she would have much of her life force back. She couldn't beat Van Doren without it.

"No!" Van Doren screamed from beneath Knox.

Clover took the blade in both hands and pressed hard. Cracks began to show bright as the sun in the surface of the soul flint, and when the blade broke, the snap echoed deep into her mind. The flash blinded her, and she felt utterly and completely weightless.

Chapter Twenty

IT WAS like breathing for the first time. A constricting grip released Clover's lungs and her head felt light as the familiar pain burrowing through the top of her skull stopped. The cold liquid feeling came to the center of her chest, and she let it envelop her entire body. This was no magic from the forest—this belonged to her, and her alone, and it was powerful.

Clover was flat on her back with the two halves of her spirit blade in either hand. The cold feeling was fading, and she was able to sit up on her own. As she did, she saw Van Doren and Knox still fighting. They had managed to get on their feet, but Van Doren was stronger. Knox drove Van Doren into a stone counter covered in ancient bottles and books.

Clover stood and went to Soleil, who was still trapped in the cage. The cold magic crept through Clover's veins and strong roots and vines shot down from the ceiling, wrapping around the iron cage and lifting it. Soleil snaked along her belly from under the cage.

"The son of my filthy human half-brother." Van Doren

lifted one foot and kicked Knox hard in his injured leg. There was an audible snap and Knox fell to the ground screaming as Van Doren laughed. "Your human bones break so easily!"

"Knox!" Soleil shouted.

Clover heard the rushing of water. It flooded down from the ceiling in a torrent and began swirling around the room. It closed in, rapidly passing over her, Soleil, and Knox and sweeping up the doctor before he could bring his foot down on Knox's head.

Dr. Van Doren went flying. He smacked a stone wall and slid down, landing on his front between the bodies of her mother and Grant. Clover and Soleil went to Knox.

He was breathing hard, tears streaming. "I knew you liked me."

"Silence." Soleil looked at his leg. It was broken, badly—even if Clover couldn't see that, she had definitely heard it. This had to stop. She couldn't let her friends keep getting hurt. The truth was, this was between her and Van Doren.

"Soleil, get Knox out of here," she said. "Don't argue with me."

Soleil didn't. A resolve grew in her eyes. She knew what Clover was doing and seemed to agree with her decision.

As the doctor stood, Clover heard Soleil dragging Knox out of the chamber, so it was just the two of them. Her goal was clear: she had to get her mother's knife and make Van Doren break his own knife—only somehow, he had to do it willfully.

"I can't wait all day." He rushed toward her.

Clover didn't want to move, fearing more of the spike traps. Van Doren reached out to grab her as he came close, probably intending to knock her to the ground. She inter-

cepted him, her hand wrapping around his wrist. He struggled, like he did the day Knox stopped him.

Clover gritted her teeth and shoved him back, knocking
him off his feet. He went sliding across the stones.

Shocked, she looked at her hands. Was she stronger? Or
was he weaker?

What did it matter? She couldn't waste any time. She
needed to get her mother's spirit blade.

Clover rushed for Van Doren and began feeling along his
pockets for her mother's knife before his hands came up and
wrapped around her throat. Her air cut off and she panicked,
grabbing at his solid hold. He was crushing her throat, so
Clover reached forward and dug her fingers into his eyes. He
screamed but didn't let go. She couldn't breathe and her head
was pounding.

Then she heard a whisper and felt Cypress's dagger
thumping against her side. She drew it out and sliced it
savagely across Van Doren's wrist. When he still didn't let go,
she kept sawing until he finally did. He shoved her away and
she rolled before crawling, gasping ragged, desperate breaths
through a burning throat.

Through the noise of her struggle, she could hear Van
Doren advancing. Clover turned and with a clenching of her
fist and teeth, a massive rock fell from the ceiling between
them. He leapt out of the way.

Clover got to her feet, still dizzy from lack of oxygen. She
saw her mother's head roll from side to side. Clover was going
to leave this chamber with Grant and her mother, or she was
not going to leave at all.

She clenched Cypress's dagger harder as Van Doren got to his feet. His white shirt was ripped and bleeding from both forearms.

"You belong to me," he said through his teeth. For the first time, Clover noticed that he looked...older. His hair was grayer, and the lines on his face were more pronounced. The dim, green, upward light of the candles wasn't helping—but she noticed the difference. Without her spirit blade, he could no longer feed off her power.

Clover held out the blade. "No, I don't. Let us go and I won't kill you."

"You would sacrifice your light for them?" he asked. "Do you think they will still love you afterward?"

"Yes," she said. "I do."

She had no choice but to believe that, because it was becoming more and more apparent to her that the only way she could beat him was to kill him. He was never going to stop, and she was running out of options.

Van Doren spat at her. "You're pathetic." He reached into his pocket and pulled out Torryn's spirit blade. "I can still end your mother's life."

Clover took out his own spirit blade, and with Cypress's dagger in her other hand, she now held two blades of darkness.

"Kill her and..." She could threaten his life. She had all the power to end him right then and there—but then she remembered her other tactic. "...and you'll never know what true power feels like."

Her body felt the strain of the lie as soon as she said it, like an itch at the center of her chest. She pretended to wince at the injury in her hand, which was still throbbing and bleeding down Cypress's dagger.

"Tricks and games, girl. Don't forget, I know you can't lie for very long," he said.

"Why lie when I have the upper hand?" she asked. "I don't suppose you thought your endless books and guides knew the truth behind these blades." She forced her voice to remain steady through the lie. She had to make him believe he had been misled. "My knowledge comes straight from the fae...light and dark alike."

The itch began to grow, surging through her bones. She wanted to throw herself down and scratch her skin raw, or else let the truth come pouring out. She held on, she held on for dear life, thinking of Grant and her mother.

"See this?" She gestured to Aviana's necklace. "You know what this is, don't you?"

Dr. Van Doren growled. "Where did you get that?"

"It was given to me. By Aviana."

"Aviana died years ago," said Dr. Van Doren.

Clover arched an eyebrow. "Suppose you read about that in a book? I guess anything can be written in a book—but she seemed alive and well to me."

His eyes cast to the floor in thought before returning his hateful glare back to her. She was planting the seeds of doubt in his mind—if the books were wrong about that, then what else were they wrong about?

Clover continued. "Well, I went to her about my problem and she let me in on a little secret."

"And what did they tell you, superior being that you are?" Van Doren was mocking her, but Clover could tell he was truly curious. She had struck his most vulnerable chord—his pride. He liked knowing more and being capable of more than everyone around him. It irked him that there was even a single card in Clover's hand.

Clover put away Cypress's dagger and held Van Doren's spirit blade in both hands as though to break it. "She said that if one of the bound spirits breaks the blade of the binder, then the binder will die…"

"And if I break it? Don't suppose that would be in your favor, would it?"

"No, it wouldn't." Clover put a little pressure on the blade and a single crack, shining bright white light, streaked across the void-like darkness.

"You're bluffing," he said.

Clover smirked. "Am I?" She gripped the blade a little harder and another crack appeared.

Van Doren held out a hand. "Stop!"

She did and her jaw relaxed; the itch was fading but it was still present. The truth lurked at the back of her throat, like stifling the urge to cough.

"Perhaps we could make a deal," said Van Doren.

Clover held the blade in one hand. "I'm listening."

"I'll let you have your mother's life. You both leave in peace, and you give me the blade." He reached for it.

She stepped back and checked to see if she was standing on another spike trap. There was one nearby.

"Not nearly good enough."

He smirked. "You can't have the whole world, girl."

"My mother, her blade, Grant, and you release the town of Veritas."

He scowled. "He is my son."

"Don't pretend as though you care about him now!" snapped Clover. His sudden possessiveness of Grant enraged her. He had never loved Grant. Grant was just a trophy for him, an object that ensured his legacy. "When he wakes up, he'll still love me…then what would his *affectionate* father do? Kill him for real? I'd bet my soul on it. You will give me what I ask." Clover held his knife once again in both hands, ready to snap it in half. "Don't play games with me, doctor. I've got nothing left that I'm not willing to lose."

"All right." His expression relaxed from one of annoyance into a mask of neutral stone. "Both of them, Veritas, and the blade."

And Clover knew then that there was no deal. He was never going to let her walk away with anything, so she knew what she had to do.

Clover held the spirit blade with her injured hand and with the other made sure Cypress's dagger was in her pocket where she left it. Van Doren held up her mother's blade and cautiously, they approached one another. When they were standing close enough apart to grab the other's blade, he dropped Torryn's and reached behind him, so Clover did the same.

She didn't remember what happened to his dagger after they had tumbled to the ground the first time, when he'd been on fire and her hand had been skewered—but he must have recovered it, because he had it now. He brought his upward toward her middle, while she shoved hers downward toward his heart.

Neither of them made their mark, for they both caught each other by the wrist barely in time. Van Doren was still strong, but now she matched him power for power.

"Perhaps I underestimated you."

Clover strained, pushing all her focus into keeping his blade from reaching her.

"No—you *definitely* underestimated me." She pressed her own dagger down toward his heart, and this time, he struggled against her, but it was becoming clear that neither of them was about to gain ground.

Then Torryn woke up.

***

"Roan!" Torryn screamed through her tears.

Clover had been caught off guard enough for Van Doren to turn them both and see what the commotion was. He saw Torryn and an evil smile twisted his lips. Torryn would be defenseless against Van Doren, and so Clover had no choice but to take her mother out of the picture.

She closed her eyes hard, and her cry of resolve and pain began before she even let go of Van Doren's wrist and let his dagger plunge deep into her middle. The blade wasn't iron, but it stung, its sharp sides slicing right through her. Her scream continued as Van Doren was surprised by the sudden change in the fight. His hand that held her wrist slackened and she shoved her own dagger forward. The shift in his balance caused her dagger to stab into the top of his shoulder, rather than into his heart. Then Torryn was there, pushing and screaming.

"What are you doing to him?! Roan! He's burning! Let him go! You monsters! All of you!" she screamed. She managed to shove Clover and Van Doren apart, but Clover didn't let go of Cypress's blade like Van Doren had with his dagger.

As Clover stumbled back, she grabbed her mother so Van Doren wouldn't hurt her, and they both fell to the ground. Every twist, every turn caused the blade in her side to dig into something new, but she wasn't dead and so she wasn't about to give up now. Clover grabbed hold of the dagger and ripped it out, clenching her teeth and holding her breath. She held it tightly, and now armed with two daggers, Clover pushed herself up, expecting Van Doren to advance—but he wasn't even paying attention to them. He was kneeling on the ground, holding his spirit blade in both hands. He looked at Clover with a twisted smile blazing with darkness.

"You lose," he said, and he broke his blade in half.

The light blinded Clover and instead of the snap simply echoing in her own mind, it echoed around the chamber, it shook the ceiling and the ground, and she was sure that it could be heard for miles—maybe even all the way to Veritas.

When the light faded, Clover was left in pitch darkness. The candles around the room had blown out, so she created her own light, a blazing fire pushed to the center of the room, and it spread, re-lighting the candles with just a thought. Warm light flooded the chamber. Both her mother and Van Doren were on the ground, unmoving.

Clover reached beneath her coat and felt her stab wound. It was bleeding at a steady trickle, and beginning to seep into the cracks of the stones around her and her mother.

Clover rolled Torryn over and pressed her good hand to the side of her mother's face. Torryn's heart was still beating, and color was still in her skin. Her face twisted like she was having a nightmare before her eyes opened. She looked confused, like she still didn't know who or where she was, or who was in front of her.

"Mother, it's me, Clover," she said, already in tears.

Torryn shook her head. "No, my Clover is just a child." It was a sentence, a full, coherent string of words—something she never thought she would hear from her mother again. And her voice was so steady and calm, just like Clover remembered. Her chest grew tight as her stomach twisted into knots.

"It's me. I swear, it's me."

"How long have I been asleep?" asked Torryn.

"A long time…a very long time," said Clover.

Torryn sat up, and for the first time in over a decade, Clover saw true clarity in her mother's eyes. The defenses Clover had put up between her and the world, and between the world and her mother, were beginning to crumble. As soon as the first heaving sob broke from her, she couldn't stop the wave of them from rushing out of her. They shook her body down to her core, the ragged, gasping cries of a girl who was weary from being a protector. Her mother held her as her crying quieted and though that moment seemed to stretch on for miles, deep down, Clover knew her conflict with Van Doren wasn't over.

VAN DOREN STIRRED. CLOVER AND TORRYN TURNED TO HIM as he shakily pushed himself up. His hair was white as snow and thinned down so Clover could see his scalp. When he turned to them, his face was aged beyond what Clover expected.

"You! What have you done!" His voice was wavering and craggy, a sharp contrast from the steady boom it normally was. He had shrunken within his clothes, his hands and arms and legs frail.

Torryn stood and helped Clover stand as well. Clover picked up both the daggers, willing the world to stay in focus.

"Impossible!" Van Doren choked out. "You can't lie! You *can't lie!*"

Clover didn't answer him. She just studied him, this shell of a man she once feared, that had held her and her mother prisoner for nearly two decades, and now that she was free, she felt...sorry for him. Just like she had for Benjamin.

Dr. Emerson Van Doren had caused her pain and misery. Years of her life were spent toiling for him, years she would never get back with her mother. Bitterness and anger swelled in her, but as though in a dream, she saw the rest of her life stretch out before her, like a path through the forest. And it was utterly and completely empty, blank but waiting for her to fill it.

She could end it all right now and take Van Doren's life. He wouldn't even be able to fight back. She felt stronger now than she had even after breaking her own blade. But darkness was like a boulder rolling down a steep hill. Once it started, she would never be able to stop it.

So, she stepped forward, and the frail and defenseless Van Doren flinched as she moved past him and stood in front of Grant. He was still sleeping, the preservation spell still there, but it was a sheer cloth compared to the iron blanket that had laid over Marvin Hallows.

Clover removed it on her own, pulling it back with a single hand, starting at his head and ending at his feet. Like Marvin, Grant had gray hairs creeping up around his temples—but otherwise, he seemed fine. Maybe his life would be shorter now, but she didn't care. She'd take whatever she could get.

Clover pressed a hand to her bleeding wound and sat on the edge of the stone table he was lying on. She leaned forward and laid her head on his chest, closing her eyes. The pathway revealed itself once more, but it grew dimmer, shorter with each breath she released. Grant seemed to take one and she could feel his heart beating.

His arms came up and wrapped around her and she breathed him in and brought up her hand, blood covered as it was, to hold onto him. If everything didn't hurt so much, she would wonder if she was in some sort of twisted dream. But this was no dream. She felt an enormous weight lift off her shoulders.

Grant sat up and she held on even tighter, letting her eyes open to see her mother sitting nearby and watching.

"I knew you'd find me," said Grant.

Clover smiled. In spite of everything, her familiar annoyance at Grant's ability to make her smile in the worst moments was welcomed back. He lifted one hand and saw her injury before gently pushing her back and lifting one side of his coat that she still wore.

He quickly took off his own coat and rolled up his sleeves. His face grew stern with focus, but he still paused to give her a small smirk. "I hope you know you're in for a scolding once I save your life."

"I'm looking forward to it," she said, still smiling.

Chapter Twenty-One

DR. VAN DOREN died of natural causes. While Clover was reviving Grant, Dr. Van Doren had fallen asleep, and he didn't wake up. Grant and Torryn moved him to one of the stone tables and laid him to rest under the blanket Clover had brought. Being the gentleman he was, Grant let Torryn have his coat.

"You've gotten so tall," said Torryn.

Grant smiled. "Well, you and your daughter took good care of me."

Torryn smiled back at him, and after a moment, a distance set in behind her eyes. Clover knew her mother was slipping into memory but now Clover wasn't afraid. The Breaking had cost her mother part of her very being, something she couldn't get back, but it didn't mean she was completely broken.

Grant had ripped off part of Clover's skirt to make a bandage for her hand and to tie around her waist to help stop the bleeding so she could get back to the manor in one piece. She was lightheaded from losing so much blood, so while

Grant carried her, the best she could manage was a small flame to light their way.

"You're too light. You haven't been eating enough."

Clover leaned her head on his chest. "I was busy looking for you."

"I can't believe I missed the Blood Solstice."

Clover smiled; she knew he was trying to keep her talking. "We can have another celebration...just for you."

They came to the second landing and passed carefully over the skeleton and up the second set of stairs.

"So...what happened exactly?" asked Grant. "One moment I was in the library, then suddenly I've woken up in some kind of ritual chamber and my father is passing."

Torryn stopped walking. "I believe that's my fault."

Grant stopped too and turned to her. They were standing in the mausoleum now, surrounded by Van Dorens. Clover let her flame fade, since the ones in the bowls were lighting the room just fine.

"Under Dr. Van Doren's power, I couldn't control my thoughts. They would pass back and forth from memory to the present and sometimes reach a sort of between space where time no longer existed." Her voice got tight. "Ghosts of my past would wander back and forth before my eyes until I never knew what was real. I would say things, speak to my memories. I saw you both that day in the forest. Engaged to be married and I...I'm so sorry."

Clover tried to lift her head but couldn't really. "It's not your fault."

"I don't blame you for a second," said Grant. "I blame my father."

Torryn nodded, but her face was still downcast like she didn't truly absolve herself from any blame. But she would, someday. Grant put an arm around her. Torryn had raised both of them—been the only presence of maternal love in their lives. Clover was sure he was as glad to have Torryn back as she was.

"What is this place?" asked Grant. "These are all Van Dorens."

"Yes...I don't..." Clover couldn't bring herself to answer so many questions. Her mind was becoming muddled, not with memories, or words, but she just didn't know the answers anymore.

"All right, I hear you, let's get you out of here...as soon as I find the exit."

"The water," Clover breathed. She forced herself to stay awake, she forced herself to stay alive. She wanted to fight but it seemed impossible, like something was pulling on her, pulling her away from Grant. She held onto the white cloth of his shirt with equally white knuckles.

GRANT FOUND THE WATER AND DIDN'T HESITATE TO PLUNGE into it, adjusting her so her head remained above water. Torryn came behind them, all of them breathless but determined to leave that terrible place. When they made it out to the open, the bright white of the snowy forest blinded Clover for a moment before her eyes adjusted and she saw Soleil and Knox on the shore of the pond.

"Thank the forest you're all right," said Soleil, rushing through the water and pulling out the three of them. She had started a large fire where Knox was leaned up against a tree, pale, but awake. It was nighttime now and being out of the water had them all gasping, so they took a moment to warm themselves by the fire. Soleil pushed Grant aside, much to his protestation, as she looked at Clover's wound and the blood.

"Eat this." Soleil shoved something slimy into Clover's mouth. Clover grimaced, trying to spit it up, but Soleil pressed a hand over her mouth and pinched her nose. Clover had no choice but to swallow the putrid ball of mush. It tasted like dirt, and leaves, and something bitter. But immediately she felt her energy return to her. She coughed and gagged, but she was still too weak to move. The blood flow from her wound slowed.

"I don't want to know what that was," said Clover as Grant pulled her to him again.

Soleil nodded. "No, you don't. That will only last so long."

Clover grimaced.

"Warner? Good to see you." Grant sat up straighter at the sight of his cousin. He reached out and they shook hands, which was the most either of them could do in their current conditions.

Soleil narrowed her eyes. "Who is Warner?"

"Warner is Knox's real name; he and Grant are cousins," said Clover. Her mother sat next to her, and the fire began to drive the ache from her bones.

Soleil glared at Knox and threw snow at his face.

"Hey!" he cried out.

"You lied to me about your real name, this is vile and offensive," Soleil growled.

Knox threw snow back. "It's called a nickname; I did not lie to you."

But Soleil didn't seem convinced, and she sulked by the fire.

"What are you doing here?" asked Grant.

Knox sighed. "My mother sent me here to try and rescue me from my life of danger."

"I thought you were a reporter?"

"Every job comes with its own dangers," said Knox with a shrug. "And you should feel lucky I did come, or this one would have never found you."

Clover narrowed her eyes. "I had to dig up a grave just to convince you he was alive."

Grant gave his cousin a look and Knox shrugged.

"Knox, this is my mother, Torryn Grimaldi," said Clover.

Knox frowned, not knowing what she meant, but Torryn held out her hand.

"It's a pleasure to meet you, young man."

Knox shook her hand, shocked at her presence of being.

Torryn went on, "If you're anything like Grant, then we'll get along just fine."

"They're both trouble," said Soleil under her breath.

Grant lifted up the edge of Clover's coat, looking at the blood which was continuing to flow. "We better get you back to the manor. I don't know what she gave you, but I still need to patch this up, and if we stay out here much longer, we may freeze to death."

SINCE NO ONE WANTED TO FREEZE TO DEATH, EVERYONE gathered themselves and made for the manor. Soleil helped Knox, and Grant helped Clover and Torryn. Halfway to the house, Clover began to flicker in and out of consciousness. Her legs failed her, so Grant picked her up and she let herself drift into oblivion. She remembered cold and a bit of stinging pain but when that

faded, the dreams took hold. The sting of iron and Van
Doren's blade wandered into her sleep and she found
herself standing in the forest with Cypress's dagger in her
hand.

She heard a sigh.

"I thought we had a deal."

Clover whipped around and saw Cypress.

"I figured I would exhaust all options before following
through. No offense intended. I have questions, though."

Cypress smirked. "Go on."

"Why Dr. Van Doren? He wasn't human."

"The fact that he was dark fae only would have made his
heart sustain me longer. But to tell the whole truth? His
mother had a hand in…" He gestured. "How you see me now.
She owes me a heart, and since her bones are lying in a ritual
chamber along with her son, I suppose my thirst for revenge
must go unquenched. No thanks to you." He raised an
eyebrow at Clover.

Clover narrowed her eyes. "You don't think knowing he
was dark fae would have helped me in any way?"

"Was I ever really interested in helping you, is the better
question."

Clover sighed before holding out the dagger.

Cypress's smirk turned to a sad smile as he took it from her.
"You would have made an excellent dark fae."

"I'll do my best as a light fae," she said with a smile. "I bet
you would make a good light fae, too."

"Maybe someday, little Clover, maybe someday."

The dream ended and Clover woke with a start. She was
in one of the hospital rooms. Light streamed in through the
window, and she had been changed into a green dress. It was
knee length and warm and if it hadn't been for the bandage

around her hand, her waist, and shoulder, she would have thought she was still in a dream.

She moved off the bed and her feet touched the frozen ground. Her whole body ached and her middle stung and burned, echoing out to the tips of her nerves, but she needed to see Grant. A coat was draped on the end of her bed, and she put it on before leaving the room. Her mother, Knox, and Soleil were all asleep in the remaining rooms. Clover jumped across the gap in the middle of the house and checked Grant's room. No one there. A speck of worry grew in her mind but there was still one more place to check.

Clover's teeth chattered as she made her way into the attic, up the ladder and into the tower. Grant was sitting in his usual place, asleep, head tilted against the wall and a blanket around his shoulders.

Clover moved into her own place and made a small fire between herself and Grant, heating up the small space. She stretched out a hand and her fingertips brushed along his cheek; he was real. What would they do now? They couldn't stay here, that was certain.

Grant stirred in his sleep and when he saw her, he grinned, closing his eyes.

"Making sure I don't vanish again?" he asked.

Clover smiled. "Even if you did, I'd find you."

He rubbed his eyes and sat up. "Sorry I wasn't there when you woke, I just—it sort of hit me all at once."

"What did?" asked Clover.

Grant's charm melted away. "Everything. What my father did, what he was."

"You're not anything like him," said Clover. "He chose the darkness, and I know that—however small the fae part of you is—it's good." She sniffed. "Your father can't hurt anyone anymore. We're free. You're free to be the good doctor you are, and I have the potential to be anything I want."

Grant's eyebrows went up. "Well, this is new."

"I've learned a lot, mostly that you were right about a lot of things," she said.

"I told you—"

Clover pressed her hand over his mouth. "Ah! Not *everything*, just a lot of things." She could feel him smile under her hand and she took it away, but he grabbed it and pressed her palm to his cheek.

"So you're ready to run away with me, then?" he asked. "I was thinking a house on the edge of Hirane. The city's a bit crowded for a country boy like me."

"I wouldn't mind being close to the forest," said Clover. Before all this started, her future seemed so far away—but now it was her next step, and she couldn't keep the smile off her face. "When's the wedding?"

"The warmest day in spring," he said dramatically.

Clover laughed. "You were never much for planning. Spring, then. Suppose we should tell the others."

"We should...but unfortunately, you're in my tower, and the price of release is a kiss," he said, grabbing her but being mindful of the wound in her side.

"A kiss, that's all?" Clover pressed her forehead to his.

He smirked. "The price of admission goes up after the initial deal is struck—to benefit both parties."

"How generous," said Clover, and when they kissed, all the missing time melted away like thawing snow. There was no more need to hide in the dark or behind closed doors—all plans, all wants and needs and their future were out in the open. Just like it should be.

CLOVER WAS DOWN THE STAIRS OF THE ATTIC BEFORE SHE gestured to her dress questioningly.

Grant smiled. "Late Blood Solstice gift. I'm surprised you didn't see it when you went into my closet."

"Must have had my mind on something else," she said with a mocking grin. They got to the stairs leading down to the main hall.

Grant whistled. "We better start packing. We don't have much but the road to Hirane is long. It'll take us all day to walk it."

"You're right. I'll make us something to eat, you should wake everyone up." She started to lower herself down gingerly from the stairs and make her way to the kitchen but Grant caught her by the elbow and turned her around.

"That dress wasn't just a gift. It was also a request."

Clover's brow furrowed. "What for?"

"I don't ever want you to wear the color gray again." He took her by the shoulders. "Please."

"Happily obliged," she said, smiling.

And by the end of the morning, they were all packed. Most of them could fit everything they wanted to take into a pillowcase or a sheet tied together at the corners.

"I will be traveling with you," said Soleil. They were standing at the door leading out of the servants' quarters, ready to leave, all of them with their things. Knox was sporting a crutch, but he could still carry some of the load.

"Really? Don't you live around here?" asked Clover.

"I live in Thea Serin. The fae guard the forest, we turn and shift around each other, always moving. And so where you will go, I will go—as long as it's close to the forest." Soleil was thoughtful for a moment. "Is it close to the forest?"

"That's the plan," said Grant.

"Ha!" Knox laughed. "Guess you're not rid of me yet."

Soleil scowled. "That would be more your benefit than mine, I assure you. Now we travel the Fae Road?"

"Not yet," said Knox. "There's someone in Veritas that we need to pick up...uh, the rest of you can wait outside"

Clover smiled. "Your fiancée?"

"I haven't asked her yet, but essentially, yes," said Knox.

Grant threw his arm around his cousin's shoulder. "I knew you'd get her back; you just have to use that charm you...only seem to lack around the woman you love."

Knox laughed, pushing him off, and Grant took Clover's hand tightly. With her other hand, she pulled his coat more closely around her. They made their way down the lane to the front gate before Clover looked back. A cold swelled through her blood and the candle in the tower came alight. She smiled before turning and following everyone out the gate. Grant closed it behind them.

The path of Clover's life was new and unclear, but brightly lit and welcoming. Clover Grimaldi was ready to walk that path, to take new turns, backtrack, and start over. She was ready to wander and get lost and find her way back because now she was free. They all were.

Thanks for reading!

Word of mouth is the best way for an author to connect with more readers. If you enjoyed *The Grim and the Grave*, would you be so kind as to leave a review on Amazon or Goodreads letting others know what you thought of my book?

Thank you!
Sami Eastwood

Acknowledgments

This story spawned from a dream I had about three years ago, and I began this project, which I can't believe is finally here.

I would never have completed this story without so much support from the people around me. Thank you to my family for their love for me and this book. To user Wonderburg on 99designs for creating the cover, and Sekcer on Fiverr for drawing the map.

About the Author

Sami Eastwood was born in Northern California and grew up all along the West Coast. She now resides in the Pacific Northwest with her large family and their dog, Pepper.

Also by Sami Eastwood

Blackstone Asylum

CPSIA information can be obtained
at www.ICGtesting.com
Printed in the USA
LVHW081108020922
727314LV00010B/298